PRAISE FOR
LET'S SPLIT UP

"*Let's Split Up* is a bingeable page-turner full of fun, frights and friendship. Compelling, original and twisty, I devoured it in one sitting. Bill Wood is a fresh and exciting new voice in YA."
—KATHRYN FOXFIELD, AUTHOR OF
GOOD GIRLS DIE FIRST

"Full of lovable characters, fun action and creepy atmosphere—I loved it!"
—AMY MCCAW, AUTHOR OF
THE *MINA AND THE UNDEAD* SERIES

"A fun, fast slasher as full of heart as it is hijinks."
—SARAH UNDERWOOD, AUTHOR OF
LIES WE SING TO THE SEA

"A thrilling, heart-stopping debut. High stakes, mysterious ghouls, and a group of teens who I wish I was part of back when I was in school. A show-stopping horror mystery that you will devour in one sitting. Just incredible."
—BEN ALDERSON, AUTHOR OF
A BETRAYAL OF STORMS

"An unmissable love letter to the spooks of *Scream* and *Scooby-Doo*, this is a deeply atmospheric, tense, and propulsive debut fueled by horror."
—LUCY ROSE, AUTHOR OF
THE LAMB

"Holy hell, this is magnificent! I am unwell. The friendship group, the haunting, those twists! Seriously, my heart can't handle it. What a perfect homage to the best of '90s horror. I'm obsessed."
—ROSIE TALBOT, AUTHOR OF
SIXTEEN SOULS

"Iconic and gripping."
—ANDY DARCY THEO, AUTHOR OF
THE LIGHT THAT BLINDS US

"Creepy, mysterious, and fun. It brings big Point Horror energy to a new generation."
—KAT ELLIS, AUTHOR OF
HARROW LAKE

"An absolute MUST for fans of *Scooby-Doo* and '90s/'00s horror movies. With characters you root for and a mystery that gives you chills. A thoroughly entertaining ride!"
—KATE WESTON, AUTHOR OF
MURDER ON A SUMMER BREAK

BE RIGHT BACK

BILL WOOD

Scholastic Inc.

If you purchased this book without a cover, you should be aware that this book is stolen property. It was reported as "unsold and destroyed" to the publisher, and neither the author nor the publisher has received any payment for this "stripped book."

Copyright © 2026 by Bill Wood

All rights reserved. Published by Scholastic Inc., *Publishers since 1920.* SCHOLASTIC and associated logos are trademarks and/or registered trademarks of Scholastic Inc.

First published in the United Kingdom in 2025 by Scholastic UK: Westfield Road, Southam, Warwickshire, England CV47 0RA.

The publisher does not have any control over and does not assume any responsibility for author or third-party websites or their content.

No part of this publication may be reproduced, stored in a retrieval system, or transmitted in any form or by any means, electronic, mechanical, photocopying, recording, or otherwise, or used to train any artificial intelligence technologies, without written permission of the publisher. For information regarding permission, write to Scholastic Inc., Attention: Permissions Department, 557 Broadway, New York, NY 10012.

This book is a work of fiction. Names, characters, places, and incidents are either the product of the author's imagination or are used fictitiously, and any resemblance to actual persons, living or dead, business establishments, events, or locales is entirely coincidental.

Library of Congress Cataloging-in-Publication Data available

ISBN 979-8-225-00619-8

10 9 8 7 6 5 4 3 2 1   26 27 28 29 30

Printed in Italy   208
First edition, March 2026

Book design by Cassy Price

To the readers who always guess the ending—
you've officially made me paranoid

PROLOGUE

It wasn't like any other night.

The skies hummed a melancholic song as the trees whispered with restless disdain, yearning for the embrace of amber skies. However, inside the manor, none of that mattered. The walls were an unyielding force, sealing out the world beyond. But it was only a matter of time before the tendrils of darkness slithered through the manor's barrier and infected the rest of Sanera.

Amber's breath echoed in the darkness, her feet rooted in place on the aged floorboards of the secret passage. Up here she couldn't move; her mind wouldn't let her. Finding this hiding spot was by chance—one wrong step and everything was lost.

"We can't stay here all day," Jonesy whispered, so

quietly his voice could be mistaken for a breath. Buffy gripped Amber's arm tight.

Jonesy was right, of course. They couldn't delay: Cam was relying on them. The blood trails on the staircase had told a grim story. His stitches had either torn, or new wounds had been inflicted. Either way, Cam needed their help. They were alone. No one was coming. It was up to them.

The secret passage felt cramped and claustrophobic. Amber leaned forward, her eyes peeking through the peepholes they'd discovered in a portrait of Robert Carrington, the manor's original owner, its eyeholes cut out. It was like something straight out of an old mystery television series.

She peered into the darkness.

Nothing.

It felt like a dream, as if they'd somehow stumbled into the wrong haunted manor on the edge of town. The silence was suffocating. Only the creaks of the house settling broke the stillness.

Then, a sudden jolt.

Another pair of eyes, inches from her own.

A gasp caught in Amber's throat as she tumbled backward, only to be caught by Buffy's soft hands.

"Run!"

As they sprinted blindly down the passage, the painting suddenly swung open. The Carrington Ghoul, a shadow emerging from the dark.

The gang slammed into walls as they frantically tried to escape. They didn't stop—they couldn't stop. Or else they'd share the same fate as Brad and Shelley. The ghoul had known this entire time where they were hiding. They were clearly just pawns in their twisted game.

Amber risked a glance over her shoulder. Through the shadows, she caught sight of the Carrington Ghoul, their form looming in the dark. A glint of a butcher's blade, pointed directly at them.

They all barreled through a painting that was nothing more than a hidden door, into another dark room.

"Where are we?" Amber whispered, expecting Buffy or Jonesy to answer, but instead, another voice responded.

"That you?" Cam's shaky voice cut through.

They turned and, as their eyes adjusted to the darkness, there he was. Cam was bound to a chair, each limb tied tightly. Blood ran down his face, slowly trickling from his forehead.

"Cam . . ." Jonesy's voice faltered as he clambered to his feet. His first instinct was to try to untie him, and he ran to the chair. His fingers worked fast but Amber knew it wasn't enough. They didn't have the time—

Cam's expression shifted, his eyes suddenly wide with terror. "BEHIND YOU!"

TO BE CONTINUED

serial_queen 20 mins ago

Nice work. But the order is all wrong. The gang knew that Mr. Graham was the killer at this point.

cluesmind24 19 mins ago

The paintings were entrances to the tunnels, is that right? I don't remember hearing about them in the reports I've read. And how many secret passages were there?

serial_queen 16 mins ago

We know there's a secret passage downstairs. There's bound to be more, but yeah . . . not confirmed.

mysterychic 13 mins ago

Please post more! I can't get enough of this.

fallback2841 6 mins ago

If you're going to write something, do some research first. This is riddled with inaccuracies. This forum was created for dedicated fans of *true crime*. Stick to the tv shows.

1

CAM, 2002

"Everyone out!"

I hover at the locker room entrance with one hand on the doorknob, the other rapidly ushering the freshmen out. We're already thirty minutes late because I'm too soft on them. They begged for extra time on the track before tryouts tomorrow, and I caved. I get it, I've been there. But Coach never would've allowed this. I'm almost certain it's against some kind of school policy. As I've discovered since I started working at Sanera High, there is *always* a school policy.

One by one, the kids file out, offering small murmurs and the odd fist bump until the final kid—Dean—stumbles through the door, his backpack hanging on for dear life. The bag is half his size, so no wonder he's struggling. It's clearly too big for him. A quick glance tells me that the bag is most likely a hand-me-down. The stitching on the straps has clear signs of wear, and that's not to mention the fading on the base of the—

I breathe deep. *Observant as ever, Cam.* I do miss using those skills. Memory and recall is my thing—being able to remember key details to connect past clues to present ones. Problem-solving—that was Jonesy's and Amber's strength. And when it came to reading people, Buffy was in a league of her own.

I was always the most patient of the group. I'm even more so now—after all, whether you're solving mysteries or handling teenagers, patience is a vital part of the job.

"You managing there, Dean?" I motion to the mass on his back.

Less than enthusiastically, Dean nods. "It was this or nothing." He readjusts, getting the backpack somewhat under control. His dark hair tumbles into his face, but with both hands occupied, he makes no move to push it aside. "Thanks for letting us stay longer, Mr. Cotton. We needed it."

Mr. Cotton. I laugh at the formality. Like I'm a proper teacher. It makes me feel way older than I am. I was a student here less than five months ago. I had the chance to leave like everyone else—a scholarship and everything—but something about it didn't feel right.

"Please. Cam is fine," I say. "And what's this about *needing* it? You guys are going to kill it tomorrow!"

He smiles. "You *have* to say that. You're a teacher."

"A *teacher* might have to say that." I follow him out, close the door and lock it. "But I am not a teacher, I'm a coaching assistant . . . If you were a lost cause, I would say so."

Dean squints his brown eyes. ". . . Thank you?"

Another kid joins us. Harry. Dean's best friend. His face carries the same nervousness about tomorrow. It's a big day, and at that age, it's everything. I can't blame them.

"Look, guys," I say as we make our way to the exit. "Tryouts can be scary—they *are* scary. No doubt about it. But the more you worry about them, the more those nerves take hold. And trust me, that never ends well."

Dean looks away. "I guess."

Harry nods, though. "He's right, Dean. We've got this."

"That's the attitude! Get plenty of rest tonight. Have a big breakfast in the morning. Eggs, bacon, all of it. Something hearty. Then just go in and give it your best. You've got this."

Oh my God. I *sound* like a teacher.

We reach the parking lot, where Dean's mom is waiting for them both. She's parked at the closest sidewalk with her arms crossed, clearly less than impressed with me as she taps her fingers impatiently on the steering wheel. Her judgmental glare feels like it's burning through me.

I throw up my hand in a halfhearted apology. With one final "thank you," Dean and Harry scurry toward the car. I watch them go.

Teenagers. Who would want to be one?

Sanera is alive as I head home and the town trades sunlight for something more artificial. Warm yellow hues mask the street and guide me on my travels. While my hands may find a home in my pockets, my guard is never down. That's something eight months of mystery-solving taught me. *Expect the unexpected.* I know that all too well.

As I pass through the streets, it doesn't escape me how busy it is. Sanera used to be a ghost town year-round, but even more so once summer faded. But ever since the showdown at Carrington Manor last year, and Rick Field's reporting on the incident, the town's popularity has exploded. True crime enthusiasts, urban legend fanatics, even school history field trips have all come to Sanera. People are flying into the nearest airport, which, let's be honest, isn't exactly close, then driving for hours just to visit the home of the Carrington Ghoul. And that's not to mention the media explosion.

Townsfolk think it's strange, but the stats are undeniable. Sanera's economy is booming. New businesses are opening up, which has been great for the local kids finding their first jobs. A lot of them have been working for Mayor Gomez's latest venture, which opens tomorrow. Sanera Hallowed Fall Fest. A three-day celebration to honor those lost—murdered by the Carrington Ghoul, or, rather, Mr. Graham. According to the mayor's statement, Sanera Hallowed Fall Fest will also raise money and bring "new life" to Sanera. Poor wording, to say the least.

Plenty in town disagreed with the festival. It has only been a year, after all. People are still grieving. But nobody can deny the publicity has rejuvenated the town. I can see that as well, even if I, and many others, think it's too soon. I wouldn't have been offered the assistant coach job if the school hadn't had an uptake in enrollment. For the first time in who knows how long, people are moving *to* Sanera, instead of leaving as soon as they get the chance. It's a double-edged sword.

The library comes into view on my left. A dark figure is hovering near the front door, seemingly fiddling with the lock. My stomach lurches at the sight. The shadow is ominous, hunched low. What are they doing here? The library has been shut since—

Without thinking, my slow pace quickens into a light jog. But as I get closer, it appears my panic was, perhaps, a little premature.

A young Asian woman, probably in her midtwenties, is fumbling with a familiar set of keys. Mrs. Adler always had them on her. You could hear her wherever you went, those jangling keys. So this must be . . .

I clear my throat, making my presence known before I get any closer. Of all people, I know better than to sneak up on someone, especially when it's dark. "Need some help with that?" I call out, trying to sound friendly.

The woman turns to me, and it takes little time for her eyes to widen, but with interest rather than fear. Her dark hair looks like it's been hastily thrown into a ponytail, and her forest-green jacket is only half on. She's clearly leaving in a rush. "Oh my gosh, you're—"

"Yeah." I cut her off, the word coming out a little quicker than I intend. Being recognized by strangers never gets less awkward, so I've learned to speed up the whole process at the start. I know by now that it's easier if I get ahead of their questions, and I slip into the monotonous voice I've grown used to putting on. "Yeah, it's me. Cam. One-fourth of the Sanera Four."

"I'm sorry, I'm sure that gets repetitive. I'm just trying to close . . ." With a large tug, she tries to finish the job. It doesn't work—the keys are still jammed in the lock.

She releases a deep sigh before introducing herself. "I'm Cassie." There's a softness to her features, made even more striking by the warm glow of the streetlamp casting gentle light across her face. It's almost ethereal. "I'm the new librarian, if you couldn't guess. I started today and I cannot get this door to cooperate . . . It's been a day."

"I had guessed as much," I reply. "I have to say that you have some big shoes to fill. Mrs. Adler's passing really hit the town hard."

It was a shock, but at the same time, expected. I'm almost certain Mrs. Adler was the oldest Sanera citizen still living here. Sure, everyone knows everyone in Sanera. But *everyone* knew Mrs. Adler. I'm glad I got to spend some more time with her earlier this year. Our little gang got some phenomenal history lessons. Mrs. Adler was a fixture in this town for so long.

"So I hear!" A tight, unsure smile crosses her face. "I've only just moved to Sanera, so I sadly never got the chance to meet her." She glances at the jumble of keys still poking through the keyhole. "Do you mind?"

"Oh, for sure." I lean forward and yank the key toward me until the clank of a lock sounds. It's easier than I expected. "Maybe you should look into a new lock."

"You might be right." She accepts the keys when I pass them back. "Thank you for your help. Are you coming to the event tomorrow?"

She points at the poster right in front of my eyes, pinned to the library door. I hadn't noticed it before. I blame the light—the poster is almost obscured by shadow. But as I squint, I can make out the image. There he is, arms crossed, digitally placed in front of Carrington Manor, with bold letters beneath him.

RICK FIELD RETURNS TO SANERA
AN INTIMATE AUDIENCE WITH ONE OF THE BOLDEST INVESTIGATIVE REPORTERS WORKING TODAY, RIGHT HERE IN SANERA . . .

As my eyes skip through the text, a mixture of emotions pulses through me. I don't know how I missed this. Mr. Rick Field. So-called investigative reporter. He's always somewhere doing something—as long as it's in his best interests, of course.

"I had no idea he was coming back," I say.

The last I saw of Rick was the day I left the hospital. Word of my discharge had leaked to the press, so it was chaos. And right there, front and center, was Rick Field, shoving an obnoxious microphone in my face. I'd told him to go to hell, but, conveniently, *that* wasn't publicized. He'd done enough damage in Sanera.

He tried to contact us all after that, but we not-so-politely ignored him. After the way he handled the murders—more focused on getting a story than letting people grieve privately—we decided it was best not to associate with him. All the same, *The Carrington Secret* was a bestseller before it was even published.

Cassie nods excitedly. "He's doing an event here to kick off the Hallowed Fall Fest. I think his publisher suggested the bookstore as the location, but Rick insisted the library was the perfect place. So it's been a lot of prep today." She lowers her voice. "He's apparently revealing some *exclusive* information too."

My brows knit at that news—what exclusive information? But there's no point in questioning Cassie about it. She won't know anything. "Rick can be a lot," I say.

"Yeah, tell me about it. I had his PR team emailing me before I even moved here," she says. "Have you read it?"

Cassie is asking me the same question I've been asked countless times for the past two months. Have you read it? The book all about how you *almost died*? The book where the author has made himself a bigger part of the story than he actually was? Well, they don't ask that last one. No one has bothered to fact-check Rick.

"Can't say I have," I say plainly.

We've been asked for *our* side of the story too, of course. But we have yet to divulge the actual truth.

Until now.

In fact, we're doing our first interview only this weekend, a year after everything. Just to set the story straight. Now that Amber, Jonesy, and Buffy are at college, they want a fresh start, but that proves difficult when the public has a million questions and rumors are still circulating. So, when the opportunity arose for an interview this weekend—with a journalist we all agreed on—we made the decision to do it.

I think Cassie senses my aversion to the topic because she stuffs the keys into her pocket and steps back, giving me some space. "Well, thank you again for your help. Feel free to stop by the event, if you want?"

"It was my pleasure," I say, ignoring her invitation. I already know that would be a disaster. The last thing I want to see is Rick Field showboating. "Anyways, nice to meet you. I work up at the school, by the way. And I'm sure our paths will cross again. Sanera is pretty small."

With a tip of her head and a swift goodbye, Cassie heads off downtown. Her dark green jacket soon becomes a blur in the streetlights and then she's gone. She seems like she'll fit right in to Sanera. Friendly, hardworking. Plus, she's young. The mayor will be pleased—he's made it very clear that he wants *young blood* to stay in town, rather than move away at the first chance. It's Sanera's future, he says.

I glance back at the library door and pull on the handle. Definitely locked. Weird that Cassie was struggling with the lock when I pulled the key out so easily.

I'm sure it's nothing, but all the same, I notice a strange feeling in the pit of my stomach.

What with staying late with the freshmen and chatting with Cassie, the evening is slipping away all too fast. I still have to make dinner, call the gang, and check I've got everything together for work tomorrow.

I take a shortcut through the alley by Main Street. Saving a few minutes whenever I can is almost mandatory at this point. If 2001 taught me anything, it's that every minute counts. And time is moving fast—too fast. It's only been two months since I started at the school, but it feels like a lifetime already. It's like my life is slipping right through my fingers. The others have plans—Jonesy and Buffy are at college; Amber is studying nursing. But all I want to do is be with my friends. Investigating cases together, using a different part of my brain, doing something I never thought I'd be good at.

Sure, our investigative agency was short-lived. We never had a case like the ghoul again, nothing as exciting. But it was still *fun*. The feeling of finally cracking something is euphoric. By the summer, though, it seemed that only I felt that way. I was the only one who was still invested. One by one, the others left. A tough pill to swallow.

We're still close, of course, and I can't wait to speak to them tonight and see them—in person—this weekend. Especially Jonesy. Even thinking about him brings a flush to my cheeks and a pang to my heart. Long distance sucks.

The alley is narrow. Aged red brick encases me for at least sixty feet, only disrupted by a dumpster midway down. I've passed through here countless times and, despite how busy Sanera is, this alley always seems to be empty. Almost as if it's visible only to my eyes.

For some reason, my senses become heightened. Every single bone in my body goes cold and my hairs stand on end. Amber taught me many things about horror movies, and a big survival tactic is that you don't go down dark alleys, which applies to real life too. *Don't do it.* So why am I?

I'm too far gone to turn back now, so I speed up. If someone *is* hiding behind the dumpster to murder me, I don't see them because I practically close my eyes and let the wind take me. Gone in a flash. By the time my eyes are fully open again, I'm out on the other side of Main Street. It's quieter down this side. More residential, and most people are tucked away for the evening.

I resist the urge to glance back as I step out of the alley and onto the dimly lit street. A few cars pass by me, their headlights bright beams that momentarily provide a level of comfort. But it's fleeting. I cross the street.

The thought of calling Jonesy, just to keep me company, comes to mind—but I've been learning not to pester him too much. He's living it up at college, in his element. Perhaps not at the frat parties, but definitely in the science lab. Possibly at the cafeteria too, if he's feeling really wild.

I grasp the hard outline of my phone in my pocket but retract my hand. No. Let him live his life. We're all having a call tonight anyway—to discuss the plan for our interview. We're going to have little time to talk properly when they get here. It seems like this weekend is going to be full steam ahead with events and people.

There's one last alley and then I'll be home in two minutes, tops. I stand at the opening, peering down. *I could still go the long way round*, I think, already knowing what my decision is going to be. I never said I was smart.

I set off. My feet are fleet and my eyes are constantly flicking to the things around me, especially behind. It's only now I realize why I'm anxious—the alley reminds me of the passageways at Carrington Manor. Those dreaded passageways. My memories of inside the house are mostly a blur. Perhaps because I was unconscious, or losing blood, for so much of it. I had dreams about it at first, but they've faded for the most part now. The therapy has helped, of course. All our parents paid to get us help. And thank God they did. But I remember the passageways.

Halfway.

And that's when I see it.

I sense it before I fully comprehend what I'm looking at. I skid to a halt. A presence, shadowed but drenched with familiarity. Lights flicker in the alley. Decorative lights for the festival, I presume. They seem to change color every few seconds. The silhouette takes me back to that night in my home, when I was attacked. Jonesy had left. I got that call. And then the security lights fluttered on and off, bathing everything in red.

It's hard to forget your first killer.

The obscured lights turn red, and I'm transported back.

At the end of the alley stands the Carrington Ghoul.

Charred clothing, torn fabric hanging down like rags. Everything in me screams to turn and run. But there's a nagging voice, most likely Amber's influence, reminding me that would be a death wish. *Never turn your back*, I can hear her saying. In a horror movie, this would be the moment when another killer materializes from either side, trapping their victim in the alley. Or sometimes the killer magically teleports (because, let's face it, the writers got lazy).

The ghoul is unmoving, eerily so. Not even a tilt of the head, like Michael Myers. My eyes are drawn to the knife in their hand—Carrington's signature. It's hard to make out clearly, but I'm almost certain there's a dark liquid dripping from the blade, pooling slowly on the ground beneath it. My stomach tightens.

I can't believe I'm back here again. A year on and here I am. I've imagined this, of course. Even though Mr. Graham was dead, I was afraid the ghoul might come back somehow. But then the anniversary passed and I thought we were safe. Or did I? I've seen enough movies to know never to let my guard down fully.

Weirdly, I'm angered more than anything. Terror fills my veins but it's clouded by rage. I'm sick of being scared to walk in my own town, fearing dark alleys.

"Now what?" I yell. The volume of my voice takes me by surprise but I'm not going down with a whimper, not this time.

The ghoul remains motionless.

I've had enough.

I step forward with determination. "I dare you—"

And then they move.

"Oh shit." Instinctively, I jump back. But they don't come closer; they take a step away, putting distance between us. I take another cautious step and they move again, still deeper into shadow.

I swallow. "Screw this." With a newfound courage flooding through me, and without truly thinking it through, I sprint down the alley. The moment I do, the ghoul steps backward into a mass of fog.

I barrel out of the alley, stumbling and landing hard on the sidewalk. I clamber to my feet in an instant, pushing through the pain. My fists go up in defense and—

The ghoul is gone.

My heart is racing, beating a mile a minute, as I cautiously tow myself back to the alley, my eyes unwavering. I barely blink until I reach the opening again. *Where are they?* It's like the ghoul vanished into thin air. I can't see where they would have gone. I have to remind myself that this is real life. People don't just *vanish*. That would be ridiculous. We've been here before and there is absolutely no room for supernatural nonsense.

It's only now that I realize the fog isn't fog at all, but steam billowing from a nearby pipe, forming a perfect veil of smoke, ideal for a swift escape.

I hear a *squelch*. Damnit. I lift one foot and I realize I've stepped right in the blood that was dripping from the blade.

A frown creeps onto my face. "Great," I mutter to myself, knowing I'll have to explain to Sanera's new sheriff how I've managed to tread in evidence.

The pooled liquid refracts the light. I bend down and inspect it more closely.

I'm sure of one thing.

This is not blood.

2

JONESY

"Jonesy, isn't it? Jonesy Shaw?"

Startled, I look up at the origin of the sudden voice. Studying in the one place you're forced to be quiet is the last place I expect a jump scare. Yet here we are.

"Yes?" The face before me isn't a familiar one. Perhaps I've seen him around, but there's only so many faces one can remember at college. I can't even begin to count how many people I've met this semester already. An introvert's worst nightmare. "Have we met?"

A boy stares back at me. Another student, I think, about my age. Long dark hair is greasily plastered to his head, falling flat over his shoulders. He wears a Stanford sweater, zipped all the way to the top—definitely a student, not a stalker. But then again, being a student doesn't necessarily rule out the possibility of stalking. Reports indicate that the average age of stalkers has lowered since the rise of the internet . . . I'm overthinking this.

"No, no," he says. "You don't know me. I just wanted to say how much of a fan I am of you and the rest of the Sanera Four . . ."

As soon as those words leave his lips, my mind blocks out his voice. It's like a defense mechanism at this point. It feels ridiculous to have *fans*. We solved a mystery, sure, but there's no need to make us heroes.

An awkward smile finds its place on my mouth as I nod away while he talks. And talks and talks. I glance back to my work, hoping he'll take the hint, but he doesn't. I've entertained hundreds of these conversations since I enrolled—but finals are calling. Every minute matters.

"So what do you think?"

I snap out of my trance at his query. I blink. "Sorry, what was that?"

The boy chuckles. I still don't even know his name. It's weird. These people seem to know everything about me, and my friends, and my situation, but I know nothing in return. "My media assignment. Can I interview you?"

"Oh." The four of us have had countless interview requests this year and have declined them all—until this weekend. But I've never had to say no to someone's face. It's hard to come up with an excuse. I'm a bad liar as it is. Lying was always more Buffy's area of expertise, and I mean that in the nicest way possible.

Hopeful eyes bore into me.

"I'm sorry" is what comes first, then, "I'm going home tomorrow so I can't—"

"Of course. For Sanera's Hallowed Fall Fest, right?" he interrupts. "That's okay. We can do it when you're back."

What do I even say? Something in me won't let me simply refuse. I have to be nice, and agree, and be approachable all the time. I can't help it. I glance away to try to catch my breath, and hopefully think of an out, when I spot Buffy at the library entrance. I shoot her a pleading look. We've been through this enough now that I think she understands immediately what's going on.

"Oh no," I manage. "My friend is here. I forgot I have a thing." My limbs move fast as I pack away my stuff. "It's a . . . really important thing, sorry."

The guy looks over to the door and spots Buffy for himself. His face lights up. "No way . . . Is that Buffy Allen?"

Shit. "No, no," I insist. I start walking with my bag barely zipped up. "Buffy's hair is, like, way more ginger." When I reach her side, my *fan* following me, I motion to her hair. "This is . . . Daphne."

Buffy raises an eyebrow. "Is her hair really ginger?" she mutters under her breath. I nudge her to play along. She glances at her watch and widens her eyes—like I said, she's always been excellent at lying. "Jonesy, have you seen the time? We *really* have to go."

"You're right," I say, before nodding to the would-be

interviewer/assailant. "Come find me another time!" I raise my hand as a gesture of good faith, knowing with absolute certainty I will try to avoid him.

The boy opens his mouth to protest, but we're gone before he can pin us down. If it weren't for Buffy, I would've unwillingly agreed to a three-part special. And I *would* like to help another student. But I dread the idea of being blindsided by questions I don't want to answer.

That's why we agreed to the interview this weekend—because we get control of it all. The internet is a wild place and there are plenty of people right now falsifying what *really* happened. Rick Field included. But this weekend we get to set the story straight.

"Was that your second weirdo of the week?" Buffy asks as we step outside into the night that's only now creeping in. The sky is just darkening, so I presume it's around six. I lose track of time when I'm at the library. A whole afternoon, it seems.

This is what most days have been like since I started, and honestly, I don't hate it. College, I mean. The freedom feels like a breath of fresh air, even if my mom is on my mind multiple times a day. I remind myself that she's an adult, that kids aren't supposed to worry about their parents. But how can I not? She hadn't been sober that long when I left. She always reassures me that she's fine, but can I be sure? I've seen horror stories;

I've seen TV shows. I'm obviously going to worry.

And then there's Cam. It's clear, as much as he tries to dance around the topic, that he's unhappy in Sanera, but all I can do is encourage him to follow his heart. The problem is, he doesn't quite know what his heart wants yet.

"Third," I correct her. "Why do they not get you?"

Buffy guffaws. "Oh, they do. But I tell them where to go." She says this with impressive nonchalance. When Buffy first joined Sanera High, she was cautious after what happened at her last school. She was afraid to be herself. But that seems to have gone out the window. And honestly, good for her.

"We're here to learn, not to relive the past." Buffy looks upward. The trees have lost a lot of their leaves. "We're just like trees, you know?"

"Old and slightly rotting?"

"That was such a Cam answer," she says, running her hands through her fair hair, the loose curls gently wrapping around her fingertips. When her hair falls back down over her shoulders, she continues. "Trees shed their leaves and grow new ones. But the tree trunk, the heart of the tree, stays true. That's like us."

My brows rise. Color me impressed. "That was quite profound."

"Is it that obvious that I just had a philosophy lecture?" Buffy asks. We laugh together as we head toward the dorms, discussing our day. It's nice to have human contact. My roommate is lovely, but our schedules are way out of sync and we rarely get any time to talk, let alone grow close. And Buffy and I have been through something together—we're bonded now. We're unlikely friends, but it works.

After a while, Buffy eventually asks the inevitable. "Are you nervous about this weekend? Going back, I mean."

My stomach sinks. The thought of returning to Sanera isn't scary—Mr. Graham is dead and so is the Carrington Ghoul. But the people who are visiting for Hallowed Fall Fest might well be. This festival is bound to attract some . . . interesting personalities. People who are obsessed with this deadly case. I understand that morbid curiosity is a natural instinct—I've read my fair share of true crime books. But when your own life *becomes* a true crime story, it stops feeling like a harmless intrigue.

"I am cautiously pessimistic," I say.

"That is so not a phrase."

"It is now. How are *you* feeling about the weekend?"

"Eh," Buffy says. "I'm ready to see my mom. It feels like forever. And I think *she's* excited to meet Patrick."

I smile. The way Buffy says her boyfriend's name is telling. Her syllables get lighter and her eyes practically beam at the sound of his name on her lips. The honeymoon stage if I've ever seen one.

"So he's meeting your mom. Big step. How long's it been? Two months?"

She nods. "Wild . . . A first-day romance was not in the cards for me at all."

Wild, indeed. A bunch of kids run past us, faces painted the red and green of Stanford's logo—they've clearly been at the game. They're also clearly as high as a cloud on something.

"Want to get something to eat before we call the others?" Buffy asks. "Patrick's visiting his parents, so it's just me and you."

"Sure." I smile. I really like Patrick, and I like seeing Buffy happy even more. But I'm glad he won't be around for the call. This weekend is just about us. Anyone else won't understand and will only complicate things. And I've had enough of complicated.

The sun has long set by the time we get back to my dorm. Our call is a late one because Amber doesn't finish class until seven—that's nursing for you.

We step inside my dorm room and Buffy flicks on the light. The room comes into focus, with all its familiar clutter.

It's almost comical how divided the room is. My side is definitely more lived in than my roommate's. Like Amber, Tommy is taking a bunch of medical classes, which means he spends most of his time in the library. Probably even more than I do. When I'm not there, the science lab is my second home, something that's obvious from the stack of research papers piled high next to my bed. Alongside it, my wall is covered in Polaroids and stickers, little pieces of my life scattered haphazardly.

I sit down on my bed, and my eyes land on a photo of the four of us that I tacked up. Buffy, Amber, Cam, and me. *The Sanera Four.* It's from this summer, right before we all went our separate ways. We did a big road trip around California as one last hurrah. Without thinking, I reach out, my fingers brushing over Cam's face. His head rests against mine in the picture. He's always been taller than me. Just slightly.

Something lands in my lap with a thud. A pizza box. Leftovers.

"Stop reminiscing," Buffy says with a short laugh. Then she jumps onto the bed, right next to me, settling in quickly before snatching the box back from my hands.

"Am I not allowed to remember the good old days?"

Buffy looks up from the box that she's already cracked open. Below, half a vegetable pizza sits, the melted cheese starting to solidify again. Still, my appetite returns.

"The good old days being"—she pauses for dramatic effect—"two months ago?"

I scoff, half laughing myself. "Just eat your damn food."

Sure, maybe it's a little too soon to be reminiscing, but it feels like a lifetime since I've seen the gang face-to-face. Going from spending every day with your favorite people to not seeing them at all . . . it's a weird adjustment.

Eventually, it's time to make the call. God, I don't know what we'd do without the landline in here. The pizza is mostly gone, except for the crusts that Buffy has left behind, and I'm completely stuffed.

"Hello?" Amber speaks first. There's a noticeable tiredness in her voice, which doesn't surprise me at all. She spends more time working than I do, always pushing herself past exhaustion. I can imagine she's tucked into bed already.

I dial in Cam, and he elongates his greeting. "Yo! Yooooo!"

Buffy and I greet the others in unison as we lie stomach down on my bed.

"What's new with everyone?" Cam asks. That question is always the first thing out of his mouth. Forever wanting to know about our days, about college, but he won't divulge his own without a push. Like I say, I worry about him. And today, there's a quiver to his voice. I wonder why.

"Well, I saved Jonesy from a fan." Buffy nudges me and giggles.

"Another one?" Amber says.

"I can't help that I'm approachable," I reply, throwing my hands up, as if any of them can see. "I have a friendly face, I don't know."

"You're too kind for your own good, Jones," Cam

adds, which makes my lips curl upward. I feel lighter whenever he speaks. There's hours between us, but hearing him talk transports me home.

Once Cam got out of the hospital, we wasted not a single moment making up for all the lost time. We saw each other almost every day and now it's phone calls only. It's weird.

I sigh. "I just don't want to be rude. You know?"

"We know, babe."

There go my cheeks now. Hot and flushed. Warm to the touch.

"All right," Buffy interrupts. "Amber! How is being a nurse?"

"Being a nursing *student* is great," Amber corrects her. "Lots of studying, so it's been hectic. But I'm excited for a break this weekend."

"You deserve it," I say. "Speaking of, do we still want to discuss . . ." I don't even finish my sentence because the others know what I'm referring to. It's the whole reason we're talking tonight. Our upcoming, first-ever interview. "Thoughts on how we handle it?"

There's a moment of silence before Cam chimes in. "I guess there are some things we might . . . *not* mention."

"Like the *treasure*," Amber says.

"Exactly," Cam replies. "You bring up the mysterious treasure hoard that might still be buried somewhere at Carrington Manor and then there will be more think pieces on us than there were before. We're trying to shut down rumors, not make more."

He puts it the best. Some of the stories circulating are completely ridiculous and untrue. I even saw one claim suggesting that we orchestrated the entire situation, framing Mr. Graham as a ploy to steal the treasure for ourselves. *News flash, we don't know where the treasure is.* There are probably plenty of other wild theories out there too.

Rick Field hasn't helped matters either. In fact, his book made everything worse. I haven't read it, but from the publicity you'd think not only was he one of the ghoul's intended victims (untrue) but that he was the one who tipped us off to return to Carrington Manor (also untrue).

"I think I should talk the least," I admit, mostly as a joke, but there's some truth to it. With the questions and all the attention, I'm unsure how I'll cope.

"You'll do amazing, Jones," Cam says. "As always." I can almost see his face as the words leave his mouth. That's partly the reason I agreed to the interview. It's a chance to see Cam. It will be my first time seeing him in two months and I can't wait. I'd say that I'm beginning to forget what he looks like, but that's not true at all. It's hard to forget his crystal-blue eyes.

Amber moves on. "Are you sure this journalist is decent? What was her name again?"

"Juliet Lopez," I say. "And yeah, I think so. She's an

independent reporter so hopefully will have less of a corporate MO. And she's written some really interesting investigative pieces for major newspapers. Didn't any of you read the attachments I sent?"

"Nope," Buffy says. "I'm sure she's great though."

I sigh. I'm praying this interview goes well. Plus, the mayor wants to put us on the front cover of the *Sanera Daily*. He's insistent. Juliet must have gone to him for a quote, and he jumped the gun. None of us told him we were finally sitting down with a reporter.

"I hope we're doing the right thing," Amber says. "What if we mess up the details? Make the rumors even worse?"

She's got a point. But people are already talking. At least if we play our cards right, we'll be able to get the story straight. With Juliet, we have some insight into the kind of things she plans to ask. She sent over a bunch of sample questions, and they look straightforward enough. How we ended up tangled in this mess in the first place, why we chose to go to Carrington Manor alone to rescue Cam. That's all fair game. But we've also made it abundantly clear that we won't be delving into any traumatic or sensationalized conspiracy theories. She's assured us she wants the truth and that's all.

We chat more about the interview, going over our stories and making sure we're all on the same page. After everything we've been through, and the therapy since, some details have inevitably become blurred. For the better, mostly. If we don't want to talk about something, we'll say so and back each other up.

Eventually, we agree to call it a night. After all, we have a long day of travel ahead of us tomorrow.

Amber signs off first, and Buffy follows soon after, heading to bed early, and leaving just Cam and me on the call. Our group get-togethers normally end like this.

We chat a bit longer, but I have a strange feeling. Cam seems fine, laughing even, but there's something off, I'm sure of it.

"Cam, I feel like something might be wrong," I say at last, picking my words carefully. "With you."

"Why do you say that?" His response is quick, his tone almost too casual.

I let a pause settle between us, just long enough to make a point. "Cam." I say his name firmly, leaving space for him to fill. He doesn't. "I know when you're hiding something. You can try to act as normal as you want, but I know."

Silence. I wonder if he's been lonely. Making new friends after school isn't exactly easy. Not that he needs new friends because we're still here. But we're not in Sanera anymore. Sometimes, you need someone to talk to face-to-face, not as a voice coming through a phone.

"Is it weird with everyone gone?" I ask. "Have you tried to meet anyone outside of work? Even if it's just for a coffee—"

"It's not that." He sighs. "You won't believe me."

His voice sounds low, almost defeated, like he's already convinced himself.

That immediately sets off alarm bells. Cam isn't the dramatic type. He's normally the one to downplay a situation with wisecracks. Something's up. "I'll believe you. I promise."

Cam hesitates. "I saw—" He stops himself. I can just imagine him shaking his head. "I . . . I was walking home from the school, taking a shortcut through the alleys . . . and when I looked up, there was . . ."

His voice trails off. I notice his breathing has quickened, grown unsteady.

"What did you see, Cam?"

"The ghoul," he says. "The Carrington Ghoul."

I lean forward, my body practically hanging off the bed, and grip my phone hard. Am I hearing him right? Because Mr. Graham is dead.

"Are you sure?"

It doesn't make sense. Theories roll through my mind. Sanera is a busy place nowadays, especially with the festival this weekend. It must be someone dressed up for the festival. Tastelessness has never stopped anyone. It's 2002, after all. The world has seen more bizarre things.

"I know what I saw, Jones." Cam's voice comes out more certain now, a little more agitated. "I chased them down the alley, but by the time I got to the road they had disappeared. Vanished into thin air."

"You chased after them? Cam, why the hell would you do that?" I shouldn't shout but it's hard not to when I'm already worried about him. I don't need him chasing down potential bad guys as well.

"I was angry!"

"So you decided to chase after a—"

"I said I was angry, not smart!" Cam says indignantly. "I've only just stopped checking under my bed every night, so sorry if I was not being logical . . ." he murmurs. "It doesn't matter. It was just some bozo trying to be funny."

"How do you know?"

"The ghoul was holding a knife dripping with something. Blood was my first thought, of course, but it looked more like paint." He sighs. "It's pretty weird in Sanera right now. All the horror fans descending. Rick Field doing his tour . . ."

There's a tired note in his voice. He's fed up. I wish I could wrap him in my arms and tell him it'll be okay. But I don't even know if that's true. Someone in Sanera, dressed as the Carrington Ghoul. A whole festival to commemorate the events of last year. Journalists. Tourists. And at the center of it is us—the Sanera Four.

Fair game.

3

CAM

The paint stain is gone.

It's the day after I saw the ghoul and, against my better judgment, I decide to pass back through the alley. There's a couple of kids making their way to school, taking the same shortcut, and I feel a lot better about doing so. But I can't stop thinking about the vanishing stain. Did the rain wash it away? Surely it would've left some residue or remnants of its presence. *Unless it wasn't real to begin with.*

"Stop it, Cam," I mumble to myself. But maybe I *am* seeing things. Given everything we went through, and now losing my support system, it's possible.

No, I think. *I know what I saw.*

My feet take me to Sanera Coffee Co. I'm here most mornings because the long school day calls for caffeine. And today is the first day of the Hallowed Fall Fest—which is going to bring with it some challenging reminders.

The ever-so-familiar bell rings as I step into the café and a few heads turn to me. I get the odd wave too, but I'm old news now. I'm sure it would be different if the entire gang was here but the customers and staff see me every day—shit gets boring after a while.

"Same as usual?" Kelly asks me from behind the counter. She's dyed her hair since yesterday. It's bright red, almost the color of a fire truck. The bold hue stands out sharply against her fair skin and freckles. Her eyes narrow when I don't respond right away, and her hand reaches for her head. "Oh no, is it bad?"

"No!" I quickly say. "It's great. Bold. I like it."

"Bold," she repeats. "Just what every girl wants to hear."

"I didn't mean it like—"

"I'm messing with you." She heartily guffaws as she starts scribbling on an empty cup. "Dyeing it this color and *not* expecting it to be bold would be kinda stupid of me . . . Same as usual?"

"Please."

She's already pushing the cup over to the barista, knowing what I'd want. I think I've only ever gotten the same drink. "Are you looking forward to this weekend? Hallowed Schmallowed Whatever Fest?"

A perplexed shrug is my first reaction. "Are *you*?"

Kelly shrugs back at me. I had that coming. "I mean, I guess so. Horror isn't exactly my forte and it's a bit weird, right? Celebrating *murder*?" Then her eyes light up. "The Séance Sisters are playing tomorrow night though, and they're gnarly. So I'll probably go see them—solo, it looks like. I wanted my mom to come with me but apparently duty calls."

"The Séance Sisters?"

Kelly shakes her head. "I don't know what rock you've been living under but they're a great local band and they're getting pretty well-known too. You should catch them at the festival."

"Yeah, I'll have to check them out," I reply. "I'll see if the rest of the gang wants to go." Then I add impulsively, "Hey, if we make it, come hang with us. If you want to, I mean."

I've known Kelly for a few months now and we've never spoken outside our morning interactions. But I've been telling myself, and Jonesy has been too, that I need to make new friends. Now seems as good a time as any.

Kelly's expression is surprised, but a smile percolates beneath it. "Are you sure? Your friends don't know me."

"Nobody knows anyone when they're born—and babies make friends just fine . . ." My words trickle out into an awkward silence. It sounded better in my head. Maybe I'm losing my humor. *Great.* I'm seeing things and becoming an unfunny hermit. I guess I'll just waste away. Without my regular bubble around me, I'm getting rusty at the only thing I'm good at.

But Kelly is grinning. "Babies making friends? That was an awful analogy."

My name gets called at the end of the counter, which pulls my attention away. I go to grab my drink, nod my thanks, and turn my attention back to Kelly. "I will look out for the bright red head in the crowd."

She smiles, giving me a little wave. "Have a good day, Cam."

I wave back at her, a similar smile on my face. A good start to the day—for once. For a brief moment, I don't think about this weekend, or reliving the past in the interview. But as soon as the crisp outside air hits my face, I hear someone calling my name and it all comes rushing back.

"Cameron Cotton."

I don't even need to turn around to recognize the voice.

". . . Is that you?"

I turn. When my gaze meets Rick Field's, it's accompanied by a forced smile, one that I know doesn't quite reach my eyes. This man is a fraud and I despise him. But I am not the type of person to lash out at someone on the spot—even if they've decided to profit from my almost-death. I'm too restrained for my own good . . .

unless my friends are involved. Then it's a different story.

"Rick," I say flatly. "How are you doing?"

"Not bad. Strange being here for the festival, of course—when we've been through what we have, horror movies aren't exactly a joke." The words roll off his lips like butter. No hesitation. No acknowledgment that I know the truth. Mr. Graham never targeted Rick. It's as if he's lied so much over the past year that the line between fiction and reality has completely blurred. He doesn't know what's real or not anymore.

He goes on. "So glad I could catch you today, Cameron."

Oh, here we go. He wants something—of course he does. "What do you want, Rick?"

"Right." He nervously laughs. "I'm sure you're aware but my final book tour stop is tonight at the library. The opening event of the festival, no less." He gives a modest laugh. "We'd love to have you there. A fellow survivor of the ghoul. And, well, it'd look great for the press."

And there it is. Exactly what I expected. "Rick—"

"You don't need to answer now," he interrupts. He digs through his satchel and pulls out a thick wad of business cards. Carefully, he selects one and it soon finds a place in my back pocket.

"Call me if you have any questions, but we'd love to see you there. *All* of you. I heard the rest of the Sanera

Four are coming back too, so the invitation is open to everyone."

There's something in his voice that makes me pause. Desperation. *He needs this*, I think. But why? The Sanera Four back together and endorsing *The Carrington Secret*? That would generate some headlines, sure. But his book has already gotten plenty of attention. From what I've heard, sales are great too. So why does he want us there so badly?

"We'll think about it," I lie.

I nod as kids pass the finish line while I note their completion time. Running a straight mile can be tricky if you're not trained. I cracked five minutes last year but that took years of practice. And I must admit, I much prefer being a spectator now. My scars aren't too forgiving.

Dean passes the finish line with a time of six minutes and twelve seconds. Extremely impressive for his age. As soon as he catches his breath, he looks over to me and Coach with an uncertain expression and I give him a reassuring smile. He beams proudly, running back to the locker room with a skip to his step.

The rest of the kids finish their mile. Most of them will make the team, though the stragglers will have to find somewhere else to spend their spare time. Something tells me they won't be too bummed though. Lots of kids sign up and then never show. I frown down at my clipboard. There's only one missing today. Harry. Harry

Lanz. Which is weird, now that I think about it; I remember him and Dean raring to go yesterday. He must've had a change of heart. If there's one trait that seems universal among teenagers, it's indecisiveness.

I consider mentioning Harry's absence to Coach, but he's too busy backslapping and high-fiving. So I swallow the thought and head to the locker room.

Maybe Harry just decided track isn't for him. I only stumbled into it myself and then was surprisingly good at it. Mom was so proud, which made it even harder to quit. My whole life seems like that. One thing leading to another, never entirely by choice. And now, here I am, stuck in high school, stuck in Sanera . . .

"Mr. Cotton!" Dean's voice calls out for me as soon as I close the locker room door behind me. He's already showered and changed. His dark hair is wet and plastered to his skull but I don't think he could care less. He's on a high. "I think I can go faster. I think—"

"Whoa," I interrupt. A chuckle escapes me. "That was fast enough for now. It's good you have something to aim for. Really impressive today, Dean. I told you it would go well."

"Thanks, Mr. Cotton."

"That goes for all of you." I raise my voice and direct it outward, to everyone. A bunch of needy eyes bore into me. Not intimidating at all. "You should be proud of how you did today. Good job, guys."

"Cam's right," Coach says, joining us, a pair of glasses teetering on the bridge of his nose. He only ever wears them when he's looking at paperwork, so he must be reviewing the times already. "Some of the best tryouts we've ever seen. We'll let you all know who's made the cut next week."

The room descends into a cacophony of teenage noise. If I wasn't used to the locker room volume, I think I'd have gone deaf. I swear the sound bounces back ten times harder on the tiled walls.

"Enjoy the festival, Dean."

"You too, Mr. Cotton!"

Dean heads out the door, but something nags at me. I call after him. "Hey, Dean."

He turns on his heel. "Yeah?"

I glance at the clipboard of names in my hand. "You haven't seen Harry, have you? He was supposed to be here."

Dean frowns slightly. "He forgot his sneakers, so ran home earlier. But I haven't seen him since. I assumed he got sick or something. He was more excited than me."

A flicker of unease washes over me. I nod, though, masking it with a smile. "All right. Thanks, Dean."

He gives a quick wave and heads off. Soon enough, more and more freshmen trickle out of the locker room until it's just me and Coach. The fog-like mist from the showers still hasn't dwindled and I can't lie, not being able to see the other side of the locker room totally creeps me out. The steam is almost opaque.

"I'm gonna head out," I say to Coach, who is stacking paperwork.

"Hold on a minute, will you, Cam?" he says. "I need to speak with you."

"All right." I glance at the steam again and shiver, thinking of the alley. "I'll wait outside."

As soon as I step out of the locker room, I'm hit by the sight of hundreds of kids, all in costume. It's between classes so that's not surprising, but the costumes are. Halloween isn't until next week but this damned festival has got the town acting like the holiday has come a week early.

Halloween always used to be my favorite, but the events of October 2001 have soured my perception. I'm sorry, but seeing a severed arm, even if it is fake, isn't funny to me now.

While I wait for Coach, I tune in to multiple passing conversations. They're brief but mostly all about the festival.

"What are you wearing?"

"I'm so excited for the Séance Sisters."

"I'll meet you at the diner."

The crowd slows to a standstill—hallway traffic is a real thing—and one particular conversation sticks out more than the rest.

"I haven't seen him," a Michael Myers says beside me.

A DIY Pinhead replies. "He's probably just . . ." His voice tails in and out. The occasional shout makes it stupidly hard to hear. I squint my eyes as if it'll help me hear the muffled words. "I'll text . . ."

"I've tried and nothing. He was . . ." Damnit. ". . . at practice yesterday. He was . . ."

At practice yesterday. Instantly, my mind goes to Harry. It's most likely a coincidence. But my mystery senses are tingling. Despite my better judgment, I turn to the kids to ask more, when the crowd seemingly comes alive. Like a wave, it crashes forward, nearly taking me off my feet. It turns out I wasn't safe by the locker room doors. And the kids are now too far ahead to hear me. *Shit.*

As fast as I possibly can, I weave through the multitude of horror characters after them, narrowly avoiding a faceplant into the back of a Nosferatu. I make it halfway down the hall before I lose them around a corner.

"What happened to waiting for me?"

It's Coach. He's strolling easily now that the crowd has dispersed.

"Sorry, got caught in the wave," I say.

Coach gives me a sharp look. After a beat, he reaches out and takes my arm, his grip firm but not unkind. Without a word, he guides me to the side, away from the others, creating a small pocket of space out of earshot.

"Cam, I've been a bit worried about you lately. That's

what I wanted to talk to you about. You seem quiet, preoccupied. Is this about the festival?"

"Oh..." I shift from foot to foot. "No. I mean, it's a bit weird, but it's okay. *I'm* okay, I mean."

"You don't *have* to be okay."

I frown. "What's that supposed to mean?"

"C'mon, Cam... what you went through wasn't fair. You're a kid, for God's sake."

Not this again. I thought I was over all this promising I'm all right stuff. I know he means well, but hearing it over and over for the past year takes its toll. "Really. I'm fine."

Coach narrows his eyes. "Are you sure? You look pale. Cam, I know there's a lot of—"

"I'm fine," I interrupt. I end up laughing through all the nervous energy. "I just thought I heard..."

I freeze in my tracks. I can't even finish my sentence. Through the crowd, at the foot of the stairs, within the hustle and bustle, is an awfully familiar figure. Not again. Is this someone's idea of a joke?

The Carrington Ghoul, looking right at me.

"Cam?" I hear Coach's voice as though it's underwater. "Cam, what's wrong?"

The figure stares in my direction, unmoving, just like last night in the alley.

Are they a student? Is this their idea of a sick joke? Or could it—

The second bell rings.

The hallway erupts into even more chaos and I try to keep my eye on the figure. I find myself on my tiptoes, occasionally catching glimpses of a burnt scarf, but when the crowds die down my stomach lurches. Gone.

"What the . . ."

I turn back to Coach, whose face is a mass of confusion. "Cam, what's going on?"

"Did you not see that?" I ask.

"See what?" Coach says with a shrug and knitted brows. He looks over now, but it's too late. There's nothing there. Only an empty space, haunted by the memory of what I saw.

I stare at the hallway, as if the ghoul will magically reappear before me. Or did I imagine it? Coach never saw them. And no one but me saw the ghoul in the alley . . .

"Hey," says Coach more gently. "I've got this last period free. Let's go back to the locker room for a minute—"

"No, I—I just realized I left something in the teachers' lounge," I lie. I need to get away. The gang will be here soon. Thank goodness. They'll be able to make sense of this. They always do.

Prank or not, I've spotted the Carrington Ghoul twice. And that's not something I'm going to take lightly.

4

BUFFY

Sanera is exactly as I remember, albeit quite a few degrees colder than what I'm used to. It's normally just the right amount of warm, but now there's a light wind. The drive was long—four hours or so—but at least it wasn't me behind the wheel. Patrick gallantly offered to drive the whole way and I wasn't going to say no. That, plus Jonesy said he didn't trust me. I've only had *one* fender bender.

But I think Jonesy knew Patrick would pick us up bearing gifts—evidence being the empty wrapper where the breakfast bagel used to be. Patrick's thoughtful like that. Always picking up the tab. Helps that his family's totally loaded. So much so, he flat-out refused to let us pay for gas—not even for a drive that required a multi soundtrack and snack rotation.

I glance at Patrick now, who's taking in the scenery,

his eyes curious. His black curls peep under the red baseball cap perched on his head. A large *S* for Stanford is emblazoned on the front in the largest font possible. He might be dressed like a total jock, but his oversized glasses at least soften the look, hinting that he's really a nerd at heart. That's what drew me to Patrick in the first place. He's different.

Patrick took me a while to figure out. He's got the easygoing charm of a jock, but there's also a warmth to him. A sincerity. The kind that comes from someone who can get easily lost in a stack of comics or a movie marathon. He doesn't care if it's seen as nerdy. It's one of the things I admire most about him.

He isn't your classic prep school rich boy—although he's all those things. Patrick is dorky and sweet and generous and shy and . . . well, let's just say I've got it bad.

He catches me looking and grins. "What?"

"You're dressed like a walking ad for Stanford," I tell him.

"Hey, what's wrong with a little school pride? Besides, it's comfortable." He beams, then unleashes the biggest yawn known to man. "What about you?"

I feel a little bad. He's tired, I can see it in his eyes. He didn't get enough sleep. His family lives closer to Sanera than Stanford, so he doubled back just to pick us up. But, of course, he wouldn't take no for an answer, and we set off basically the moment he arrived.

I glance down at my branded Stanford crewneck. "Oh yeah. I'm a hypocrite."

"A beautiful hypocrite," he says. He frowns at the road. "This it?"

"Yep. The second one to the right," I say as we turn into my street.

The car radio blares "Goodbye to You" by Michelle Branch—*ironically*, I think, since here I am returning to Sanera. But, still, I catch myself nodding along as the wind tousles my hair. Pure music video magic.

We pull up outside my house. We dropped Jonesy just down the street so he could see his mom as soon as possible. And Macey, of course. He has not shut up about that gorgeous bundle of joy all semester.

As I stare out at my neat front yard, a weird feeling strikes. Here I am again. Like I never left.

I turn to Patrick, who's seemingly analyzing every single detail of the house, his eyes scanning back and forth, from window to window, brick to brick.

"So?" I ask. "What do you think?"

He shrugs. "It's bigger than I expected."

Not the answer I was anticipating. The house isn't small by any means, but it's not exactly the *Home Alone* mansion. "What were you expecting?" I tease. "A shack?"

Patrick rolls his eyes. "You said Sanera was a small town!" he says. "I didn't know *what* to expect."

I sigh. Patrick would rather die than show off about his

background, but it slips out all the same. Because he's *always* lived in a mansion. A real *Home Alone* mansion, in fact. I've seen it in person—I almost cried. He doesn't mean to be insensitive. He just seems vaguely surprised that not everyone has a massive yard, eight bedrooms, and a yacht.

"Are you sure you'll be okay in the hotel this weekend?" I ask. I knew Mom wouldn't want him staying here. And Patrick booked a hotel without asking. Which is nice of him.

"Of course," he says, squeezing my hand.

From the corner of my eye, I see the front door open. I texted Mom that we were nearly there when we dropped Jonesy off; knowing her, she's been at the window waiting like a vulture, ready to assess my newish boyfriend. She's very protective of me. For good reason, I know, after what happened last year. I had a tough time convincing her to let me move across the state. The only way I managed to sway her was scheduling phone calls every other day. I know Amber was in a similar situation with her parents.

But when I forgot one of our Sunday night catch-ups, I didn't hear the end of it for two weeks. Never again.

"Okay," I say, turning to Patrick with a slight smile. "This is it. The moment of truth." There's a hint of mischief in my voice, but I'm serious too because I want this to go well. It's the first time I've ever brought someone home. "Don't say anything stupid," I warn him.

"Hey! What's that supposed to mean? You think I'm stupid?"

"No, I don't mean that!" I say as I catch a smirk cresting on his lips. He's messing with me, I know it—Patrick is one of the top students in his class—but I still flap my hands, searching out the right words to say. This is all new territory. Sure, it's only been two months with Patrick, but considering the amount of time we've spent together, it feels a lot longer. Spending every day with someone will do that. And I don't want Mom to take one look at his preppy exterior and get the wrong impression. She won't be impressed by stories of yachts and country clubs and vacations—the opposite, if anything.

"I want her to like you," I finally say softly. My finger gently brushes a stray lock of hair from in front of his glasses, making sure he knows I'm serious. I want him to see me clearly, and for me to see him too. "You're the first guy in a while I haven't hated, you know?"

"Wow, I'm touched," he replies. Then his voice softens. "I don't hate you too, Buffy. A lot."

I feel my cheeks flush, but I'm still aware that Mom's staring at us. So I compose myself. "Seriously. She's going to love you, so be yourself, but also . . . beware."

Before he can ask for clarification, I open the car door. Mom is now standing at the front of the house, practically wriggling with impatience. I forget Patrick as I sprint into her arms. Warmth embraces me and I can't help but sigh with relief. I knew I missed my mom, but I didn't realize *how* much. Spending eighteen years under the same roof and then suddenly never seeing her takes its toll. I think I've been so busy that it's distracted me. Until now. A tear forms and I let it fall.

"Oh, honey, I've missed you so much," Mom says under her breath.

My cheek is crammed into her shoulder and I've never been as comfortable with discomfort in my life. "I've missed you too." The smell of sandalwood and vanilla blankets my senses. I don't want to move. But then I remember—

"And you must be Patrick." Mom kisses me on the forehead before pulling away to greet him. "I've heard a lot about you."

Patrick steps forward, offering his hand in greeting. He looks slightly nervous but his voice is clear and confident. "It's lovely to meet you, Mrs. Allen."

She takes his hand in hers, shaking it tightly. When they part, she turns to me with an impressed look on her face. It seems Patrick knows how to shake a hand.

"I hope you're letting my daughter study," she says sternly.

"Mom!"

"I sure am, Mrs. Allen," Patrick says firmly. I'm almost certain his voice is deeper than normal. "Buffy is super focused on her work. As am I."

"Mm-hmm." Mom makes an enigmatic noise. "Well, you kids come inside. I'll make us some tea."

I turn back to go grab my bags but I'm stopped by Patrick. "I'll get these," he says with a nod, followed by a quick blown kiss. "You go on in." He winks. "I want to impress your mom, don't I?"

My lips upturn. I kiss his cheek quickly and he goes pink.

"He's not what I expected," Mom whispers as we go inside and walk down the hallway.

"In what way?" I ask.

"I just thought he'd be taller."

"He's five foot ten."

"Yeah, and I'm Pamela Anderson."

"Mom, can you please be—"

Before I can finish, Patrick hobbles into the house, his arms weighed down by my, I admit, excessive luggage. His face is strained as he pauses just inside the doorway, adjusting his grip on the handles. "Er, shall I take these upstairs or . . ."

"Leave them there," Mom says, fighting to keep a straight face. "I don't want you to pull a muscle." He exhales and lets the bags fall to the floor with an audible thud. His shoulders relax, and for the first time since stepping inside, he gives himself a moment to take in his surroundings. His gaze drifts from the living room to the staircase, then he peeks down the hall into the kitchen.

"You have a lovely home, Mrs. Allen," he says politely. His eyes land on a photo of me in my prom dress, taken earlier this year. It feels like a lifetime ago already. So much has happened since then.

It *is* a lovely home. Warm, cozy, simple. As I follow his gaze, I spot subtle differences from before I left. The odd photo placement, new coasters, very minor additions. But still . . . it's different. Most people wouldn't clock them, but to me, they stick out like a sore thumb.

Mom is the one to break the silence. "Let's get you kids something to drink. I'm sure you're exhausted after the drive."

Patrick follows her down the hallway. "That sounds great, Mrs. Allen."

In the kitchen, I notice more change. Mom has completely gutted the old tiles and replaced them with a dark green mosaic.

"Well, this is new," I say. To be fair, the old tiles were outdated—they were the one thing she wanted to change when we moved. But then a serial killer came to town and we almost died. Life got busy, in other words. I take a seat at the kitchen table, closely followed by Patrick.

Mom smiles as she opens the fridge to reveal a large pitcher of iced tea. "I got bored with you being gone and all."

"I like it," I admit.

Patrick chimes in. "It looks great."

"Thank you." She grabs cups and pours him a hearty measure. "Where are you originally from, Patrick?"

"A little town called Shiverville," he replies. "You may have heard of it? We're actually only about an hour west."

"I think I might have," Mom says, passing me a glass. "Is it the town that goes all out for—"

"Halloween?" Patrick finishes for her. Then he nods. "It's a big thing. Pretty sure that's where it got its name."

Mom chuckles. "Go figure . . . So, what does your family do for work?" she asks, like she hasn't already grilled me about it.

"My parents own a home security company," Patrick replies. "Oh, and my older sister is a makeup artist. She helps out with the parades—does the kids' makeup and everything."

Mom pours her own tea. "Wow, quite a contrast there. Do you plan on doing that too?"

Patrick nods with a straight face. "Yeah, I practice my eyeliner on Buffy all the time."

His joke lands perfectly, making both Mom and me laugh. I'm relieved to see him loosening up and letting his personality shine through.

He sips the cold beverage before continuing.

"But for real, I don't know," he says, pausing for a moment. "My parents have always made it clear I should follow my own path, you know? So I'm just enjoying college life right now. Studying. Hanging with friends, movies. Although I can't usually persuade Buffy to come with me."

It's my turn to laugh now, shaking my head. "Patrick's a horror fiend and I've had enough horror in my real life. I don't need to go sit in a dark theater for two hours to be traumatized for *fun*."

Patrick grins. "Which is why I took you to see *Spy Kids 2* instead of *The Ring*."

"Such a gentleman," I say sarcastically.

My eyes meet Mom's and they're warm. There's a small smile on her lips.

"Well," she says as she swirls the ice in her glass. "It sounds like you two are really getting along."

"We really are." Patrick squeezes my leg under the table. A small gesture that says a thousand words. "I know it's only been a couple of months, but we're having a great time."

It's the way he says it with no hesitation or second-guessing. Just certainty. My heart warms.

"Time is a construct," Mom says. But I catch her looking at him, an unreadable expression on her face, and I wonder what she's thinking.

We sit around the table for over an hour, the liquid in the glasses slowly dwindling as we catch up and share stories. For such a short time away, I have so much to tell Mom about. Parties, school, friends. She sits and listens intently as I tell her about life, as though she hasn't heard any of it before, a soft smile never leaving her face.

Given not only the events of last year but what happened before that, Mom knows these past two years have been hard. And honestly, I think, more than anything, she's just happy that I'm happy.

"I think I'm going to go check into my hotel," Patrick says.

My eyes shoot to the clock. Just a little past one p.m. "You sure?" I ask. "We're not meeting the others until five thirty."

Patrick stands up and stretches his arms out wide. Then he politely pushes his chair in. "Yeah, I'll let you and your mom catch up without me. I paid for early check-in, so I can explore the festival a little bit before tonight."

"If you're sure . . ."

He leans down and kisses me on the top of my head. "Of course I am. Where exactly am I meeting you?"

"Luigi's," I say. "Big bright red spot on Main Street. You can't miss it." I smile. The last time I was at Luigi's was the final meal I had with the rest of the gang before we left for college. We squeezed into our usual booth, laughed until closing, and tried to have one last good time.

I can't wait to see them all together again. We've spoken a lot but it's never the same. Nothing compares to the chaotic energy friends have when they're all in the same room. I imagine we'll pick up right where we left off, as if no time has passed at all.

"Got it." Patrick throws on his jacket that I didn't even realize he'd taken off, and turns to Mom. "Thank you so much for having me."

Mom is already guiding him to the door. I'm able to make out some words from the hallway. "It was lovely to meet you, Patrick."

She makes her way back to the kitchen. For a moment we sit in silence; she's making me wait for her judgment. When she finally speaks, my heart unclenches a little.

"He seems like a lovely boy." She lets out a soft laugh, then fakes a serious tone. "And he smells great. What on earth does he wear?"

"You don't even want to know," I say, knowing it's more expensive than we'd ever dare pay for some aftershave. When I first went to his house, I slipped away to call Mom because I was so overwhelmed by the sheer grandeur of everything.

Mom's eyes widen. "Well, I'm glad he's not making you watch scary movies... You really like him, don't you?"

I nod, a smile tugging at my lips. "He'll do."

"Well, I think he'll do too." Mom laughs at my sarcasm. "Only the best for my girl." I can hear the fondness in her voice. She's telling the truth, I think; she really does like Patrick. I don't know why I was so scared to bring him home. Maybe it's just the unfamiliarity of the situation, but now I realize I had nothing to worry about.

Mom's smile fades. "Your interview is on Sunday, right?"

I nod.

"Okay," Mom says with a sigh. "Buffy . . . are you sure you want to do this?"

"Of course," I say confidently. "I've spent a lot of time thinking about it. We all have and we decided it was best to do it now. Rick Field's book is reigniting the case, and it's also spinning some harmful headlines. People love to run with the wildest claims because it gets them attention. It's time for us to tell our own story for once."

Mom nods, but her expression is worried. "But, Buffy, what about . . . what happened in Connecticut?"

My stomach flips. I hadn't thought about that. Connecticut. Nancy. *I did nothing wrong*, I think. "What about it, Mom?" I say, keeping my voice steady. "The story is out there. I don't have anything to hide."

"I know, I know." She looks down. "*We* all know you're innocent, but the internet is becoming a scary place. The media is brutal. You say something wrong in that interview and you don't know what that journalist can spin."

She's right: We've seen how the media can spin things all year. But the idea that they might rake up my past didn't even occur to me. Now that I think of it . . . of course they would. The papers and the public love to see people crash and burn, even if it's unjust. Drama sells.

I swallow. I've never told Patrick about what happened with Nancy. Instant turnoff, being investigated in relation to your best friend's death. Even if I was officially cleared of any wrongdoing, it's something I'd rather keep buried. The image of Nancy materializes. Her ever-smiling face. Her light freckles. And then—the blood.

My mind reels as I go through every outcome in my head if Patrick finds out. Not many of them are positive. Then I wonder—what if he knows already?

No, I think. Sure, Google exists, but if Patrick knew, he would've told me by now, right? Still, the thought of him finding out from anyone but me feels completely wrong. It's a pretty big secret to keep. Should I tell him, I wonder, before someone else does?

Mom squeezes my hand, which pulls me from my distressed state. Spiraling is the last thing I need to do right now. I can't undo all those months of therapy. She puts her arm around me.

"You know I'd do anything to keep you safe," she whispers into my ear. "Anything at all. You've been through enough. Please be careful."

I nod. "I'll try," I whisper back.

5

AMBER

"You're kidding. You got *ninety-seven percent* on your first test of the year?"

"What, like it's hard?" I throw my hands up, doing a perfect Elle Woods, knowing Jonesy won't catch my reference. He's not a movie guy. A ninety-seven and I barely tried. Yes, I'm proud of myself. I won't shut up about it. I think Mom and Dad got tired of me pointing it out every other day on our calls. Kind of funny, considering how much they used to be on my case about grades.

"It seems college is working out, then?" Cam asks. There's a sort of somber tinge to his voice that he's trying his best to mask but can't fully. It's got to be hard. His whole friend group got up and left him. We're all still in the same state, but with hours between us. It's not like we can visit every weekend.

College *is* working out. It's going great. I feel like I can finally be myself, finally live outside my parents' shadow. Their expectations were always sky high—they always acted out of love, but it was a lot. All the time. Now I can breathe properly for the first time ever.

It's not all roses, don't get me wrong. My roommate does not clean up after herself and I've been kept up one too many times on a school night. But I've taught myself to have a little bit of sympathy. I'm not the only one who's moved to college, who's experiencing these things for the first time.

"How about you, Cam? How is work?"

Cam hesitates.

"C'mon," Jonesy presses, his right arm reaching around Cam and pulling him closer. "You can't avoid the question forever. How is it being able to boss everyone around?"

That gets a chuckle out of him. It seems like he really needed it. "It's nice that you think I have that sort of authority." Cam sighs and succumbs to Jonesy's grip. He leans close, relishing it. "I enjoy it. Do I want to coach track for the rest of my life? Debatable. But for now, it's great. Most of the kids are fine; I don't mind driving them to the weekend games and stuff."

"You don't?" I say. "Doesn't that eat into all your free time?"

He shrugs. "It's not like I've got much else going on."

Cam forces a smile. "Life is just a bit . . . quiet, that's all— Oh, hey. Look who it is!"

He waves at someone behind us. Jonesy and I exchange a concerned glance. Something is definitely up with Cam.

I turn to find Buffy entering the restaurant. She's as effortlessly dressed—yet somehow perfectly put together—as ever in a Stanford crewneck, blonde ponytail bobbing. She always carries herself with a confidence that makes it work.

I wait for her to take a seat next to me before I wrap my arms around her. "Hello, gorgeous."

"It's been *too long*." Buffy elongates her words to emphasize *how* long—like I haven't felt it either. After a moment or two, we pull away and she quickly shuffles out of the seat again to hug Cam.

"Okay," Cam says when they break apart. "Where is he, then? The mystery man?"

Buffy glances at her watch. "Not sure. I thought he'd be here by now. He said he was going to go explore the town a bit, so he's probably lost . . . Anyways. Before Patrick gets here, is there anything we need to talk about? You know, without him?"

Nothing comes to mind—but when my eyes catch an odd look between Jonesy and Cam, my interest is piqued. And suddenly I'm nervous. I don't know if I can take any bad news. I stepped foot in Sanera three hours ago. I'm not ready for anything to go wrong.

"What is it?" I ask uneasily, glancing between the boys.

"You have to tell them," Jonesy says, looking firmly at Cam.

God, something actually *has* happened. A flurry of hypotheses enter my mind and none of them are good. The possibilities cause a twist in my stomach.

"Tell us *now*," says Buffy.

"It's probably nothing," Cam assures us, rather unconvincingly. The lack of conviction in his voice is impossible to ignore. "Honestly. Probably a prank by some freshman with too much time on their hands." His words sound hollow, like he's trying to convince himself as much as he is us.

"Spit it out, Cotton!" I say.

Cam stretches and covertly scans his surroundings. Then he lowers his head and urges us all to gather in closer. "Last night I had a run-in with some goof dressed as the ghoul—I wasn't hurt, they didn't even attack me. They ran off as soon as I chased them."

The ghoul.

"What the fuck" is all that comes from Buffy.

And "Cam" is all that I can muster. I should've known that this damn festival would drag some weird shit in with it.

Jonesy picks up the story. "They left a pool of *blood* behind, but it was only paint. Looks like a prank."

Buffy scoffs. "A shitty prank if I've ever seen one."

"That's not the only thing," Cam adds under his breath.

Jonesy sits forward, his posture and knitted brows making it clear that, whatever Cam is about to say, he's hearing it for the first time too.

"I saw them again earlier." Cam stares at his hands as he talks. "Most kids were dressed up at school today. They were excited. But there was a Carrington Ghoul. They kept staring at me, the same way as last night. And then they just seemed to *vanish*."

We look at each other. Then Jonesy places his hand on Cam's. "Cam, I hate to ask, but . . . are you sure you definitely saw them?"

Cam hesitates. "Yes . . . No . . . I don't know," he admits, frustration flickering all over his face. "I was with Coach but he didn't see them."

"If you saw anything, it was someone messing with you," I say firmly. "I've been here for a few hours and I've already seen every costume available at Party City."

Cam nods slowly, but his expression is worried. He looks around the table, then lowers his voice. "There's more . . . I think a kid has gone missing. I overheard these kids talking about their friend. They haven't seen him since yesterday. *And* someone was missing from tryouts today."

My heart aches for Cam. He's clearly scared; I can see the tension in his features. But the return of the ghoul?

A missing kid? That feels like a stretch. I want to believe him, I really do. But I worry that, in his panic, he's connecting dots that aren't there and grasping at loose, unrelated threads. It's almost Halloween; it's Sanera's festival. Of course someone dressed up as the Carrington Ghoul.

Yeah, it's insensitive as hell. But that's real life. People don't always care about other people's feelings.

"This kid probably just lost interest in the tryouts. I've signed up for a ton of things and then never actually followed through with them," I say, trying to reassure him.

"You're probably right, but I can't help thinking . . ."

"You worry too much," Jonesy says, but the moment the words leave his mouth, he laughs. "I realize how rich that sounds coming from me." He shakes his head. "Do you know the kid's name?"

"Harry Lanz."

"Well, I bet you that on Monday, Harry Lanz will be in school, safe and sound. He changed his mind, that's all. You can even ask him why, if you need to."

Cam nods again. He doesn't look completely satisfied with our reassurances, but I think he accepts them. We all have enough on our plates and plenty going on this weekend. Still, I recognize the feeling he has. Sometimes that uncertainty gnaws at you. And now it's starting to gnaw at me too.

"That's what we get for coming back," Buffy says. It's true, but I wish it wasn't.

At least we're all together. Stronger as one, or whatever they say.

The bell at the front of the restaurant dings and Buffy's head almost dislocates from how fast she turns around. "There he is," she says, waving someone over.

I glance that way to find a guy. Average build, black hair that peeks out from under a red baseball cap. He's breathing hard, sweaty as all hell, and clearly flustered, like he got lost on the way. It wouldn't surprise me. Sanera isn't big, but the streets can be a bit of a maze. *So this is Patrick.* Buffy's new boyfriend. He looks the type—good-looking, preppy. But his expression is sweet and earnest.

"Hello," Buffy says as Patrick reaches the table.

Patrick leans down, pressing a kiss to Buffy's head. "I asked someone to point me in the direction of Mario's . . . ended up on the other side of town. Apparently, I picked the wrong Italian brother." He wipes his brow and puts his hands on his knees, flashing a rueful grin. "*Sorry.* Not the first impression I planned to make. I even left early, can you believe that?"

Buffy flashes a warm smile before scooting over to make space for Patrick in our booth. "It's fine, you're just on time. Besides, Sanera isn't exactly cut out for this many visitors. The streets are overrun. *Okay,*

Patrick, this is everyone, and everyone, this is Patrick."

"Cam. Nice to meet you."

"And I'm Amber!" I chime in with a grin. "Buffy has told me a lot about you."

Patrick smiles shyly as he shakes Cam's hand across the table and then mine. "Good things, I hope?"

"Mainly that I now have a worthy competitor if we ever have a horror trivia night," I say. "Well, *worthy* may be a little strong . . . You get the idea."

Patrick's brows rise. His eyes behind his glasses are dark, wide, and kind—but with a glint of humor in them too. "Is that so? That sounds like fighting talk to me."

"Well," I say. Smug. "Believe it. Test me if you want."

A small smirk tugs at the corner of his lips before he takes a deep breath. Then: "What year was *A Nightmare on Elm Street* released?"

"Eighty-four."

"What was *Halloween* originally titled?"

"*The Babysitter Murders*. Supposedly."

"Where did they get the mask—"

"It was a William Shatner mask that was painted white," I interrupt with a grin. It was an obvious question: the most well-known bit of *Halloween* production trivia. "There *are* other movies, you know?"

"Okay, well . . . you try me, then, if you're such an expert," he retorts, his grin widening.

I waste not even a second. "Since you're so *Halloween*

inclined, name two more horror movies starring Jamie Lee Curtis."

"*Prom Night* and *The Fog*." Patrick lists them off effortlessly, without even a second thought.

Cam claps, impressed.

We ignore him though, focused solely on the game. I'm having the most fun I've had in a while. College has shriveled my movie time to practically nothing. I barely have time to watch anything between classes, assignments, and everything else.

I raise a brow. "That was a warm-up."

"You two are such nerds," Buffy says under her breath. But it's clear that she's amused. "Can we talk about—"

"No," Cam says. "I'm enjoying this. It's not often Amber gets some competition."

"Yeah, keep going," Jonesy says. "I'm curious to see who'll win now."

Patrick looks at me again, a mischievous look in his eye. "So, what book was *Hellraiser* based on?"

"Clive Barker's novella *The Hellbound Heart*," I fire off without having to think.

Great film. Buffy hated it.

"I hated that one," Buffy confirms my thought. "Too . . . gross."

Patrick gasps indignantly, but I interrupt his train of thought.

"First ever slasher film?" I ask. The question is

open-ended. Every person will have a different answer, which makes it the perfect question. Surely, it'll trip him up. Or at least make him second-guess himself.

But Patrick laughs in my face. "Nice try," he says. "There is no *official* first. But *Halloween*, *Black Christmas*, *The Texas Chain Saw Massacre*, *Psycho* . . . You could make an argument for any of them."

I nod, impressed. He knows his stuff. "After three, state your favorite. Three, two, one—"

"*Black Christmas*," we say in unison.

I burst out laughing. I look to Buffy, who looks understandably bemused. Me and her boyfriend only met two minutes ago and we've already had a horror-off. I'd still win in a battle but I have to admit it—Patrick knows his movies. "Buffy, you chose well. He's a keeper."

"I think so," Buffy says.

"Why, thank you," Patrick says, his voice softer as he looks at Buffy. The rosiness creeps up his face as he tries to play it cool. He's smitten, I can tell.

"I'm glad you're all getting along," Buffy says.

A waitress approaches our table. I glance at her name tag; it reads JOANNE. She's a larger white woman, her blonde pin curls resting neatly on the shoulders of her pale pink uniform. The soft color complements her gentle expression, giving her a welcoming appearance.

I don't recognize her.

Sanera has always been one of those stereotypical small towns where everyone knows everyone. But in the two months I've been gone, there has clearly been a lot of change. Now that I think about it, as I scan the room, I don't recognize *a single person* working here. Mayor Gomez's push to bring new blood to Sanera seems to be working just how he wanted.

That or people are so obsessed with the case that they've moved here, hoping to get close to whatever mystery lies beneath. On paper, that sounds wild, but honestly, it wouldn't surprise me in the slightest.

We place our orders. Joanne saunters off and we're once again left to our own devices.

"Cam," Patrick says, "Buffy tells me you work at Sanera High now?"

As much as Cam doesn't like to talk about his job, he doesn't show that on his face. He's making an effort, for Buffy. "I do," he says pleasantly. "Assistant coach."

"For?"

"Every sport, really. Track tryouts were today so a lot of that right now," Cam replies.

I wish I could see him at work. It must be weird to go from being a student to faculty in only a few months. I wonder how it's been socializing with the teachers. I can imagine it's . . . odd.

"Do you know what you're going to major in, Patrick?" Cam continues.

Patrick releases a puff of air. "Probably history. But I've been having doubts."

Buffy cranes her neck. Clearly this is news to her. "You have? Why?"

Patrick shrugs. "It's not the sort of history I enjoy. It's lots of military and political history and I prefer more cultural. I love stories, you know? History so rich that it feels like fiction."

"Like legends?" Jonesy asks.

"I guess so." He looks up, pondering, but soon gives up on his thought. "My mom keeps telling me to do whatever major that will help me with eventually taking over their company."

"And you don't want to?" I say sympathetically. I know what it's like to have the burden of parental expectation. And I remember Buffy saying his family was seriously loaded. I glance at her and see she's biting her lip. I wonder if the difference between them is a problem—but it's only been a few months.

"Not really," he says sheepishly. "I know I'm lucky to have the opportunity . . ." He trails off, smiling.

I smile. "You shouldn't be unhappy though," I say while glancing at Cam, hoping he'll heed my words. His own job is clearly only a stepping stone.

Cam ignores my meaningful look. "Speaking of stories," he says. "Rick Field is in Sanera for his tour. I had the *absolute pleasure* of bumping into him this morning."

The sarcasm practically oozes off him like honey.

Jonesy's head shoots up. "You did?"

Cam nods. "Yep, he invited us to his lousy book event."

"Ugh, no way," I say. "Waste an evening to hear him tell a pack of lies? No thank you."

"He's that journalist I told you about," Buffy explains to Patrick. "You know how I feel about that loser. Stealing our story for his own gain. Making it all about him."

"Maybe you should go." Patrick pushes his glasses up the bridge of his nose. "Tell your side of the story. Show him up for what he is and make a fool of him." He gestures around the table. "You guys are the Sanera *freaking* Four . . . You're heroes."

"No way. It's a terrible idea," Jonesy says. "No offense, Patrick."

"None taken."

"We're going to tell our story, just not tonight," Buffy says to Patrick. "That's what our interview is for."

"That's true," says Patrick. "I just hate the idea of that lowlife saying whatever he wants about you. You guys risked your lives and that fraud took all the glory. Who knows what new stories he's conjuring next?"

"He did say he was revealing an *exclusive* at the event," Cam says slowly. "Cassie, the new librarian, mentioned it. I have no idea what it is though. Probably more made-up BS, knowing Rick Field."

I can see the cogs whirling in everyone's eyes. What new falsehoods is Rick cooking up?

"I guess there's no harm in sneaking in just to hear what he has to say," I suggest. "We can stay hidden at the back. No one will even know we're there."

Buffy sighs. "I don't know . . ."

"Yeah, I am not sure this is a good idea," Jonesy agrees.

"I get it," says Patrick. "But this is your life. Your experiences. Your bravery. It's time you took your story back."

Buffy laughs. "That's a very stirring speech." She ponders for a moment. "Maybe you're right. We don't want to get blindsided by some new reveal of Rick's, so we might as well see what this exclusive is about."

Jonesy sighs, his head dropping into his open hands. "It's asking for trouble."

I can't help but feel for him because he always gets outvoted. One day we'll listen to him.

Without moving, he mumbles through his fingers. "Fine. I guess I'm going too." He looks up. "What could go wrong?"

6

JONESY

This always happens to me. I'm quiet and risk-averse—or, rather, *sensible*—and that means I get outvoted.

In the case of avoiding Rick Field's launch, I genuinely believe I'm right. I can already see this turning into a whole can of worms. And when it does, I'll make sure to enjoy my "I told you so" moment.

Buffy, Amber, and Patrick lead the way while Cam and I follow. The streets are a sight to behold—I've never seen Sanera so alive. This is only the first night of the festival and it's already like Halloween night in the movies.

"And this is the florist," Buffy says, gesturing toward the unmistakably flower-filled store. The girls are giving Patrick the tour on the way to the library, where Rick's book event is. There's not much to see normally. The festival, however, is making the place seem a lot more impressive than usual.

Lines of market stalls stretch along Main Street, offering everything from hot food to crafts to all kinds of homemade goods. I'm pretty sure I even spotted a Sanera-themed gift shop a little farther back. I can only assume Mayor Gomez had a hand in that.

While I'm looking around in amazement, Cam seems fearful. His head continuously flicks back and forth as the myriad colorful lights hit his face.

"Cam, relax," I say as I nudge him. "Nothing's going to happen out here. The worst thing that's going to happen is getting recognized at this stupid book launch and having to deal with a ton of Carrington fans."

Cam scowls at me, his lips pursing and brows scrunching. "You're the one who has a problem with getting noticed, not me."

I shake my head. "It would *become* a you problem, because I wouldn't let you forget you agreed to this. I don't like making a fuss like that." A smile creeps onto my lips, which is matched by Cam's laugh. We may have spent two months apart but we still know how the other works. I know humor is his medicine, and my medicine is his happiness.

"Very funny," Cam says.

"I learned from the best."

He pushes me away playfully. "Okay, suck-up." His

words are encircled with chuckles and almost immediately he's pulling me back in. "Thank you for cheering me up. I've really missed you."

Our eyes meet when I look up. Cam's only a few inches taller than me but it suddenly seems like more. His hair is almost white in this light, stark against his dark eyebrows and light eyes.

"What are you looking at?" Cam asks, raising an eyebrow. I've been staring for a little too long. It's hard not to get lost in perfection. "You know, a photo would last longer."

Amber shouts back at us while I'm mid eye roll. "C'mon, you two!"

They're all in line to get into the library. By the time we reach their side, they're at the head, standing right before the guy working the door. He looks our age, maybe a little older, with dark freckles that contrast perfectly with his bleached hair with dark roots already creeping in. It should look strange, but he pulls it off.

"Name?" he says at the same time he glances up from his clipboard. Instantly, his look of disinterest melds into one of shock. Eyes wide, grinning nervously. "Wow. Um. It's really you . . . They're about to get started." He pauses, then nervously adds, "Can I just say something real quick?"

"What is it?" Buffy asks.

I look down at his name tag, which reads LIAM. When I raise my gaze again, I catch the beginnings of a blushing smile forming. His words come out in a jumbled mess. "You're all so, so great. *Really.* I'm a huge fan. I've read all about you on the forum—"

"Forum?" asks Cam.

"Yeah!" Liam nods excitedly, then notices our confusion. "The forum. Like a fan site, you know? There's a ton of stories that people have written about you. Like . . . fan fiction, you know? They come up with alternative stories or add new monsters. I read one the other day that was all about you four dealing with Bloody Mary. Some of them are fun. People like to make up their own endings . . . insert themselves into the story . . ."

Insert themselves into the story. Doesn't that sound familiar? I glance at the poster of Rick Field, beaming, on the side of the library. So smug. It makes me wonder if a particular journalist has been lurking on this very website to draw *inspiration*, shall we say. The thought of there being even more people out there theorizing on true events makes me quite uncomfortable.

"It's happening with all types of media nowadays," Patrick says, trying to explain. "TV shows, movies, books . . . real-life cases too. Apparently."

I sigh. This is the reality of the modern age we're living in. Information, whether it's true or false, spreads faster than ever, and all it takes is one person with the right audience to morph it into fact. With any luck, our interview will solve all that.

"Thank you for the support, Liam," Cam says. "Maybe we should get inside now."

"Sure, of course! Enjoy the night!" Liam replies, ushering us in.

We all offer our thanks as we trade the sharp (for California) weather for the instant stuffiness of the library. As my eyes adjust, I take in the altered layout. Bookcases have been pushed aside to create a larger seating area, making room for the crowd that has already gathered.

Instinctively, I keep my head down so as to not draw any more attention. The others, however, clearly didn't get the memo because they're on their tiptoes, craning their necks to see over the crowd.

"This is amazing," Buffy says. "I'm so used to seeing the library . . . empty."

"Aren't we all?" Amber replies.

A woman I'm not familiar with braves the makeshift stage, positioned where Mrs. Adler's desk is normally situated. It looks to be the same stage they use for theater productions at Sanera High.

There's a timidity to the woman's step as she walks to one of the two empty seats facing the crowd and sits down. With a shaking hand, she reaches for one of the microphones resting on the small table beside her. She gives it a gentle tap and a roar of feedback echoes through the library, silencing the crowd in an instant. Her cheeks flush. For a moment she hesitates, then finally brings the microphone to her lips.

"Sorry about that," she says, her face now resembling the Sanera Sabertooths' mascot. Bright cherry red. "I want to thank you all for attending tonight. My name is Cassie Liu, head librarian here at Sanera Public Library, and I am incredibly honored to be interviewing Rick Field tonight to kick off the inaugural Hallowed Fall Fest. A few safety precautions before we begin . . ."

"I met her yesterday," Cam whispers to us. "Mrs. Adler's replacement. It's literally her second day on the job."

"Then this is a tall order," Amber replies. I glance back at Cassie, who's talking, still visibly nervous.

"Right," Cassie says once she's concluded her safety spiel. "And now, without further ado, I would like you all to give a grand Sanera welcome to one of your own . . . renowned journalist and the bestselling author of *The Carrington Secret*, Rick Field!"

The room erupts into an absolute riot. Any hopes that Sanera might have seen through Rick are drowned out by the wave of cheers and applause that fills the library.

A scrawny, redheaded figure in a smart suit appears, striding confidently onto the platform with a cocky ease, his tweed tie swinging. With a theatrical flourish, Rick takes a long bow in front of everyone, drawing even more cheers from the audience. Then, straightening up, he flashes a wide grin before taking the empty seat and reaching for the other microphone. He does so with a casual familiarity—he is a journalist, after all.

"Hello, everybody!" Rick says. It's clear how much he loves this. How much the attention is fueling him. He stares out at the audience, cameras flashing light on him from every direction.

"Thank you for choosing Sanera Public Library for your last tour stop, Rick," Cassie says. She still grips the microphone tightly, and now with two hands, as if to anchor herself. I can't help but notice the way her legs are crossed too. Knees locked with a tapping foot beneath. Trying to appear composed while every nerve in her body is vibrating.

"So, Rick," she says with a smile. "You must be exhausted. How many dates was this tour again? Fifty?"

"Fifty-one," Rick corrects her, accompanied by a smile. "'A date for every state' has become a little catchphrase for me and my team. But of course we had to add an extra date in California for you guys." He points to the audience, who roar again. It's like they're puppets being told when to applaud. Cassie laughs. My friends and I watch along awkwardly.

Patrick is also clapping, clearly caught up in the energy of the room. I watch as Buffy nudges him with her elbow, leaning in.

"Chill. You're literally not from Sanera," she says, low but slightly amused.

"Oh," says Patrick, lowering his hands, embarrassed. "Right. It's just so wild to be here."

She rolls her eyes at him. I don't blame him for being fascinated. Any reasonable person would be when they discovered their girlfriend was not only the target of a serial killer but also one of the people who brought his murderous spree to a halt.

The applause dies down and Cassie speaks again. "You were born in this fantastic town, right?"

"I was. Born and raised until college."

"What is your favorite thing about Sanera?" asks Cassie. "Because I have to say, as a new resident, the love and resilience in this room is palpable. It's special."

Rick looks out at the crowd again. He seems to have this whole thing down. What to do, say, how to work the room. This is everything he's wanted and he's not going to mess it up.

"*Special.* That's exactly it, Carrie."

"Um, it's . . ." she begins to correct him, but her voice fades as he keeps going.

"Sanera is a town like no other. I've moved around a lot for work but never have I found a place so tight-knit, so persistent. Through hardships, we always bounce back, and I cannot be prouder to call myself a Sanera resident. I can't wait to move back now that the tour's done."

"He's moving back for good?" Amber's lip curls. "I'm going to throw up."

"He might as well be wearing an 'I Love Sanera' T-shirt," Buffy adds.

"So, *The Carrington Secret* . . . what a triumph and huge success for you," Cassie goes on. "Ten weeks and counting on the *New York Times* bestseller list is no easy feat. Were you ever expecting *any* of this?"

"Never," Rick replies simply. But obviously he's not done. "I wrote this book as a way to cope with the events of last year. I never expected for it to be published, let alone hit the charts. It's been a very surreal few months that I've just been floating through."

Oh please. The faux modesty is off the scale. If I could eye roll without being seen, I would. Amber's face is in her hands, presumably to hide her laugh. All Rick does is spew lies. We know he only wrote the book after he got an offer. His publisher saw his countless articles about the murders and thought they'd cash a check. We should know—they asked us first.

"Writing it must have been a way for you to process your own difficult experience," Cassie says sympathetically. "Is that what it meant to you?"

Rick thinks briefly. "Oh, for sure. A way of processing, like you say. And to honor those lost, *of course*." His teeth flash in a bright smile. "And they'd want the story out there, so every copy helps."

Applause again.

Clockwork.

"He is sick," Cam says.

"Sick doesn't even begin to describe it," I reply. Using the victims to sell his book is a whole new low. People he didn't even know. "Let's get out of here."

Amber nods, clearly also done with it. She turns around, but as she does, she makes direct eye contact with a middle-aged woman beside her. A gasp from her turns into a multitude of points and whispers, which soon outperform the cheers. One by one, every single head in the room turns to us.

It isn't long before Rick catches on. "Is that who I think it is?" he says, his eyes lighting up. "The Sanera Four, everybody! So glad you could make it! Get them up here!"

"No, it's okay!" I blurt out, but we're already being nudged forward. In a panic, I grab on to Cam, who's right behind me.

"Calm down," he whispers, but the words glance off me. Little can calm me right now.

In no time, we're being pushed onstage and blinded by the same lights we were on the other side of a moment ago. Buffy loses hold of Patrick's hand in the shuffle. I can feel my legs shaking underneath me and it must be visible because Amber hooks her arm through mine.

"Well, would you look at this?" Rick says, with the biggest grin known to man. "Thank you all for tagging along tonight. If we'd known you were coming, we would've made sure to grab you some seats!"

Cassie mumbles through her mic. "Oh, I could go get—"

"No need," Cam cuts in smoothly. "Hi, Cassie. What a turnout! Is everyone having fun?" He turns to the audience and brings his hand to his ear, working the crowd just like Rick was. Cheers.

Why is Cam so good at this? He's beaming out at everyone like he's a talk show host. Meanwhile, I'm here trying to stay upright and ignore the fact that my feet feel like they're made of lead.

Cam turns to Cassie. "Now that we're here though, do you have any questions?"

I glare at him—*what is he doing?*—but he catches my eye and shrugs.

"May as well steal Rick's spotlight," he whispers.

"Sure," says Cassie quickly. "What brings you four back to Sanera—well, you three, should I say. I know you've never left, Cameron."

Cassie passes a microphone to me as I'm closest, but I hand it straight to Amber.

Thankfully, she takes it without a blink. "Well, we couldn't miss the first ever Hallowed Fall Fest," she says calmly. "We all wanted to make sure we could be here to celebrate and commemorate with everyone. This is a *memorial* event, after all."

Immediately, Amber shifts the mood in the room. It's

like her tone has reminded them that people actually died, yet here they are, cheering about a book. Glossing over the reality of what happened. Rick's book might be more fiction than fact, but that doesn't change the truth that people were killed. *People* in this very town.

Rick nods, clearly scrambling to get back the attention. The spotlight isn't entirely on him anymore and he doesn't like it. But maybe he should've thought about that before inviting us onstage. "So true. And it's great to see you here. I know you've needed some time out of the spotlight, to start your lives. But . . ." He lowers his head and looks intently at all of us, in journalist mode. "I'd be remiss if I didn't ask—I know everyone is thinking it—are we ever going to see more of the Sanera Four?"

The question silences the entire room. Not even a breath is audible. It's like we're in a movie and Rick just pressed pause. Smiling awkwardly, I look to the others to assess their reaction. Amber bites her lip. Buffy puts her finger to her mouth in a playful manner, as though thinking about it. And Cam—

Cam stares out at the crowd, his expression fixed. There's a look on his face I haven't seen in—well, in a year. He blinks once, and then again. Until he's blinking rapidly, over and over, like something is stuck in his eye. But his focus doesn't shift.

"Hey, look," he mutters. There's dread in his words as he raises his hand. "Do you see what I'm seeing?"

I follow Cam's pointing finger through the crowd, past most of the confused-looking people, toward the back. At first, it's all a blur and I can't make out anything. People are shadowed, except for the occasional flash of a camera. Most are in costume, each one embracing the festival with a different kind of flair. Horror characters, classic Halloween-type costumes. Witches with their pointed hats, vampires and their pale faces, the whole nine yards.

What is it that Cam has seen? Has he actually seen *anything*? Or is he making a fool of himself in front of the entire crowd?

But suddenly I see it.

"Is that . . ." Amber says, her voice right by my ear. Her grip tightens on my arm.

In the back row, so unassuming, stands a dark figure. Charred clothing hangs off its frame like rags. The clothing still resembles an old three-piece suit, but only barely. A scarf, mottled and singed, covers any semblance of a face. *It can't be.*

I falter back, breaking from Amber's grip, which I instantly regret. My legs tremble beneath me once again, forcing me to hold on to Rick's chair for stability. He looks bewildered as a commotion builds.

Not again.

Not again.

Not again.

A scream sounds from the back of the room and soon

everyone is screaming. The library quickly descends into terror. Scrapes of chairs on wooden floor muddle between yells. Burning fills my nose, but I'm sure it's my imagination. I see no fire. Nothing. The smell is a memory almost, faint but clinging. *Just my imagination.*

"It's him, it's the ghoul!"

"It's back!"

"Runnn!!!"

A hand grabs mine, then I see Cam's face. "Are you okay?"

I don't answer right away, scanning the crowd. Eventually, I manage some words. "Where did they go?"

People are clamoring for the exit, but the ghoul is gone. That's great—they come back to frighten the shit out of us and then disappear. What a gentleman. "Let's get out of here" is all Cam says.

Cam pulls me off the stage, right behind the girls. We bound through the swarm of panicked people, heads down. The chaos around us feels endless, and something tells me our presence isn't the biggest talk of the night anymore. Behind us, I can hear Rick's voice shouting our names, but we ignore him, pushing forward. I've always liked the library, but I don't want to spend another second in here tonight. I've had my fix for at least another year.

The brisk air is welcome relief when it hits my face. People don't congregate; instead, they flow into the busy streets. The unaware festivalgoers glance at the gaggle of attendees, their faces blank and uncomprehending. They have no idea what just happened. For them, this is the first night of costumes, fun, and celebration.

Soon, though, word will surely spread of the ghoul's appearance. I wonder if people will be scared—or thrilled. After all, that's why they're here. They're horror fans. True crime fans maybe. I wouldn't be surprised if they were waiting for something like this to happen.

"There you are!" I look over to find Patrick fighting through the crowd toward us. He looks as confused as everyone else. "I thought I'd lost you when everyone rushed out. Everything was going fine until . . . it wasn't. What happened?"

"The Carrington Ghoul," Buffy says angrily. "That's what happened. God, we've only been back for six hours."

Patrick's face is a picture. "Wait. The *ghoul* was in there? Are you for real?"

"Why would I kid about this?"

"Oh my God." Patrick looks thoroughly freaked out, like the fun ghost story he was enjoying had stepped off the page. Then reality comes crashing back. "*Oh my God. Are you okay, Buffy?*"

Cam rolls his eyes, his voice sharp. "She's fine. C'mon. Keep moving." Without missing a beat, he takes center stage, leading us ahead, his hand still tightly woven around mine. If anything, his grip has only hardened since we left, like holding me is keeping him anchored. "My house is closest, we'll go there."

The words are almost a command, and none of us argue. Right now, anywhere but here is a better idea. I don't know how many more Michael Myerses and Chuckys I can stand.

Funneling through the crowds is like playing Snake. Luckily, we get through the busiest part of Main Street with only a few bumps and nudges. When we reach the alley we would normally cut through, Cam stops abruptly. I can already tell what's running through his mind before he says a word. His shoulders tense, his gaze flicking toward the darkened passage.

"Cam . . . isn't this where you saw the ghoul first?"

Cam blinks. His voice wobbles. "Look. If we go the road way, that's another twenty minutes."

There's a prolonged silence as we exchange glances. Patrick looks clueless. He hasn't been here before. He hasn't dealt with what we've dealt with.

"There's five of us now," Cam goes on. "Whoever it is, there's only one of them—"

"Fine," I blurt out. My voice is more forceful than I intended. "I just want to get home."

Buffy grabs both Patrick's and Amber's hands as she glares at Cam. "If we die, I am *so* blaming you."

7

CAM

"I can see people on the other side," I say as I take the first step. "We'll be fine."

It's amazing how one foot in an empty alley can feel like another world. Narnia feels less like fiction now. A cold breeze crests the back of my neck, instantly making the hairs on my body stand at attention. Jonesy is beside me and we all shuffle in an uneasy cluster. I'm sure we'd look like complete turkeys to anyone watching—if anyone *were* watching.

It's deathly silent aside from our footsteps. Every so often the silence is broken by the noise from Main Street but for the most part it's muffled. A faraway dissonance. Then—

"Ow!" Amber yells. I can't help but also let out a small yelp. "One of you stepped on my toe."

My racing heart quickly settles. *Thank God.* But

also . . . we went from solving mysteries to . . . whatever this is. Being scared in alleys? We have every right to be a little jumpy, but this is ridiculous. We're the Sanera Four after all. That name seems so silly now.

Slowly but surely, we close in on the dumpster that still sits halfway down the alley. When I was walking alone, I fully expected something to jump from behind it, but now it seems fine. That is, until . . .

"Please tell me you're seeing this too?" I stop in my tracks and the others successively crash into me. The feeling of everyone right with me, their bodies close, comforts me somewhat. But it doesn't change what I saw: There is something behind the dumpster.

In the movies, it would be a monster that would jump out at us. But this time . . . something tells me what I can see isn't going to jump out at us.

Jonesy leans closer—his face is mere inches away from my own. "Is that a . . ."

"I think so," I whisper in reply. With a deep sigh, I loosen my grip on Jonesy's hand and look around at the others. "Wait here."

They stare back at me with scared faces. Wide eyes and hollow cheeks. I know they want to tell me to "stay" and that "we're a team," but they don't stop me. Fear can make you a prisoner in your own body. I know that more than anyone.

"Be careful," Jonesy whispers. His fingers brush mine

but I don't let them linger. Onward is the only way. I watch my every step in disbelief that this is my life again. Just hours ago I was at track tryouts, helping kids pursue their dreams, and now . . .

I'm at the dumpster now. Fear prohibits me from taking that final step. I know somehow that if I do, there's no going back.

But there's no choice.

The ground echoes beneath my feet in the narrow alley. My eyes lock on to what's on the ground. It takes me a moment to register what I'm looking at. It's dark, after all. But slowly, my eyes adjust, and I see it.

A body, the face bloody and bruised. A boy. I don't even need to check the pulse to know he's dead. His skin is almost blue, which tells me he's been dead for a while. Then I see his jacket, with the Sanera High colors.

I stumble until my back hits the cold brick wall. Instinctively, I throw my hand up, signaling my friends to stay put, but they don't listen. In no time, I feel them beside me—and then the screaming commences. The sound rips through the night. I can't blame them.

Everything I feared has come true. The Carrington Ghoul is back in Sanera.

It's the only explanation.

The last few days rush past me as I relive my sightings of the ghoul. It was real all along. It wasn't a prank. I wasn't seeing things. Coach simply didn't see the ghoul when I did. Someone really was out there, waiting. For us. But if it isn't Mr. Graham—and we know it can't be, we saw him die—then who is it?

"Everyone breathe" is the first thing I think to say. But no one is listening. Everyone is too busy panicking. Everyone deals with shock in different ways, but right now . . . panic is a shared experience.

"What do we do?"

"Oh my God. Oh my God. Oh my God."

"Who is that?"

"Shit!"

"Calm down!" I say loudly to stop the spiraling. Thankfully, this time it works. They stare at me, silenced by the command. Only Patrick hasn't made a single noise. He's frozen in shock, his eyes unmoving from the body. Horror is written all over him.

"Patrick?" I say gently. He hasn't been through this before. I imagine he's never seen a dead body before. It's not exactly a normal occurrence for the regular teenager. "Patrick, stay with us."

He blinks. "He—he's . . ."

I dare to look again at the corpse at our feet. We need to tell the police. They weren't exactly useful before, but Sheriff Rogers resigned a few months back and they hired someone new. Someone from outside Sanera. Maybe it'll be different this time.

"Let's go," I say. "We need to call the police and—"

But as I turn, my insides freeze over. I see it. The Carrington Ghoul right there in the flesh, staring ominously. A flicker of rags, the smell of smoke. The knife at their side . . .

"Nobody panic," I whisper as I grab Jonesy's hand again. It's instinct at this point. "Move very slowly."

They all turn to look where I'm staring and someone—Patrick, I think—lets out a whimper. The rest of the group stands frozen. The tension builds, threatening to shatter at any moment.

"Has anyone got something we can use?" I say in a low voice.

"Use?" Amber questions.

"A weapon, a sharp object, any object. Something. *Anything.*"

But we have nothing. We're alone, and we have nothing to defend ourselves with. Once again we're playing a losing game. But unlike last year, I am sick of this shit. The same feeling I had the other night in the alley overcomes me again. A feeling of pure rage that's only heightened by the presence of my friends. I am not letting them get hurt.

Without a word, I drop Jonesy's hand and bound forward, toward the ghoul. Jonesy calls out to me, but I ignore him. I am not playing this game of cat and mouse any longer. Finally, I had started to feel safe in Sanera again. I refuse to go back to that awful place.

My feet fly beneath me, the alley a blur as adrenaline courses through my veins. The ghoul disappears from view, just like before—but this time I'm not letting them escape. No tricks of the mind, no convenient smoke. I quicken my pace until I'm nearly back on Main Street. Sweat breaks out on my forehead as I burst out of the alley. I can see the ghoul, sprinting down the road.

A clatter of steps sounds behind me, so I know the gang isn't far. I don't wait for them. Screeches from passersby sound as they spot the ghoul for themselves. Thankfully, the crowds disperse for me. They're not taking any chances. If this ghoul is anything like Mr. Graham, they have a violent vendetta and are not to be messed with.

As I run, I feel the gap between us closing. Years and years of track practice is finally paying off. Suddenly I have a newfound appreciation for the sport. I'm glad the job has kept me in shape for this moment.

I'm gaining on them. Pumping my arms with everything I have and propelling myself forward, I fly through the air. I make contact with the ghoul, fling my arms around their neck, and let my weight take them down. The feeling of a solid body under the flimsy material proves to me that, once again, the ghoul is very human.

The Carrington Ghoul breaks my fall but I can tell I'll be bruised tomorrow. I recover in an instant and pin their arms down. A struggle ensues, the ghoul thrashing beneath me. I grit my teeth and use every ounce of strength in me, refusing to let go.

Right as my muscles are screaming for me to give up, Patrick joins me, his weight crashing down onto the ghoul, making them grunt in . . . pain?

"Are you hurt?" he asks as he practically sits on top of the ghoul. They can wriggle and struggle as much as they want but there is no chance they're getting away.

"I'm fine."

"I can't believe this," Patrick gasps. "I can't believe this is happening—"

Join the club, I think.

At that moment, Jonesy, Buffy, and Amber arrive with police in tow. A crowd of festivalgoers surrounds us now that the danger is contained. I've never been this happy to see law enforcement. Patrick and I let them take over restraining the figure and stumble to our feet.

"In . . . alley," I wheeze. "Ghoul."

One of the cops kneels down beside the now-limp impostor. With heavy hands, he unravels the singed scarf around their head. A weird nervousness floods through me. Part of me wonders if it's Mr. Graham, and somehow, impossibly, he survived last year's ordeal. I realize it's preposterous. But who else could it be?

The scarf falls to the ground and the ghoul's identity is revealed.

"Who the hell is that?" Buffy asks.

A young boy lies there with a frightened face. His lip trembles as the police officers drag him into an upright position. He must be no older than sixteen, if that. What on earth is a child doing in this costume, flouncing around dressed as a serial killer?

"I . . ." the boy says. He gulps. "I . . ."

"Speak up!" one of the police officers shouts. "Do you think this is some kind of joke? Scaring folks after what happened last year is totally thoughtless."

"I'm innocent!" he screams. "I've only . . . been paid to . . ."

Whispers fill the air as the crowd mutters crossly. They don't know about the body and think that at most this is a tasteless joke. But it doesn't make sense. This *child* killed that kid in the alley? Weirder things have happened but it really seems too easy. Nothing is ever this easy. I'm about to open my mouth to question him for myself when a voice sounds through the crowd.

"Er, excuse me, folks. Coming through."

In the next moment, Mayor Gomez appears, pushing himself through the crowd. His dark hair is slicked back, a mirror of his tailored suit. As soon as his eyes land on the handcuffed ghoul, his face sinks and the color drains from it. "Oh my" is all he says.

"Some kid has been fronting as the ghoul," says an officer. "Probably just trying to scare people and cause trouble, but you can't be too careful. I'm going to take him in for—"

"Oh, that won't be necessary," the mayor replies. He looks to the ground, then back. Clears his throat. "You see, I . . . can explain."

My brows rise. That is not at all what I expected him to say.

"What do you mean, *you can explain*?" I take a step closer.

"This ghoul is . . ." Gomez stops himself. I notice a member of his staff appear at his side, shaking her head, telling him no. But he brushes her away. What the . . .

"This ghoul is a fraud."

To my surprise, Jonesy speaks up. "Mayor Gomez, you seem to know a lot about this."

"Yes. The thing is . . . I—I hired him. It was meant to be a publicity stunt, to promote the festival," the mayor admits, his voice wavering. It's clear he's embarrassed to announce this ridiculous marketing ploy. "I realize now it was a mistake, but—"

"Wait," I blurt out. "Did you have this kid dress up as the Carrington Ghoul to follow me around these past few days?"

Again, I relive the sightings. The first encounter in the alley. The sighting at the school, and how quickly the figure disappeared. He was a student—of course he blended right in.

Mayor Gomez nods. He steps toward me but I falter

backward. How could someone be so malicious, so heartless?

"Why?" I ask simply. "Why would you do this?"

The heads of the watching crowd flick between the mayor and me, trying to make sense of the chaos unfolding before them. Mayor Gomez was there through Mr. Graham's reign of terror. He saw it all. And he still decided *this* was a good idea.

"I was worried the festival wouldn't perform well," Mayor Gomez says weakly. "I've put a lot into this. I wanted it to be a success. The ghoul . . . well, forgive me, but the Carrington Ghoul has done so much for Sanera . . ."

I stare at him in disbelief, my frustration rising. "You set this up?" But then a thought breaks through. I freeze, narrowing my eyes. "Wait. This *can't* be fake."

Mayor Gomez's face distorts with confusion. "But it is. Like I said, I hired this kid to—"

"No," I say sternly. The murmurs of the crowd continue. My friends stare at me, realization clearly striking them at the same time, all at once. The same thought is running through our heads. Because this is no harmless publicity stunt.

"Why do you say that?" the mayor asks, bewildered.

I blink twice, my eyes dry and stinging. My voice feels heavy when I finally speak.

"Because . . . there is a body in the alley."

8

BUFFY

We're waiting by a police car stationed not too far from the alley. I can't believe we're back in this situation again. We thought everything had returned to normal. But no, life *had* to throw a curveball. It seems Sanera's Hallowed Fall Fest is off to a less than great start.

No one has talked in what feels like hours. The "ghoul" is in custody now. Even if the mayor insists he was only hired to follow Cam, the newfound body complicates things. A lot.

Patrick left a while ago, looking shaken—we sent him back to his hotel room and told him to make sure he locked his door. The police got his statement but asked us to stay behind. For obvious reasons.

Patrick asked me about a thousand times if I'd be okay without him, but I think he was glad to go. I despise the fact that he's had to experience this. He's barely had a minute to settle in, and he's already been confronted with . . . this. Maybe it was naïve of me to believe I could move on from last year.

The police have taped off the entire street so people can't pry into what's happening—and so we can't disappear. We were targeted by the ghoul last time; they're not taking any chances. And Cam walks home through this alley every day.

"How long do you think they'll be?" I ask, eyeing the alley where the police are presumably still examining the body.

Amber scrolls through her phone, showcasing the stream of angry, confused, and worried texts from her parents. "Hopefully not too much longer because my dad is three texts away from coming here himself to *have a word*."

"They'll have to send us home soon." Cam checks his watch. "It's nearly two a.m."

"I am so tired," Jonesy says, resting his head on Cam's shoulder. The slight height difference makes it a little difficult for him, but he's making it work. That's when I notice Cam's bent knees, which instantly makes me smile. It's much needed after tonight. *He really loves Jonesy*, I think.

"Let's lay it out for old times' sake," I say. "What do we know?" As if it helps, I mime laying out cards. Sometimes it works to visualize these things. "One dead body. A teenager. A kid, really. And we find it on practically the biggest night of the year for Sanera."

Jonesy chimes in. "Whoever did this chose the first night of the festival to strike—why?"

"Sanera is busier than ever," Amber adds. "More eyes on the town. You think they killed for the attention?"

"Maybe." Cam's deep in thought. "I keep thinking about that kid who missed track the other day. Harry Lanz."

"Cam, we don't know enough yet to jump to conclusions," says Jonesy quickly.

Cam chews his lip. "But it could be."

We don't need Cam thinking he could've stopped this, or informed someone sooner. This isn't his fault. Besides, it's too early to start speculating.

Suddenly Amber gasps. "Hey." Her eyes have gone wide, looking at the alley. "I've realized something. That alley is the exact one Trevor Ward was kidnapped from."

My eyes bulge. Trevor Ward was kidnapped by Mr. Graham and framed as part of his plan—from the same alley where another victim now lies. "That can't be a coincidence—"

Before we can question it further, an officer comes into my peripheral, silencing the conversation.

"Thank you for your patience," the officer says. Her voice is calm, but I can hear the tension in it. We all can.

Her blonde hair is captured into a tight ponytail. A few stray strands have escaped.

"I don't believe we've met," she goes on, "but my name is Sheriff Myers. I'll be heading up the case and I want to assure you we're taking it very seriously."

Sheriff Myers must be close to our parents' age, with only the slightest trace of wrinkles beginning to form. They're subtle, but they hint at the fact that she's at least in her midforties. We all give her a cautious nod. Our experience with law enforcement in Sanera isn't great.

"Given that the four of you played a significant role in the previous murder investigation and now you're the ones who discovered the body . . . let's just say I do not believe in coincidences. Because of that, we're going to divulge more details than we would to most. The quicker we get this person off the streets, the quicker you can all go back to college."

"What do you mean?" Jonesy blurts out. "We have to stay in Sanera till you solve this thing? Because I have a test—"

She gives him a brief glance. "There's a killer out there, young man."

He's silenced almost immediately. Jonesy's not one for confrontation. But he hates the idea of missing a test, dropping a grade . . .

"We're estimating the time of death to be around midday. Give or take," the sheriff says. "It's hard to tell. But the body may have also been staged in the alley." She frowns. "Almost as though they wanted someone to find him like that."

"Someone? Or us." The thought sends a shudder through me. "How did he die?" I ask.

"It's hard to tell without an autopsy, but most likely asphyxiation. Blood spots in the eyes and heavy bruising on the neck point to that conclusion." Sheriff Myers clears her throat. "However, there is also a singular stab wound to the chest. From the width, most likely a large blade. It's unclear at this point whether this action was performed postmortem or not."

"Mr. Graham stabbed Brad and Shelley *after* they died," Cam says. "It could be a copycat."

"We can't rule it out . . ." The sheriff trails off hesitantly. What isn't she telling us?

Eventually, with a sigh, she reaches into her pocket and pulls out a small evidence bag. Inside, there is something white. A slip of paper. "There's also this. We found it on the body."

All four of us stare at the mysterious bag, attempting to inspect what's inside from where we stand. She doesn't let us see it too close—I can't blame her. After all, we're still pretty much kids. Something tells me Sheriff Myers is the type to stick to the rules. By the book, no risks, nothing that can get her in trouble.

"A receipt for a gas station out of town. Does that ring

any bells? If this *is* a copycat, there might be a connection to Carrington."

"No," Cam replies, shaking his head. "We never came across that in our research. Maybe the receipt belonged to the kid though? It might be nothing to do with the killer at all."

Myers doesn't exactly reply to Cam right away. Instead, she lets out an unsatisfied noise that offers nothing.

"Funny you should say that," she says at last. "Because there's also this."

With a slow motion, Myers turns the bag around, revealing a message in dark, jagged letters that stops me cold. It's almost illegible, as if it was written in a rush.

"*'Time for a redo,'*" Amber reads aloud, her voice trembling.

The words hang like a threat, the beginning of a twisted mystery. In that moment, the street suddenly feels like a cramped room. *Time for a redo.* Does that mean what I think it means?

"But Graham is dead," Cam says.

"We're aware," Myers replies. "But it's clear that . . . something is afoot."

"So it *must* be a copycat," I say quietly.

"It may be," the sheriff answers. "It's certainly worth considering."

Before we can question anything further, Sheriff Myers hands the bag to a young officer who approaches.

"Well, we'll check it out. Get some rest. We have all your details, so we'll be in touch if we find anything. Or have any more questions. Stay safe, kids."

There's no lingering. The moment Myers is done with us, she's already moving, and is soon in her car, leaving in quite the rush.

The officer is still here, bag in hand, his eyes focused on us. Now that I look at him properly, he seems somewhat familiar, but I can't quite pinpoint him. He's slightly heavier set, with enough muscle to suggest he could probably bench a hefty amount without breaking much of a sweat.

The officer fiddles with the evidence bag before finally breaking the silence. "You don't remember me, do you?"

Cam replies, "Should we?"

The officer chuckles. "I was in your senior class."

"I *knew* I recognized you," I say. "What's your name?"

"George Pérez," he answers. "I never shared any classes with you but I think you're all great. Truly. In fact," he says, blushing, "you're why I decided to join the force."

"We made you become a cop?" Amber says, frowning.

"Because I saw how useless they were in the Carrington case," George explains. "I thought I'd like to try and make a difference."

"And how's that working out for you?" Amber asks quizzically.

"Weeks of the academy were rough, and I'm still a

rookie. It has its highs and lows. But I have a great partner... who's around here somewhere..." George looks around, then down at the bag in his hands. He takes a deep breath and thrusts it at us. "Anyways, I want you to take this."

"George..."

Cam speaks up. "Are you being serious?"

"Think this through," Jonesy says. "This could get you—"

"I know," George says. "It could get me suspended or fired. But I don't want to risk a repeat of last year and I'm scared we're on that road again. You can solve this. You've done it before and you'll do it again."

I blink. The enthusiasm is flattering but we haven't done this in a long time, a year in fact. Small cases came after the ghoul, but not freaking *murder*. That was a one-time deal.

Well, until now it seems.

Amber steps forward and glances behind us to make sure no one is watching. "I don't think you should *give* it to us, George," she says. "How about we just take a look at it instead?"

George pauses briefly, as if weighing the decision, before finally settling on a quiet "Sure." Maybe he's regretting his risky offer. After all, he could lose his job for handing over evidence. If he *shows* it to us, well... Sheriff Myers doesn't need to know.

Amber digs through her bag, her hands clawing for something until she pulls out a small digital camera. "I brought this to take some photos for my dorm . . . I guess this might be a better use."

George gives her a soft, slightly uneasy smile. Without saying a word, he motions for us to follow him toward a dark store doorway. There's a crowd lingering, but they're not paying us any attention now, not here. Their eyes are fixed on the area cordoned off by police tape.

Finally, he presents the evidence bag. Amber takes it and quickly starts snapping photos, with the flash on and off. After all, there might be a small mark or clue that can only be seen from certain angles or with a particular light.

"Thank you, George," Amber says, returning the bag.

We head back onto the street, George with his hands in his pockets, attempting to act natural. His worry is almost palpable.

"Make us proud," he says, and I can hear the desperation in his voice.

I guess that's what a killer does to a small town.

9

AMBER

The library is cold as the door clicks shut behind me, a stark contrast to the warmth of the morning sun outside. The lock gleams, brand-new, like it's been recently installed. It clashes with the worn wood around it. A shiver runs down my spine, not just from the chill in the air but from the strange feeling of being back here once again. For a moment, I let myself forget everything that's happened in the past few months and it's like nothing has changed. But the illusion quickly shatters as soon as I glance toward the front desk. Because of course Mrs. Adler isn't there.

Instead, Cassie now occupies her place, hunched over a computer screen, her eyes locked on whatever she's reading. Her glasses dangle off the bridge of her nose, eerily similar to the way Mrs. Adler used to wear hers. The resemblance is unsettling. Must be a librarian thing, even if she's at least fifty years younger.

She hasn't noticed me, so I look around, forcing myself to replay last night's fiasco. The tables and chairs stand neatly in their proper places, as if nothing happened, the familiar, comforting scent of old books lingering in the air.

That's when it hits me.

The ghoul had been standing almost exactly where I am currently. Only that wasn't the killer, I remind myself. That was just Mayor Gomez's publicity stunt. I'm sure he's been let out now. The real killer is still out there—and we have no idea what their next move is.

"Can I help you?"

I look up to find Cassie leaning forward, a small smile on her face. The glow of the computer screen reflects slightly in her glasses. Draped over her shoulders is a maroon knitted cardigan. I notice that her dark hair is tucked inside her clothes too. It *is* chilly in here.

"Hi, my name's Amber," I introduce myself. "I'm meeting some friends here."

"Ah . . . AH!" Cassie suddenly exclaims, jolting up from her chair, realization in her tone. "Amber, I'm so sorry. I didn't recognize you from here. Blame the stage lights last night. Or my eyesight . . . it's as bad as my spending habits." She readjusts her glasses, then with a tilt of her head, she gestures toward the back of the library. "Your friends are already here."

I peer through the rows of bookcases and spot some movement in the back. That must be them. "Thank you, Cassie." Before I leave, I ought to strike up a conversation. She's new, after all. If I were in her shoes, I'd want someone to be friendly to me.

"How are you enjoying Sanera so far?"

Cassie's head tilts to the side. While she decides how to respond, her fingers delicately tug at her long, dark hair, pulling it free from the confines of her cardigan. It slips over her shoulders. "I don't know if *enjoying* it is quite the right word. What with everything that happened yesterday."

"Right," I awkwardly respond. "That was a silly question."

"There are no silly questions."

I beg to differ. "So how long have you been a librarian?"

"Not too long, actually. I earned my graduate degree in library science a few years ago. This is my first *adult* job, which is cool."

"That's great." I glance through the stacks again and catch a glimpse of Jonesy's curls peeking out between the shelves. "I've got to get going, but it was lovely to properly meet you."

"And you," Cassie says warmly. "Just shout if you need me—well, maybe not *shout*. I guess I should enforce that rule. You know what I mean."

I giggle with her for a moment, then pass through the rows of shelves. The first thing I notice is the dust.

Mrs. Adler, despite her age, kept this place looking pristine. I still can't believe she's gone. One of the oldest Sanera residents. She seemed to know everything and everyone. Even though I didn't come to the library as often as I should have since moving here, her death still hit me like a punch to the gut. We all started coming here more often after Cam got out of the hospital. It became a bit of a safe space.

"There you are," Cam says when he sees me. "Get much sleep?"

"Did you?" I say. The dark circles under my eyes should answer his question already. It was past three when I finally got into bed and it's only nine now, so understandably . . . we're all pretty tired.

I notice that Patrick is here, yawning into a cup of coffee. That shouldn't be surprising—he's here to be *with* Buffy, after all—but it somehow doesn't seem right. I can't help but feel that having someone outside *the Sanera Four* in the investigation might not be the best idea. But maybe I'm being overcautious.

"Not really," Cam replies. "Funnily enough, my mom's on a work trip."

I groan, and he adds with a chuckle, "And no, don't worry. I've spoken to her three times already this morning. Not taking *that* risk again."

They're all sitting around a makeshift table—books stacked high enough that they've formed an actual structure. I take a seat, my mind stuck on what Cam said. His mom's away on a work trip, just like she was last year when the ghoul struck.

And here we are now, back at the library, researching, just like we were last year. It's almost as if time has folded in on itself.

Patrick holds up a cup, offering it to me. "Decaf, right? I grabbed everyone a drink on the way here since I am kinda crashing the party. I think Buffy mentioned you prefer decaf?"

I blink, genuinely surprised. "I do," I say, touched by the thoughtful gesture. "Thank you, Patrick."

I take a sip of coffee, then say, "Don't you guys think this is all a bit weird?"

"Of course it is. Someone is dead," says Jonesy.

"I know." That is not what I meant. "It's the fact that so many things are mirroring before."

Buffy bites her lip. "So, you think we *do* have a copycat on our hands?"

I shrug. Instinctively, my fingers tap against the table. "There are similarities, aren't there?"

"Like?"

I turn to Cam first. "Well, it's a weekend when us four are back together, for starters. Your mom being on a work trip. The reappearance of the ghoul. Then there's the body being found in the alley where Trevor Ward was kidnapped."

"There's also . . ." Jonesy begins, but he doesn't finish

his sentence. His cheeks flush a deep red.

"What is it?" Cam asks, urging him to continue.

"It was just a thought," Jonesy says, voice quiet. He darts a glance at Patrick. "Maybe it's stupid. But last year, there was a new person in the group." He motions toward Buffy. "And *this* year, there's another new person in the group."

"Me?" Patrick says.

"What's that supposed to mean?" says Buffy, scowling.

"Nothing!" Jonesy twiddles his fingers, clearly regretting that he said anything in the first place. "It was a similarity, that's all. That's what we were talking about. We don't know Patrick . . . No offense, Patrick."

"None taken," responds Patrick, his voice uneasy. "I think."

"Come on, Jones." Buffy throws her hands out in exasperation. "You know Patrick! We've been in classes with him for months now!"

"You're right! But it's another coincidence. You were new last year, Buffy. And now here we are again. Someone new at the start of the case."

Cam nods. "Let's just say, there are certain odd similarities between now and then. We can't disregard the possibility of a copycat killer. Okay, let's get on with the real reason we're here. Do you have your camera, Amber?"

I nod and pull it from my jacket pocket. "My mom nearly caught me looking at it this morning, so I threw it under my pillow. I'm pretty sure she thinks I'm hiding something now—well, never mind. I am."

I turn the camera on, quickly scroll through the photos, and choose a clear one. I pull it up on the screen and turn it around for everyone to get a good look.

"Wait," Patrick says. "Is that a *police evidence bag*?"

Buffy looks to him. "You do not speak a word about this to anyone. Promise?"

"P-promise, of course." His eyes are locked on the camera. He looks half thrilled, half horrified. "So, this is *evidence*? Um, how did you get this?"

With a tight lip, I mimic the motion of zipping my mouth shut and tossing the imaginary key away. Thankfully, Patrick doesn't question the matter any further. He simply lets it go.

Maybe he'll fit in after all.

I let Cam pick up the camera first. He inspects the photo closely for a long moment, his eyes scanning every detail before speaking. "This receipt was found on the body so it might be significant. Either the victim was at this gas station—or the killer planted it on the body. I can just about make out the name—*Maven Gas*?" He squints. "Marked with yesterday's date. Only twenty dollars . . . Well, it's somewhere out of town, the sheriff thought." He looks up at Jonesy. "Jones, grab the map, will you?"

With a nod, Jonesy rises to his feet and reaches for a large, rolled-up map from a nearby bookshelf. He takes little time in pulling off the band that's holding it and unrolling it on the table. It covers the table almost entirely and I'm immediately greeted by a detailed map of Sanera and its surrounding landmarks.

"Not at all daunting," Buffy remarks. "I can't wait until there's computers in here so we don't have to do this by ourselves... What is the name of the gas station again?"

Cam peeks at the paper, trying to decipher the stamped text. "I think it says *Maven Gas*—no, *Haven Gas*. I think, at least." He offers it to me to look, but I was staring at it last night and that's exactly what I thought too.

"Okay..." Buffy begins scouring the map.

"Wait," Patrick says. There's an odd expression on his face. "*Haven* as in the lake? Haven Lake? The one here in California?"

Cam's eyes grow large. "It's like forty minutes away."

"Here it is!" Buffy says excitedly. She points at the lake on the map that's north of Sanera. The gas station isn't marked on this particular map but it's our best lead. And our only lead at that. "Good spot, Patrick."

He's looking at us, still with that odd expression on his face. "But... you all know about Haven Lake, right?" Silence. "You *haven't* heard the legend about Haven Lake?"

A bunch of blinking eyes stare back at him.

"The Lady of Haven Lake? The urban legend?" He blinks back at us. "Seriously?"

"Patrick, we have lives," I say.

"The Lady of Haven Lake is an old folktale," Patrick says. "It's, like . . . super famous. I know I'm a bit of a nerd about this stuff but— Hold on."

He stands, his gaze dancing over the surrounding bookshelves before he suddenly darts off. A few shelves away, we hear a soft thud, followed by the sound of something toppling over. Then, moments later, he reappears with an old book clutched tightly between his hands. It's leather-bound, worn at the edges: either a relic from another era or carefully crafted to look like it.

"Libraries are so rad," he says excitedly as he gently settles the book down on the table. I can see why Buffy finds him cute. He's like the perfect mix of nerdy enthusiasm and jock-ish charm.

The front of the book reads *Folktales of Old*.

"Give me a sec . . ." Patrick murmurs, swiping through the pages with quick fingers. It isn't long until he pauses on a page, his grin widening as if he's found exactly what he was looking for. "Here we are."

We gather round. The first thing I notice is a sepia-toned illustration of a pale woman with soaked black hair clinging to her face and shoulders. Water drips from her white dress, pooling around her bare feet. Behind her is a large body of water. A lake with the darkest surface that exudes an eerie, almost ominous presence.

"This legend dates back to the 1800s," Patrick informs us, his finger pointing to the caption, in faded typeface: *Artist's rendition of the Lady of Haven Lake, 1834.*

I read aloud. "'*The legend of the Lady of Haven Lake tells the story of a woman who drowned trying to save her child. It's foretold that she'll haunt the lake, waiting to exact revenge on those who did nothing to help. Drowning them.*'"

Hang on. Something about that sounds horribly familiar.

I look at the others, searching their faces for a similar reaction. "Someone who haunts the site of their death, waiting to take revenge on those who abandoned their child. Where have we heard *that* before?"

"Another similarity for the ever-growing list," Jonesy says.

"I don't like this in the slightest," Cam mutters as he stands, brushing off the library book dust from his clothes. As he does so, he catches his hand on the hem of his T-shirt, lifting it enough to reveal a glimpse of his stomach. I wince at the sight of his scars, a reminder of what he went through.

It puts everything back into perspective, because we were lucky last time. *Too* lucky, which sounds ridiculous to say. But if we don't figure this out fast, we might not get that kind of luck again.

We need to stop this before it even has the chance to begin.

10

BUFFY

There's a disturbance on Main Street.

"What now?" I say. We've barely taken one step out of the library and there's a crowd gently circulating, all facing in one direction. Some of the market stalls are still being set up, so it's not because of the festival.

"Come on." Cam leads the charge, weaving us through the thickening crowd. Ahead, a line of police cars sits parked along the street. They all seem to point toward a makeshift podium at the center of the chaos. The crowd swells, growing larger each moment.

Beside me, Patrick slows, but with a firm tug, I pull him forward before he can get lost. "Stay with me," I whisper.

We spot a row of reporters clustered at the front of the crowd, right below the stage. This is big. Cameras flash; microphones are raised in anticipation.

"Press conference?" Cam says, halting nearby.

At first, I'm surprised at the absence of a certain pale redhead among the reporters. But the more I think about it, the more it makes sense. This is all beneath Rick Field now.

I'm not the only one to notice.

"Rick's missing," Amber says.

Jonesy tuts. "He's made his riches. He's probably lounging in bed counting his gold coins, like he got the last laugh."

Mayor Gomez steps onto the stage, his presence commanding an immediate silence from the confused crowd. Dressed in a crisp navy-blue suit, his posture betrays him. There's a stiffness in his shoulders and a slight hesitation as he glances at his note cards. He's nervous.

Then, with a short breath, he clears his throat.

"Good morning, Sanera. I want to thank you all for joining me," Gomez says, then tugs at his tie. It's a small movement, but telling. "As you all know, a body was found here in Sanera last night. I made a promise when I was elected mayor that I would do everything in my power to protect the town, and I mean to make good on that."

The irony isn't lost on me. *Protecting the town.* Rich words from a man who, just yesterday, sent a ghostly lookalike to stalk one of his own people.

"A boy has been murdered," he says bluntly, sending a

ripple of murmurs through the crowd. "A heartbreaking and tragic loss for Sanera." He pauses, shaking his head sadly in a way that strikes me as rehearsed. "I can now confirm the identity to be Sanera High's Harry Lanz."

"No."

Cam falters back and I catch his arm, steadying him. This is exactly what he was worried about. The kid who never showed up for tryouts. We should've listened to him, believed him, trusted his gut. Now a boy is dead . . .

Déjà vu strikes me again. Another press conference to inform the town of the death of a teenager. More fake sorrow from the mayor, more camera flashes. It feels all too familiar. The whole situation seems to be unfolding like clockwork, like it's all part of some twisted copycat plan. The same pattern, the same steps, just with a few extra faces.

"I urge anyone to come forward if you have any information on this terrible crime. The sheriff's office has set up a special hotline. Even if it seems unimportant, the smallest details can aid the case."

Mayor Gomez peeks at the cards he's holding. He clears his throat once again. "Now is not the time for speculation; rather it's a time for unity and healing. Sanera is built on small-town values. We can get through this. Again."

The reporters explode as soon as he finishes talking. Most of them blur together, their questions simply noise.

But one question rises above the rest, and clearly the others wish it to be answered as they go silent.

"What will become of the festival in the wake of this tragic death?" a reporter asks, her voice loud and carrying. Her black hair is pinned into a tight bun on the top of her head. She points her microphone out as far as her arm can stretch.

The mayor hesitates. "Discussions regarding the festival continued through the night and we came to the conclusion that Sanera's Hallowed Fall Fest will go ahead."

The crowd erupts.

It doesn't surprise me at all, but it doesn't make me any less infuriated. The crowd seems to contain myriad emotions. Any Sanera resident is surely livid—this is disrespectful to Harry's family, to say the least. But isn't it also just ridiculously *dangerous*?

"So, the festival will go ahead in spite of the fact a killer is on the loose?" the journalist says, her voice cutting through the noise. "Is that really a good idea, Mayor?"

Mayor Gomez struggles to calm the crowd. "I want to reassure you all that this decision was not made lightly. The Plains County sheriff's office is sending additional officers as a precaution—"

"And what about you?" the reporter asks. "Do you take responsibility for your actions this weekend?"

The mayor is silent. "My—my actions?"

"You organized this festival. You hired someone to

harass kids dressed as the Carrington Ghoul. You added fuel to the fire. And now a teen is dead. Does that not haunt you?"

My brows rise at the question. She's not letting the mayor live his decisions down, and good for her. Using the visage of the Carrington Ghoul to promote your festival is the definition of abhorrent.

"My conscience is clear—I have always acted in Sanera's best interests, even if some may see it differently. There will be no further questions," he announces, his voice sharp. Without another word, he's quickly escorted off the stage. But luckily for us, he's brought closer to where we stand. We don't miss the opportunity.

"Mayor Gomez!" Amber shouts.

He turns, the color in his face draining as soon as he locks eyes with us. He scurries away, muttering, "Not now," over his shoulder. "I have a very important meeting to attend."

"This is not safe!" Amber continues as he climbs into a waiting police car. "You do not know what's out there!"

And she's right. Nobody does. Not only do we not know who the killer is . . . but, thanks to the festival, everyone is dressed up, nobody is themselves. It's like trying to find a needle in a haystack. How are we supposed to find one murderous ghoul in a sea of other monsters?

I glance back and my point is proven. A sea of people,

and at least half of them are dressed in costume. Ghosts, goblins, and all manner of unsettling disguises.

"He's putting everyone in danger," I say, watching the crowd. "Any one of these people could be the killer."

In my peripheral vision, I spot a figure moving toward us. As it gets closer, I realize it's the reporter who called Mayor Gomez out. There's something recognizable about her, but I can't quite put my finger on it.

Before we can question anything, she brushes past us, her microphone still in hand, and taps the window of the police car. Clearly, she has more questions. All she gets in response is the car pulling away. She huffs and steps back, muttering something under her breath.

"Do any of you recognize her?" I whisper.

"Not me," Patrick says.

"A little," Jonesy adds. He thinks for a minute, then realization hits. "Wait . . . Juliet!"

The reporter turns to us, looking baffled at first, but her expression clears. I realize now. She's Juliet Lopez. The same reporter and journalist interviewing us tomorrow. I think I've only seen her photograph maybe once.

"Gosh, you made me jump," she says. With one last glance at the car, she walks toward us. "Well, well, well. The Sanera Four. It's lovely to finally meet you in person." Juliet scans us all, a smile brewing on her lips, but I'm sure it dips slightly when her gaze lands on me. My heart sinks. Am I being paranoid, or is she giving me an odd look?

"How are you all?" she asks.

"Good," Cam says. "I mean, given the situation."

Juliet nods. "I know how you feel," she says. "I can't believe what Mayor Gomez has done. Getting some kid to follow you around? And letting the festival go ahead? It's ridiculous."

"Somehow, I don't find it surprising at all," Amber says.

Juliet's sharp gaze shifts to her. "How so?"

Amber tuts. "Let's just say we haven't had the best experience with authority in this town."

"Ah." Juliet tilts her head, her curiosity clearly piqued. "Maybe you could tell me about it tomorrow? This is a chance to tell *your* story, remember." She glances at me. "I need to get this to my editor but I look forward to our interview. Are we still good for the library? What did we say—ten a.m.?"

"Can't wait," Cam says.

"Great" is the last thing she utters before she walks off, the sound of her heels clicking on the sidewalk. She takes a glance back and I'm sure I catch it again. The faint trace of an odd look. It's subtle, but I don't seem to be the only one who notices.

"Did she just give you a weird look?" Amber asks, her eyes suddenly on me. "What's that about?"

I'm glad someone else saw her expression, otherwise I'm not sure they would've believed me. There's no reason I can think of for Juliet to single me out. I don't know the woman, and she doesn't know me. Unless . . .

I stare at Juliet as she walks away. *Connecticut. Nancy.* I think of Mom's warning. Could Juliet have dug up my past? All the facts are out there already—and she is a reporter, after all. They love to dig. Go deeper. Worry creeps up on me. She has the power to twist anything—that's her job.

"I have no idea," I reply under my breath. No need to bring it up now and worry the others. We have more pressing issues.

Patrick takes my hand in his and squeezes it tight. I smile at him gratefully. The closeness is much needed. Patrick. He's another reason to stay quiet. I don't want him involved. Not in this—and not in anything that happened to me before Sanera.

I have no idea what Juliet thinks she's found out about me—but I'm going to find out.

11

JONESY

"Do you think Patrick will be okay?" Buffy asks.

I look over to her as the blurred sights of the highway pass by her. We'd persuaded Buffy it was best he stayed behind today because we don't know what we're getting ourselves into. And, secretly, I'm glad. I want it to be just the four of us.

"It's for his own safety," Amber says from the passenger seat as she peeks her head around. "Did he say what he was going to do?"

Buffy shrugs. "Explore the festival, I guess."

"He'll be with crowds of people, then," Cam says, his eyes on the road. "Tons of witnesses. He's in the safest place he possibly could be."

"The safest place is *out* of Sanera," Buffy says. "But he won't go. Not while I'm still here."

"Silly boy," Amber adds.

"Yeah," says Buffy, with a shadow of a smile. She's touched, I can tell—but she's worried for him too.

There's a prolonged silence as we head north, the only sounds being the hum of passing trucks and the occasional plane overhead. The weather seems to be shifting now that we're out of Sanera—it makes me wonder if the town is just cursed at this point. The sun is shining. It shines in town too, but there's always the hint of a ghostly wind with it.

Buffy is the one to break the silence. "So, while I've got you all. Do you all . . . like Patrick?"

I blink. Luckily, Amber has plenty to say.

"About a hundred percent more than I expected," she says. "I mean, I took one look and thought, *classic simple jock*, which, let's face it, is totally your type, Buffy."

"Thanks," murmurs Buffy dryly.

"But surprise—he's actually a horror nerd with an eye for research. Who knew?" Amber beams. "*And* he got my coffee order right. I think he's perfect."

Buffy laughs. "So one thumbs-up. Cam, Jonesy?"

"We like him, Buffy," Cam says, again saving me from answering. "You two seem great together. But I think it was a good call leaving him behind today. We don't need someone new clouding our judgment right now. If he were here, we'd be worried more about keeping him safe than solving this thing."

"I understand, but I think you're all forgetting that *I* was Patrick last year," Buffy says. She turns to me. "You didn't want to let *me* in at first, did you? And now look."

She's right, I think. My anxiety about newcomers—Buffy last year and now Patrick—is silly. Unexpectedly, I smile. College has been great, and Buffy has been a major factor in that. I can't imagine it without her. If I'd been told that we'd be best friends when I first met her . . . I would've died laughing. It just proves that books cannot be judged by their covers, or a person either for that matter. Buffy might look like a classic preppy, popular girl, but beneath all that, there's kindness, and one hell of a sharp mind. I've learned not to take people at face value. Not anymore.

"You're right," I say. "But the point still stands. The four of us work best as a unit. We need to focus on getting to the bottom of this before anyone else—"

Suddenly the car bumps and jolts, rocks flying up around us as the tires struggle for grip. I look out the window, trying to see what's causing the trouble, and I'm met with the sight of a large wooden sign.

WELCOME TO HAVEN LAKE

"I think we found the gas station," Cam calls out.

A run-down building sits before us. It looks downright abandoned. The wooden paneling across the front side of the building is starting to peel off. Like Carrington Manor, the windows are boarded up with little care.

"Delightful," I say.

Cam pulls up outside and the car squeaks to a stop. We pile out of the vehicle and stare up at the gas station. HAVEN GAS, the crumbling signage reads.

"Well, that was easy enough," Amber says. She's the first one to investigate, walking toward the building without checking her surroundings first. I thought she was the horror aficionado. The rest of us follow more nervously.

Steps creak beneath her as she mounts the low wooden decking and peeks through the door's small window.

"It's dark inside," she says. Then she notices a laminated sheet of paper tacked to the wall. She reads the text aloud. "*'Reopening for spring break.'*"

Hmm. It makes sense. It's mostly day-trippers and hikers out this way, so probably no reason to keep this place open when business dries up in the fall. But someone *was* here—and recently, according to the receipt . . .

Cam steps forward, cupping his hands to shield his eyes as he looks through the small window in the door, leaning against it as he tries to see. "It's dark as all hell. I just need—"

He falls forward as the door crashes open, the sound of it loudly echoing through the quiet. The next thing I know, Cam's on the floor, wincing as he tries to push himself up. "Ouch."

"Oh God," I say as I reach for his hand and pull him up. "Are you hurt?"

Cam gives himself a quick once-over, checking his scars. He breathes a sigh of relief. "Just my pride."

"Good," Amber adds. "Your pride could do with a knock."

Buffy steps forward this time, passing the rest of us to be the first inside—if you don't count Cam's failed entrance. "It's . . . something."

We all file into the abandoned gas station. The boarded windows emit only a small amount of light, but it's enough to give us a glimpse of our surroundings. And by surroundings, I mean . . . not much. The white metal shelves are nearly empty.

But if you opened the windows, restocked the place, it would be a regular old gas station. There's a cash register and racks for magazines, all draped in thin veils of cobwebs. A few fridges stand without the expected hum, their shelves empty. Right now, the place looks like it was pulled straight out of some postapocalyptic movie, where everything's abandoned and you're fighting to survive.

"This place hasn't been in use for a few months . . . at least," Cam says. "But the receipt is dated yesterday . . . Amber, do you have the camera, so we can check?"

Amber nods, pulls it from her back pocket, and powers it on. A few quick taps, and she finds the right photo. She hands the camera to Cam.

He squints at the photo for a long moment. "Can you zoom in?"

Amber nods and turns the dial. "What are we looking at?"

"The date . . ." Cam says, eyes narrowing even further. "Tell me that doesn't look tampered with." He angles the camera so we can all see.

10/25/2002

I lean in, looking properly this time. The ten is wrong—uneven, like someone has written *over* it. That wasn't always a ten. It wasn't always October.

"This receipt is from July," I say slowly. "Someone changed it. That ten is fake."

"Exactly," Cam agrees.

Buffy glances between us all. "What does this mean, then?"

We look around. There's nothing out of the ordinary in here, not that we can tell at least. Things have been closed for months now. But someone has tampered with the date.

"Why here?" I ask.

"I say we hurry up and find some clues or something," Cam says. "Sheriff Myers is bound to be on her way. Let's check any back rooms and then outside. And for the love of God . . . *don't* split up."

Amber snorts. "I think we've already learned our lesson there," she says.

There are two rooms to the back and a door leading out to a jungle of overgrown shrubbery. The right-hand room is an office of sorts, including an old, stained couch. Rows of storage cabinets line the farthest wall. We don't even need to sift through them to know they're a maze. But we do find receipts.

"This is exactly the same as the one on Harry's body," Amber says, holding up a receipt from one of the cabinets.

"So the receipt is genuine," Cam says slowly. "But the date was changed." I swallow. It's all adding up. Harry Lanz never came here. He couldn't even drive. He was a freshman.

No. Whoever left that slip of paper was the killer, I'm sure of it.

"So the killer changed the date," Cam says, "to bring the police out here . . ."

"To see what exactly? Black mold and asbestos?" I ask as I take in the derelict building. Nothing is clicking.

Cam shrugs, leaning his back on one of the empty walls.

"What if they wanted *us* to find it?" I say. "What if whoever did this is reeling us back in, leading us right where they want us?"

"There's no reason to think the clue was meant for us,"

Buffy says. And she has a point. "We were only shown the evidence on a whim. If Officer Pérez hadn't shown it to us, we'd be none the wiser."

"Maybe the killer didn't care who found it," I say, unsure. "They just wanted someone to come looking. Why? I don't know."

"They call it a mystery for a reason," Amber remarks as she pockets the receipt. "I for one don't want to ponder the ifs and buts. I want to get out of here as soon as possible."

"Agreed," I say.

We take one more pass over the room before moving on to the last, Cam leading the way once again. I think he's feeling guilty—I *know* he's feeling guilty. He called what happened to Harry Lanz early on, and we told him to not worry. So the guilt is all of ours.

The autopsy won't be finished yet, but Harry was maybe already dead by the time Cam first noticed he was missing. There was nothing any of us could've done. All we can do is hope to not repeat history.

Cam stops at the final room. With a slow hand, he pulls down the handle, but it doesn't open. "Locked."

I step to the side. "Well, that's a shame. Let's go—"

"One sec," Cam says. He kneels down until he's at eye level with the handle, peeking through the keyhole. "There's some sort of equipment in there. A few screens, I think. A computer, maybe?"

"Security cameras?" Amber suggests.

Cam starts shaking the handle again, trying to see if force will open it. But I don't have a good feeling about this at all. Just like I didn't have a good feeling going into Carrington Manor last year. Like we're following someone else's script.

"Cam, stop." I place my hand on his shoulder. He looks up at me with those annoyingly blue eyes. They're hard not to fall into. "We're already going to be in enough trouble if Myers finds out we came here. No need to add vandalism to the list."

For a long moment, he stares up at me and I'm unsure if he's going to listen, but he eventually gets up in a huff. "Fine. The police will check it out anyway."

"Let's check the grounds and go," I say. "Haven Lake is right outside. There might even be more clues there."

12

CAM

Harry Lanz. I can't stop seeing his face. Not the bloodied one, but the excited one out on the track. Like the others, all he wanted was a shot at making the team. I can't imagine how his friends are feeling. *God, Dean* . . . he was going to text him.

Jonesy and I walk together down to the lake. The girls are a little ahead of us, their voices a mere mumble from here, and I find myself zoning out into my own thoughts.

If I had gone to Sheriff Myers as soon as I thought something was wrong, Harry could've been found earlier. He wouldn't have had to lie there in that alley alone. But then again . . . was he even in the alley the whole time? The police think he was moved—we don't know when. All we know for sure is that he was killed way before we found him.

But the idea of being able to prevent this haunts me. I know I'm overthinking it, but it doesn't make the guilt any easier to carry. It doesn't make me feel any less horrible.

I *wanted* this. I wanted the Sanera Four to get back together, and look at where it's gotten us. Well, I regret it all. I didn't want us back together if it meant *this*. I just know we've only scratched the surface. This can of worms is nowhere near done. Not by a long shot.

"Cam." I feel a nudge at my side. Jonesy. His voice is soft, but there's a hint of concern in it. "Are you okay?"

I nod and force a smile. But it's pointless because Jonesy can see through me; he always has been able to. He knows how I'm really feeling. I won't admit it aloud. I've never been that sort of person. Even when Dad died, I kept it all bottled up, mostly for my mom. She already had enough on her plate.

Jonesy's hair falls into his eyes, as usual. He carefully moves the curl from his view, inspecting me, his gaze darting across my features. "I know that look."

"What look?"

He raises his brows. "You know what look."

The girls are out of earshot. I sigh. He knows I'm more likely to divulge things when it's just the two of us. We've been through enough together. He knows that I trust him. He knows that I love him.

"Honestly, I feel hopeless," I admit. I expect Jonesy to argue but he does the opposite. He listens, his eyes true. A warm hand caresses my back, urging me to speak. "I've missed the gang. I've missed us together. I felt like I didn't have a purpose after you all left. I wanted a reason for us to work together again. Now I feel like my wish for the comeback of the Sanera Four has backfired."

"Hey," he whispers in reply. His voice instantly soothes me. It has a gentle quality, soft enough to calm even the busiest of minds. "None of this is your fault. And just because you *feel* like you don't have a purpose, it doesn't mean you don't have one." He points at my heart. "You just haven't found it yet."

I smile as I fight back an approaching tear, but I'm not quick enough. It slips down my cheek and I catch it. I manage a small laugh, trying to lighten the mood. "That was really cheesy."

Playfully, Jonesy shoves me. "Way to ruin a moment."

"Thank you," I say, locking eyes.

"Yeah, yeah, yeah." He puts his hand to my cheek. His touch is warm. "I love you so much."

I open my mouth to tell him that I love him too—

A scream pierces through the air. Sharp, frantic.

My walls come crashing down. It's Buffy. I look at Jonesy, and his face is already drained. Without a question, we both accelerate into a sprint.

Buffy and Amber are standing in front of the lake, motionless. I hadn't realized how far we'd lagged behind.

Jonesy and I fly down the pathway, our feet pounding

against the dirt. My heart hammers in my chest. I have no idea what we're about to find. Whatever it is, it's bad. I can feel it.

"What's wrong?" Jonesy asks as we reach the girls. We see their expressions first. Horror-struck would be an understatement. Their eyes are wide, pupils dilated, and their bodies are trembling, as if they embody fear itself.

They don't say a word, but motion toward the lake with shaking hands.

Something in me tells me to run, to get away from this before it's too late. But it already *is* too late. We're already in this.

My eyes refuse to take in the picture properly. I see the green-blue of the lake, the beautiful nature of the surrounding area. I see the small dock area, accompanied by an algae-covered boat. I see a bird floating in the water a short distance away. But the mound before me takes a moment to dissect.

"Holy shit," Jonesy mutters.

I follow the shape of the mound, from top to bottom, then finally make out something. A foot. I gulp. The scent of damp earth and decay curls into my nostrils, making my breath hitch.

Another body. I now realize why it took me so long to identify it—the face is obscured by tangled seaweed and pond scum. The lake's gentle movement causes it to move slightly, rocking with the waves.

I step forward before anyone else.

Edging closer brings the body into better view. I still end up crouching some distance away, so as not to disturb the area. But I quickly gather that the body is male—an older male. His pale skin reminds me of how Harry's looked—ghostlike and bruised. His dark hair is speckled with gray, though it's hard to make this out clearly due to how damp it is. It clings, sodden, to his scalp in wet strands.

"It's a guy." I notice his wrinkles and his clothing, trying to estimate his age. "Middle-aged, most likely."

The others come closer. "Maybe it was an accident. He fell in and drowned," Buffy suggests, but immediately disagrees with herself. "*No.* Too much of a coincidence."

Coincidence. There's that word again.

"Look at his neck," Amber says.

My gaze drifts upward. There's bruising on his throat. *Again, like Harry.* He was forced under. Not an accident.

"Oh man," Jonesy says. He paces for a moment. "Does this not just feel extremely strange to you all?"

"Well, yeah. Understatement."

Jonesy stops, assessing the situation again. He points at the lifeless man. "I mean, about the criminal's modus operandi?"

Amber glares at him. "Again. In English?"

"MO," says Jonesy plainly. "A criminal's pattern or method while committing their crime. Harry Lanz was seemingly murdered by asphyxiation but was additionally found with a singular stab wound. And now there's this body . . ."

I finish his sentence. "Which has no additional stab wound. This guy was drowned."

"Exactly. Which could mean something or *nothing*."

I force myself to look at the body again, to see if there's anything we've missed. There's got to be something we're not accounting for.

"Wait," says Buffy. "We've been thinking the killer meant the police to find the body. The only reason we know about this place is because George Pérez showed us the evidence, right?" She looks around at us all. "And he was *ever so* eager to hand it over. He didn't seem to care if he was caught giving away evidence."

We all exchange glances, an uneasy sensation creeping through me before settling in the pit of my stomach. "You're thinking George sent us here on purpose?"

"This all seems too obvious," Amber adds, crossing her arms. "George is too obvious. He was so nice!"

"He was," Buffy replies. "But maybe that's the point? Maybe he's not the killer. Maybe someone is using him, manipulating him into giving us the evidence—"

"Enough." Jonesy cuts through the tension, loud and firm. It's out of character for him, but if anything gets him agitated, it's the unknown. And I can't blame him. "We're going in circles. We're not about to stand here throwing around theories while there's a body decomposing at our feet."

He's right. This isn't the time or place.

The air is stale, unsettling. All I want to do is get out of here, tell the sheriff what we found, and go back to normal. But that's wishful thinking. Even if we could, we still have the festival to deal with. And the interview tomorrow.

I stand and take a last look at the man. I wonder if he is important to the case—or was he simply in the wrong place at the wrong time? I glance back at the gas station—unless he owned the station? Wait—

I look at his clothes again. Heavy-duty Timberland-like boots on his feet. He's wearing dark green shorts that I almost mistake as black due to the wet. But it's his shirt that makes me realize. A beige button-up, soaked through and plastered to his skin.

I turn to the others. "He's a park ranger."

They step closer to get a better look, practically glued together as they lean over the body. One wrong move, or an accidental slip, and they'll regret getting too close.

"Maybe he was in the way," Buffy suggests. "Saw something he shouldn't have."

Amber agrees. "Maybe the killer was at the gas station for some reason and this guy saw them. Then he had to be . . . dealt with." She squirms. But there is no pretty way to say it. He was murdered. Plain and simple.

"Wait," Jonesy suddenly says. His eyes are on the body. "Cam, there's something in his right hand."

With slow steps, I close the short gap between the body and myself. I realize Jonesy is right. There is something in the man's right fist. It might easily have been missed because it's so thin.

"Is that a wire?" Amber asks.

I grab the top end of the sharp object. It's a dirty brown color. "It sure is," I say as I, against my better judgment, pull it from the man's lifeless hand. It's a bad idea already, but too late now. It's maybe twenty-ish inches long. I find I can bend it easily.

"Oh man, I am so freaking confused," Amber says.

Buffy chimes in. "Makes two of us."

Jonesy shakes his head. "I think we've seen enough."

Normally, I'd probably contest the decision, try to see what else we could find, but I realize we've done all we can. We need law enforcement to discover the body and collect any evidence before it's washed away, if it hasn't been already.

Instead of putting the wire back where we found it, though, I keep it in my hand as we head back to the car. Something tells me it's of more importance than we realize. But I'm unsure if Sheriff Myers will think the same.

As we near the gas station, I take one last look from this angle—the side of it is equally decayed. There's a small boarded-up window, better preserved than the front ones. I almost look away but something catches my eye.

It could have been easily missed, being nearly shrouded by the overhanging roof. But its stark black casing makes it stand out a little against the wooden building.

A security camera.

I bound up the wooden decking. It creaks like hell under my weight. One wrong move and I'll be in the floor. I fling open the door and hurry inside, through to the back rooms.

"Cam, what are you doing?" Jonesy shouts after me. I didn't exactly explain my thought process, just pointed at the security camera and ran into the gas station.

"I bet everything that the computers in *here*"—I reach the locked door and give the handle a rattle as the others join me—"let you see out *there*." It's only a theory but the camera has to be linked to something.

"But it's locked," Amber says.

Buffy nods. "Yeah, you're not getting in there—"

I throw myself into the door.

I fall through.

"Fucking hell, Cam!" Jonesy yells, then a herd of footsteps ensues. I scramble back to my feet. "Do you have an obsession with hurting yourself or something?"

I chuckle and raise my hands, palms up, into a shrug. "Maybe I'm a masochist."

"You're such a—"

"It looks like you're right," Buffy says, pointing to the screens. "Perfect view of the lake."

I spin around, my gaze sweeping across the two different computer screens, both of them glowing softly with a blue tinge. There's clearly a brief delay—the left one shows a black-and-white view of me running through the gas station.

But it's what's on the second monitor that intrigues me. A view of the lake and the ranger's body. Clear as day, just not in color. "Do you think this can be rewound? To see if we can catch anything?"

Jonesy steps forward. He's the only person who knows a thing about this stuff. "It depends on their system. If it's digital, it can store footage for a week or so. If it's VHS . . . you can dream on."

Jonesy follows the wires with his fingers as he explains. "VHS tapes have to be rewound or replaced to record new footage, obviously. So this will hold maybe six hours of footage?" His wire search takes him to a large black box near the monitors.

"Well?" I ask.

"VHS," he says as he returns his focus to the monitors, already absorbed in fiddling with the settings. "Given the station has been shut, it should be footage from summertime. But the fact that it's live right now . . . someone's rewound it. Today."

The footage on-screen rewinds, the screen pixelated

with black-and-white static. I stare at the monitor, perplexed because it's unchanging.

Jonesy points at the date in the corner of the screen. Saturday, October 26. "They wanted someone to see this."

Jonesy fast-forwards through the footage. But nothing. The body doesn't move. It stays completely still until the tape rewinds all the way to the beginning. Only the sun shifts as the hours roll back. There's nothing on it.

"Then why?" Jonesy mutters, leaning back into the chair, confused. But his attention soon drifts as something catches his eye. To the right, another VHS tape. He picks it up and turns it over in his hand, not bothering to hide the bafflement on his face. "It's the only other one here."

"Put it in," I say. "Worth a shot. We have nothing else."

With a shrug, he ejects the old tape and slides in the new one. It takes a moment. A whir, a click, then the footage begins to play. No body.

My eyes drift to the date. *Thursday.* This past Thursday. Could the body have been sitting there since then? It did look worse for wear. Pale, slack, not *fresh* at all.

"It's earlier footage," Amber says, leaning in. "Fast-forward."

So, Jonesy does.

A chill creeps by, sending a shiver right through me and forcing my hairs to stand on end. The thought of the culprit standing right where we are only a few hours ago feels strange. The body has lain there, waiting for someone to find it. This footage was purposely recorded so we could witness whatever we're about to—

"Wait, rewind!" Buffy yells. She points at the screen. The body is back. We missed what happened.

Jonesy's fingers tap away at an accelerated pace. The security camera footage freezes and speeds up again. As soon as there's an unfamiliar movement he presses play and sits back. "Here we go," he whispers.

The lake is still, only the occasional ripple disrupting the otherwise-serene landscape. No body. Through the screen, it looks majestic, almost, like something from an old animated Disney movie. I glance at the time in the corner of the footage: 5:45 p.m.

The sun is soon to go down. It's not the clearest footage because there are no streetlights by the lake. But it'll have to do.

"There!" Jonesy calls out, his finger on the left side of the screen.

A figure comes out of the wooded area. It's briefly shadowed. Then, as the sun's rays catch it, the familiar silhouette of the park ranger becomes clear. He paces around the clearing, his eyes scanning for any hint of trouble. It's his responsibility to ensure everything is in order. At this point, nothing appears out of place, but the stillness of the moment seems almost too peaceful.

"Looks like he's on his rounds. Making sure everything is . . ." Amber's voice trails off. She leans even closer, her eyes on . . . I don't even know what. If anything it looks too perfect. Too calm, especially knowing what's going to happen.

"What do you see?" I ask.

"The water," she replies. Her finger lands on the screen, right by where we found the ranger's corpse. "The ripples. I swear I just saw something move there."

"Are you sure?" As the words leave my lips, I see it for myself. Something as dark as the lake itself, barely breaking the surface. It emerges for a moment, then disappears again, leaving behind a ripple that spreads outward.

It seems we're not the only ones to have noticed. The park ranger's head cranes toward the disturbance, his attention drawn. His head even cocks sideways as he tries to make sense of it. A step closer. Then another.

I gasp as the ripple turns into a dark mound, breaching the lake's surface, clawing out of Haven Lake. A person. Or what looks like one.

"Oh my God," I mutter.

The figure rises from the lake, emerging slowly. Slick black hair clings to its face, obscuring most of its features, though I catch a fleeting glimpse of the pale skin beneath. The eyes are dark and the body is bony. It stands motionless, arms low and limp. A white garment is draped over its thin frame, heavy and dripping with water.

"That looks a whole lot like the lady from the legend Patrick showed us," Amber notes, a wobble in her voice.

The ranger staggers backward, indecisive about which way to run. I'm sure they take an oath to protect the parks, but I doubt it says anything about creepy ghostlike women rising out of the lake.

"The Lady of Haven Lake," I whisper.

Everything happens in a blur. Water thrashes as the ranger is dragged under with an unnatural strength, arms around his neck. The lake looks as if waves are crashing on the shoreline as he struggles to stay afloat.

We all watch in horror, hoping, begging, praying for another ending. But we know how this ends. With terrifying strength, the woman straddles the ranger, forcing his head beneath the murky lake. Every few moments, he manages to come up for air, but it's not enough. He soon goes quiet, his body limp, and the lake settles once again. The woman stands, towering, stares for a long while, watching and waiting for the body to move—it doesn't. Her hair clings to her face, masking her features.

When satisfied, she bends and puts something in the ranger's hand. The wire, I think. Then she retreats. Into the wooded area she goes, exactly the same way the ranger came. Her soaked white dress is the last thing we see before she's swallowed up by the dark forest.

"So we're dealing with a whole new legend?" I ask.

"Why the weird wire?" Buffy adds, pointing to the wire I almost forgot I was still holding.

"Two murders, two legends," Amber says. She finally

stands upright, massaging her temples. "Are the Lady of Haven Lake and the Carrington Ghoul working together?"

I hold up the wire, still perplexed by it. "Well, this was left for a reason. The receipt on Harry's body led us here. So this wire . . ."

"Should lead us to the next killing," Jonesy finishes for me. This is already bigger than before. The mystery is complex. Someone is playing with us. Making us think that the ghoul is back, only to throw a wrench into our plans.

Amber sighs into her palms, letting out a mini scream. I think it's how we're all feeling right now. But I could yell at the top of my lungs and it still wouldn't be enough. It won't help. The only thing we can do now is solve this mystery before the death toll grows.

I can't pull my eyes from the screen. The scene before me is, once again, serene, save for the drowned body drifting on the lakeshore.

Amber leans forward and, with a decisive click, shuts off the monitor, sending the screen pitch black. "Staring at that damn screen is going to do us no favors," she says. "Let's get back to town. I have a feeling we just stumbled into one seriously messed-up horror sequel."

13

AMBER

I can't unsee it.

The black-and-white footage is permanently etched into my brain. No matter how hard I press my palms against my temples, desperate to force it away, all I can imagine is the gargling of water. It fills my head, a suffocating sound. I squeeze my eyes shut, willing myself to think of anything else, but it doesn't work. If my mind doesn't go to the lake, it latches on to some other agonizing detail of the case. It's inescapable.

"Sorry for the delay," Sheriff Myers says as she enters the interview room. An older male officer put us in here while we waited for the sheriff to get across town. She was busy with the festival, apparently. Luckily, she didn't waste any time getting back here.

She takes the seat opposite us, like it's an official

interrogation. I know we're not actually in trouble—well, I hope not—but it sure feels like it. "Okay, talk."

I don't say anything because I don't know how to exactly explain the situation. *Sorry, but we looked at some evidence and it led us to an abandoned gas station and . . . a dead body.* It doesn't really scream sanity.

Cam speaks when no one else does. His voice is calm as he says, "Before we divulge anything, I want to ask that no one gets in trouble. Us, any other officers, anyone."

Sheriff Myers's face is a confused picture. "What makes you think you get to call the shots here? Last time I checked I was in charge."

The tension is palpable. If I were Cam, I would've folded in an instant. Speaking my mind is something I pride myself on, but in front of the sheriff is not one of those occasions. God, if Mom and Dad were here . . .

I don't want George to get in trouble but I don't know if we can get around it. He wouldn't have shown us the evidence if he wasn't okay with the consequences. Unless he's the killer . . . no, it's not him, I'm sure of it. Too obvious. You don't meet the killer at the start of the story. *Well, most stories.*

Cam doesn't give in. He meets Sheriff Myers's gaze without flinching. I want to curl into a ball, so I can only imagine how Jonesy is feeling. Conflict is not his middle name. But Cam seems okay with it.

And somehow it works.

"Fine," Sheriff Myers mutters, after a long, exasperated sigh. She folds her arms. "No one gets in trouble. Now, tell me what you've got."

Cam glances to my jacket pocket. I get the memo. With slow and careful fingers, I retrieve the receipt I took from the cabinet at the gas station and place it on the table. Sheriff Myers's eyes flash.

"Is that what I think it is?" she asks, trying to restrain the annoyance in her voice.

"No . . ." Cam exhales sharply. "It's not the receipt you found on Harry Lanz's body. But it *is* one from the same gas station. We tracked down the receipt to Haven Gas, an old gas station beside Haven Lake," Cam says, and pauses, as though waiting to process the sheriff's reaction.

She nods, her neck stiff. "We were going to check it out this morning."

"Well, you're in for a . . . treat, then. When we got there, the station had been out of use since the summer. Which is interesting, given the date on the receipt. We realized someone—the killer, presumably—must have doctored the date. They *wanted* you to go to the gas station. So we went looking around at the lake and came across . . . a body."

"*What?*" At once, Myers's demeanor shifts. Any ire melts into something far gentler, like concern. "Are you kids okay?" She glances at all of us, checking us over with softened eyes. "Hold on—" She pulls her police radio to her mouth. "Dispatch to all available units in the Haven Lake area, ten-four, code three, respond to 187 at Haven Lake."

A short moment of silence fills the room before the radio buzzes with static. "Unit eleven and unit fifteen to dispatch, ten-four, en route to Haven Lake, ETA eight minutes."

Relieved, she takes a deep breath, closes her eyes a moment. A look of dread creeps onto her face. After regaining her composure, she turns her focus back to us. "Continue."

"We were going to leave there and then." Buffy picks up the thread. "We had every intention of coming straight here—but as we were walking back to the car we spotted a security camera. It was pointed directly at the crime scene. So, to cut a long story short, we found a computer in the gas station and on it . . ." Buffy pauses, clearly grappling with how to express her thoughts, a flicker of hesitation crossing her face.

Eventually, she chooses her words with care. "We saw everything."

It's past five thirty in the evening by the time we get out of Sheriff Myers's hair and grab some food. I notice that a lot of the town businesses are shut—plenty of townsfolk remember last year. But it's a futile attempt at keeping people safe. The festival is still going ahead. Soon, the streets will be filled with the innocent and the unaware, walking straight into whatever horror waits for them.

A full investigation is now underway, so we had to make statements, explain everything ten times over, all while keeping the wire a secret. We agreed on that together. The only reason we're this far in the case is because we illegally accessed evidence in the first place, so here's to another crime.

Cam shoved the wire in the back of his car, hidden beneath a blanket and some old grocery bags. It's only a matter of time before they realize we've taken it; time clearly isn't on our side. *Maybe we should have handed it in.*

Cam drives us to Jonesy's and retrieves the wire from its hiding place. We slip into the house and instantly a wave of nostalgia crashes over me. Can it really be nostalgia if it's only been two months? Maybe not, but it sure feels like it.

I lead the pack as we head to the basement. The familiar creak of the floorboards is comforting; the waft of sandalwood is welcome. It doesn't erase this morning, but at least it helps wash away the stale smell that seems to cling in my nose—lake water and death.

I feel something brush past my legs and jump, but my panic is quickly replaced with pure joy.

"Macey!" I practically screech, my voice an embarrassing mix of excitement and relief. My legs turn to Jell-O as the floor becomes my new home. The gorgeous brown ball of fur barrels into me in the most delightful way, tail wagging furiously. Her persistent piglike snorts save this day from being completely awful. It's as if she was a cute little swine in another life.

"Oh, I've missed you, girl."

Macey snorts again, which I take as an agreement from her. Shortly after, she realizes that everyone else is here too. With rampant joy, she goes around the group, forcing everyone to the floor. Macey is definitely the honorary member of the Sanera Four.

Jonesy is the first to get up. "As much as I want to stay here all day, we have things to discuss." He heads over to the couch we've spent a gazillion hours on and quickly falls onto his butt again.

Macey joins us as we convene at our seating area. Before Cam sits, he places the wire in the center of the table, its presence demanding attention. He roughs his hand through his hair, takes a seat beside Jonesy, then leans forward with his elbows on his knees, eyes locked on the evidence.

"Okay . . . what do we think?"

I shrug. "I think that no matter how hard you stare at it, it's not going to reveal its secrets," I tell him. We agreed to turn it in if we figured out what it is and if it's important to the case.

"It's all I've got right now," he replies, his gaze unwavering.

Buffy inspects the wire too. Then she leans back and

ponders aloud. "The receipt was an easy clue. Maybe now they're getting harder. Whoever is planting these doesn't want us to solve it."

"Or doesn't think we *can* solve it," I suggest.

Jonesy huffs, his hand still stroking Macey, who's already asleep at his feet. "The thrill is what drives some people. It could be the case here. They're playing with us, watching us take the bait . . . seeing how long it takes us to work it out."

"Then why make the receipt clue so easy, but this seemingly . . . impossible?" I ask no one in particular. It's more rhetorical than anything.

My horror movie brain tells me there's something here, but nothing fits into the right formula. A copycat would make the most sense with Harry Lanz's murder, but the Lady of Haven Lake has disrupted that idea completely. Is there a chance that there's *two* killers? Working together? Or competing?

Cam speaks again. "I think today has proven to us that we can't expect the expected. Last year was wild, but something's different this time around."

"You can say that again," Buffy adds.

I sigh. "Don't hate me but I'm about to horror movie you all right now." I don't wait for their reactions. "The sequel is always bigger, with more deaths, more blood, and nobody is off-limits. Take *Scream 2*, for example. Fan favorite Randy . . . bye-bye."

"Spoilers," Cam mutters.

"We literally did a *Scream* marathon last year," I contest, knowing he's joking. But still. "All I'm saying is that if this killer, or killers, can lure us out of town to play their twisted game, all bets are off. They could strike anytime, anywhere—"

Abruptly, heavy footfalls echo down the stairs, each step growing louder and more frantic than the last. We freeze, but then Jonesy's mom, Maggie, appears. Panic is written across her face, holding her features hostage. Her eyes are wide and searching, pupils enlarged, and her skin is flushed.

"Oh, thank God you're all okay. I basically ran out of the store when I saw your text." She crosses the room at top speed and practically pulls Jonesy to his feet, enveloping him in a desperate embrace. He wraps his arms around her tightly in an attempt to comfort her.

After a long pause, she finally sighs and retracts her grip. "You know what . . ." she murmurs, her British accent barely touched by her time in the States, "you're all safe, that's all that matters."

I wouldn't go that far. We're safe *for now*, maybe. But we're not safe. Not in our homes, not anywhere. No one is. That poor park ranger was just doing his job. I feel awful because we don't even know his name. His identity hasn't been revealed yet, so in his death, he's only an occupation to us.

"We won't go into details," Cam says, trying to soften the blow. "But it was . . ."

"A lot," Jonesy finishes for him, which is the best way to put it. No one should have to see the things we've seen, especially teenagers. But we got ourselves into this mess in the first place. We put giant red targets on our backs the moment we decided to play mystery solvers last year. We thought we could handle it, thought we could step away when it was over, but now I'm afraid those murders are going to follow us forever.

We're too far in. Now, even if we wanted to stop, there's no turning back. It's as if we were meant to solve this. We're finding the pieces, but the puzzle is just too complex.

Maggie takes the last free armchair, settling into our small circle. The fear on her face has faded, replaced by a different type of pain. I almost miss it as her unwieldy hair falls into her face, briefly obscuring the small, painful quirk of her lips. *Like mother, like son.* They look identical.

"I am so sorry this is happening again," she says. Her voice trembles slightly. "You don't deserve any of this. You're just kids!"

"Mom, it's fine," Jonesy says as his mom's tears begin to fall. Parents are the ones who should be comforting the child, not the other way around, which makes it extra uncomfortable when it does happen. At the end of the day, they're still human.

"But it's not!" Maggie says passionately. "It wasn't okay then and it isn't okay now." She shivers. "I'm glad I'm in a better place this time."

I watch as her thoughts take her elsewhere—to the Carrington Ghoul case, I can only assume. Maggie had her struggles back then. Well, she still does. There isn't an overnight cure to addiction. But Jonesy's told us time and time again how much work she's put in to get better. And from what I can see, she's been really committed to her recovery, not only for Jonesy but for herself too. It's truly inspiring. The strength it must have taken to get here is something I can't fully grasp.

"Well, Sheriff Myers seems more promising than what we dealt with last year," I say.

Maggie chuckles, despite the circumstances. Sometimes a laugh is necessary. Cam's taught us as much. "It's a low bar," she says.

"She sent out officers as soon as we told her what happened," Buffy adds. "They were at Haven Lake within, like, ten minutes."

"So, she did the bare minimum?"

I wonder about Sheriff Myers myself. My mind goes back to the evidence bag—why hadn't the police gone to Haven Lake before we did? Surely in a murder case, the evidence is going to be analyzed right away? She doesn't seem incompetent, so was there another reason? Or am I seeing suspicious behavior where there isn't any?

Maggie stands up, brushing off her jeans. "I know I'm being pessimistic, but I worry about all of you. And before you say anything, I know you're all adults now. But a mom is allowed to worry!"

"We only wanted to help," Jonesy explains.

His mom bends down to plant a kiss on his head, her fingers brushing through his shaggy hair before she turns to leave the room. "I'm sure there are ways you can help *without* putting yourself in danger," she says, half joking.

She pauses when she catches a glimpse of the wire still sitting on the table. She frowns. "Why do you have a broken guitar string?"

"What?" is the first thing that comes to mind.

"A broken guitar string . . ." she repeats. "What's that doing here?"

So that's what the wire is. Maggie plays a bit of guitar—how did we not realize? I look to the others, who seem every bit as perplexed as me. This mystery is getting even more confusing. Why on earth did the killer plant a guitar string on the body?

"Why a guitar string?" Buffy asks the same question aloud.

Maggie tuts. "That's what I just asked you—"

"The first clue was so simple," Jonesy says, interrupting his mom. Her brows rise but she soon realizes she's missing some serious context. "Is there a music shop in

Sanera that I'm forgetting about or something?" Jonesy continues.

I shake my head. My mind feels like a ball of yarn that I can't find the end of. It's killing me. The clue is right there, yet we have no idea what it means. Every aspect of this case feels like catching smoke with my hands. Virtually impossible.

"Wait. Do not tell me you *stole evidence*," Maggie finally says. When we don't answer, her face ends up in her hands. "You kids are going to get me arrested. I am quite literally an accessory to a crime right now."

Jonesy looks up. "Mom."

"Goddammit. I'm assuming Sheriff Myers doesn't know about this?"

We all shake our heads.

"Great. Why would she?!" Her sarcasm is off the charts. "At least she's not actively *looking* for the stolen evidence that is sitting in my house."

"Well . . . not yet," Cam says. "There's footage of the string being placed by the body . . . and us taking it."

Maggie basically whimpers at Cam's truth bomb. I know everything in her wants to scream at us, berate us for being so stupid. And I would too.

"God, why do people have kids," she mumbles, mostly to herself. Then she shakes her head. "No, it's okay. You're going to solve this thing before anything happens. Okay, a guitar string. What could that mean? Music . . .

Metal . . . Blacksmithing . . . Medieval." She fires off random words that—in her mind—must link together.

"Mom, I love you so much," Jonesy says. "But I do not think blacksmithing has anything to do with this."

"Well, I apologize for thinking outside the box," Maggie snaps. "What ideas do *you* have?"

"Not a whole lot," I say truthfully.

We sit there, pondering, for what feels like hours. The silence stretches on, like time has been slowed. Excruciating. The fact that the clue is right there in front of us, practically begging to be understood, only makes it worse. Our first clue was straightforward, almost *too* easy, but now . . . what are we missing?

"Well, I'm going to go back upstairs and leave you kids be," Maggie says. "I'm going to *strongly* suggest you call the sheriff in the next hour to let them know what you've done." She heads up the stairs before stopping, her hand hovering on the railing. "Oh, and be careful if you're going to the concert tonight. I know I won't be able to stop you kids from going—"

Cam gasps and leaps to his feet so fast he almost loses his balance. I'm pretty sure his knees crack from the speed in which he moves. "The concert? Maggie, you are a genius."

"I am?" Her voice is a mixture of confusion and . . . more confusion.

We're just as clueless, staring at Cam as he seems to piece things together in real time.

He looks around at us all. "Part of the Saturday schedule for the festival is *a benefit concert*, headlined by a local band."

"Right. The Séance Sisters," Maggie adds.

"Yeah, of course! I love them!" Buffy says excitedly.

Cam leans down and picks up the string. He drags his finger across its frayed, slightly curved length. "It can't be a coincidence. The receipt took us to the lake. A guitar string . . . it's sending us to the concert. *Something is going to happen at the concert.*"

The words settle over us, thick, heavy. For one long, terrible moment no one moves. And in that time, the realization hits. Cam is right. Something is coming.

"Could the Séance Sisters be the targets?" Buffy says slowly.

"It looks that way, right?" Cam says. "The guitar string would indicate someone in the band, surely?"

"When is the concert?" I ask, my pulse immediately quickening.

We all look around at one another; our faces are panicked mirrors. Then we turn to Maggie on the stairs.

"It starts at seven." She glances at her watch. "In fifteen minutes."

14

BUFFY

The stage is lit when we arrive.

"They're about to come on any minute," Cam says. He pushes through the growing crowd, veering for the right-hand side of the stage; we follow blindly. We were expecting a crowd, but nothing like this. The park building has been transformed from its usual state, with the stage ahead of it.

Maggie called ahead, but she couldn't get through to the sheriff, only an officer who couldn't get ahold of her either. But she said she'd keep trying. A downside of living in a tiny town. On the busiest night of the year, they're overrun.

The traffic was wild—in the end, we ditched the car and ran for it. My heart is beating out of my chest, which is not helped by the hundreds of people swarming, pushing, and shoving. It's hard to focus with the noise closing in from every direction.

I quickly check my phone. There's a new text from Patrick. Damn, I forgot all about him for a minute. Girlfriend of the year material right here.

I'M AT THE CONCERT. WHERE YOU AT?

My boyfriend, who I am supposed to be spending time with, is here somewhere. But he'll have to wait. I try my best to send a reply but I'm being jostled too hard by the crowd. I'll find Patrick once we're sure the band, and us, are safe. Hold tight, Patrick.

I don't let go of Amber's hand. Her grip is strong as we weave through the masses; I make sure I can still see Cam's bobbing head in the crowd.

Eventually, we reach a metal barrier, separating the crowd from backstage. An older man—a security guard—looks us up and down, rolling his eyes. A gray beard—or an attempt at a beard—covers his lower face, and his mouth wrinkles extend across his face. Someone clearly doesn't moisturize. "No passes, no entry."

"Something terrible is going to happen," Amber shouts, just as the crowd roars to life. An instrument blares over the loudspeaker, sending vibrations through the ground. *Shit.*

"You need to trust us!" she yells again, rocking the

barrier in frustration. The tension in the air thickens as the music pulses. It's happening. The lights flicker, casting an eerie glow, and then—*bam*—three spotlights slice through the dark. A heavy drum sounds on every fourth beat, echoing through the air. A grand entrance.

"Nice try," the guard replies. "Get back or I'll have you escorted out of here."

Then the crowd cheers again. The first notes of the song cut through the air, the band's voices filling the space in a three-part harmony. The energy is electric, but for us, it's a countdown. Time is running out and there's nothing we can do about it.

"You're making a big mistake," Jonesy says, raising his hands in a gesture of peace. "People are going to die."

The security guard scoffs at us, irritated, then leans over to look each of us in the eyes. "Have you kids been smoking? You know I can get you arrested for that?"

Is he being serious? I have to look away to hide my anger but in doing so I spot an officer a few feet away—it's George Pérez.

"HEY!" I yell. "GEORGE!"

Thankfully, he hears me over the blaring music. He frowns and hurries over. "What's wrong?"

"We found something," Cam says. "We can't get through to Sheriff Myers but we think the band is in danger—"

He doesn't need to finish his sentence before George is opening up the barricade for us to pass. As we rush through, we make sure to give an evil eye to the guard—he doesn't seem too appreciative.

"What's going on?" George closes up the barrier to avoid any more chaos.

"We don't have time to explain but we're almost certain that the killer is here. We need to get the girls offstage. Now. It's not safe." My words tumble out.

Without a word, George nods and dashes off in the direction of the stage.

As we race to catch up with him, we duck into the backstage area. As we run past, I almost miss the familiar face: Rick Field is tucked off to the side, in a VIP area, talking on the phone, gesturing—angrily, I think. His eyes flick up, curiosity sparking at the sight of us, but whatever's happening on the phone at his ear clearly matters more because he doesn't make a move to follow us.

We catch up with George, who's talking to the sound guy, who pulls a pair of headphones off his head when he notices the police uniform. "Sorry?"

"It's an emergency. We need to evacuate!"

"But they just went on!"

To my surprise, George shoots forward and yanks the power cord from the wall. In an instant, the flickering stage lights go dark, and the music cuts off mid-note. A wave of confused wails sounds from the crowd.

Before anyone can switch the electronics back on, we

rush up onstage. A sea of eyes stares out at us and I've never felt more exposed. There's no rest for the wicked.

"What's going on?" the guitarist, Jeannie, says as I grab her arm.

"We have to go, now," I tell her, and drag her from the stage. She doesn't resist. If the Sanera Four are personally escorting you somewhere, something must be up. Fortunately, the others have enough comprehension to put two and two together and the band follows us quickly off the stage.

In the thirty seconds we were onstage, the backstage area has exploded into disarray. At least ten people surround George, cursing him out for pulling the plug. "It is a police emergency!" he exclaims loudly.

"Girls! Who are these people? What the hell is going on?" A man pushes his way forward, face contorted in fury. "Let me through. I'm their manager!"

His voice is loud and unpleasant and he's wearing the most obnoxious pair of indoor sunglasses known to man.

"It's an emergency," George explains again. "Their lives might be in danger if they go onstage."

"Oh please," the man says, waving a hand dismissively. "Not more of this ghoul nonsense, is it? We've already established it was the mayor pulling a stunt. When can they go back on?"

I meet Cam's eyes. There's no way we can risk the

concert going ahead. The guitar string clearly points to the concert, and right now, these girls are a likely target. The killer wants attention and all eyes are on the band. This is the perfect storm.

Cam looks back at the stage one last time before turning to George. "Evacuate the concert now."

The girls follow us quietly. We turn into one of the building's more private hallways, which quickly muffles the growing crowd confusion. George called Sheriff Myers and she was already on it. Maggie had gotten through to her. Now the evacuation has begun, much to the concertgoers' annoyance. They don't know what we could have saved them from. And honestly, we don't really know either. Not entirely.

In the hallway, the Séance Sisters huddle together, their eyes unblinking as they stare at us. Their manager stands a few feet away and doesn't hide his scowl. I can't help but feel a little starstruck by them all.

The Séance Sisters aren't nationally known yet, but they're still headlining, which is a huge deal. Plus, their song "Spellevated" goes so hard. It's only a matter of time before they're on top of the world.

Paige, the lead singer, is the first to speak.

"Okay, can you now explain why the Sanera Four just ruined our biggest gig of the year?"

Her hair is jet black, flowing down to her stomach,

a stark contrast to her almost alabaster skin. Like her sisters, she's dressed in gothic fashion, in black scattered with deep hues of red and purple.

I look to the others to indicate that I'll explain. "You'll all have heard about the murder yesterday," I say, and they nod, eyes still fixed on us. "There was another this morning and, well, we have reason to believe the killer is here." Paige flinches and one of the others gasps. "We needed to get everyone to safety. And seeing as it's your concert, you might have been the target."

The girls couldn't be whiter if they tried. They basically freeze in their tracks, horror finding home in their faces, making their mouths resemble an O.

"Based on what?" their manager suddenly asks. He doesn't seem bothered in the slightest, like this is all an inconvenience for him. "Because canceling this gig is going to cost me thousands of dollars."

I reply timidly, knowing the reaction I'm about to receive. "We found a . . . clue."

Unsurprisingly, he outright laughs in my face, while somehow simultaneously texting away on his phone. One would think a potential murder would hold his attention for a moment or two. "Oh, the kid found a *clue*? Pipe down, Nancy Drew. This is ridiculous. They'd better be back on that stage in the next ten minutes!"

"Greg, this is serious," Raquel, the drummer, says

uncertainly. "There's been two murders. We should be safe and—"

"No!" he bites back. "What is *serious* is the fact that you're never going to book another show again." He huffs, fury basking in his eyes. "Back onstage in ten. I will be in your dressing room when you've all grown up."

Without further comment, Greg turns and heads down the hallway, phone pressed to his ear.

"What a jerk," Amber says.

The Séance Sisters all nod in unison.

Raquel eventually sighs. She pushes her bleached-blonde hair out of her eyes, exposing the dry whites. I guess that's what fear does to some people. "Big mistake on our part. But thank you for getting us out of there. I can't lie, we were nervous when we heard the concert was still happening."

Paige continues. "All Greg cares about is money. He refused to shut this down and Mayor Gomez didn't help." She grits her teeth. "Yeah, he's an asshole."

"He seems it," I say.

"What now?" Jeannie asks.

George speaks up. If I'm being truthful, I'd forgotten he was here. The past five minutes have been a stressful blur. "Sheriff Myers will be here soon. I'll arrange for some officers to escort you all home safely and make sure you have a protective detail tonight. Just in case."

"Thank you, Officer," Jeannie replies. She looks to the rest of the gang. "Do you really think we were the targets?"

"We can't say for certain," Cam answers truthfully. We don't know anything for certain at all. This whole thing is a game of cat and mouse.

"It's not worth the risk," George says firmly. "Where can we wait till Myers gets here?"

"Our dressing room. Greg will be there, but we can handle him." Paige laughs. "He may be an asshole but it's three against one." Her spunk tickles me. The band members have an almost otherworldly presence, and it surprises me that Paige is so . . . normal. I half expected her to speak in riddles.

We follow their lead, George right on our tails, as we pass through the twisting hallway. I don't want to jinx anything, but it seems something went right for once. That is, if we've interpreted the clue correctly. The thought that we might have miscalculated somehow terrifies me.

The girls stop at the door to their dressing room. Raquel turns to us before she pushes down on the handle. "Sorry for the mess." She laughs. "We weren't expecting visitors—" She shoves the door open and I see her eyes go wide.

I brace myself for the so-called mess—maybe some clothes strewn across the floor, empty glasses scattered like forgotten relics of a late night. But as the room comes into full view, my breath catches. My eyes lock on a pool of red, spreading fast across the light carpet. Just like that, my stomach hits the floor.

Time seems to freeze, then the silence shatters; we all

scream in a chaotic symphony. The girls fall backward and push George into the room in their place. But he simply stands there in terror, eyes locked on the lifeless body before him.

Greg is dead.

"Oh my God," Raquel finally says as tears flood her eyes. "What do we do?"

"George!" Cam says. He shakes the officer in an attempt to disrupt his fear-induced paralysis. "Snap out of it. The killer could be anywhere."

Something clicks inside George and he becomes an entirely different person. He shoves a wedge into the door to hold it open, then pulls his radio to his mouth. "Need immediate backup at the festival dressing rooms, we've got a deceased, requesting units for scene preservation."

I'm sure in that moment George has nothing to do with any of this. *That* was a true reaction. There's no way to fake that kind of genuine shock.

Cam steps into the room, his hands shaking. No matter how many dead bodies you see, it never gets easier. We only spoke to Greg minutes ago. Then it dawns on me.

"The killer was waiting for you," I say softly, glancing at the sisters. The band members really were the targets. Our suspicions were right. A cold shiver runs through me, freezing my veins as dread tightens deep inside. "They were going to wait in your dressing room and strike when you were done with the show."

Amber grips Jonesy's hand in one of hers and mine in the other to step into the dressing room. The sisters follow. Jeannie's entire body is shaking so hard she uses the doorframe to stay upright.

George kneels beside the body, wincing as he takes a closer look. "His throat was slit." I watch him carefully lean forward, his focus sharp. "It's a big cut. From the left carotid to the right. He would've died almost instantly."

"I can't believe this is happening," Raquel says. She and Paige join us but instinctively shield their eyes, unable to fully take in the gruesome sight before us. Jeannie looks as if she's going to throw up. They may not have liked Greg, not by a long shot, but he was their manager at the end of the day. I can't imagine how they're feeling.

"Everyone," Jonesy says slowly. "Look."

We follow his pointing finger to a mirror that covers the entire right side of the dressing room, its shiny surface marred by streaks of red. Fresh blood drips under the harsh lights, sliding in slow lines across the glass, spelling out words. The letters are jagged and rushed. The coppery tang lingers in the air and I can almost taste it. Metallic and oozing with death.

"'*Crimson Witch, Crimson Witch,*'" I read aloud, my words seeming to pulse like they're alive. They don't register in my mind properly, not at first. Then a realization strikes like a knife on hot stone. "Another legend?"

"Damnit," says Cam. "They're still playing with—"

There's a scream and I whip around. Jeannie is on the floor. A towering presence stands in the doorway, still and ghastly, head tilted, causing thick white hair to fall over its face. A white dress, stained nearly all the way to the top in deep, crimson red. Blood. And that's when I see it. The handle of a knife in Jeannie's stomach. Time slows as Jeannie's feral screams rip from her throat and her sisters watch in horror.

George snaps out of it, drops onto his knees beside Jeannie, hands scrambling to slow the bleeding, his face tight with panic.

No. This is not how this ends.

Cam clearly has the same idea because we both lunge forward at the same time. The figure raises its head and I see its face.

Black tears have fallen and stained a ghostly white face, leaving thick dark tracks. Unlike the slick and soaking hair of the Lady of Haven Lake, this hair is unkempt and unruly. The blood-written words burn into my brain.

"Crimson Witch," I mutter.

The witch runs. So do we.

"Wait!" yells George. "Don't go after them!"

But we don't listen. The killer was in the room this whole time, lurking behind the open door. The thought terrifies me. They were right there, out of sight, listening, waiting to escape. Jeannie was just in the way.

We pound down the corridor. "She's getting away!"

Cam yells as the witch veers left. He summons a spurt of speed and it's like he's been put in fast-forward. I'm glad we've got a runner on our team.

Cam whips around the same corner just a few seconds after the witch. My heart pounds as I try to keep up but my legs don't work like that. Eventually, I turn the corner for myself to see the culprit disappearing through the emergency exit.

"NO!" Cam yells. Then he trips and goes down, landing on his face. "Shit!"

I waste no time in pulling him up, noticing the warped flooring—of course. We bound across the remaining distance and burst through the door. A sinking feeling settles in my gut because I know we're too late.

Outside, the darkness stretches around us, interrupted only by the light of a single flickering lamp. An area behind the stage, away from the main road. It would be silent, if not for the faint cries of "Keep it moving." Somewhere in the dark, the crowd is still being cleared.

Minutes pass as Cam and I scour the area, never separating, always side by side. There's only two of us. Splitting up is not an option.

As the crowd's noise fades more and more, a heavy silence settles in. It's the kind that presses in, makes you think you're hearing things.

But then I do. Faint. Hard to place. It almost sounds like

something being dragged, like fabric scraping across the ground. I hold Cam by his arm, needing the comfort.

"Help me," a faint voice sounds.

We freeze. I can't see where it's coming from, but I know that voice.

"Help . . ."

My eyes dart through the dimly lit area until they land on a shadowy figure slumped in the darkness. My breath hitches.

"Patrick?" My feet take over, carrying me toward him in a frantic sprint, with Cam close behind. I drop to my knees beside him, heart pounding as I touch his cheek. His skin is clammy to the touch. Then I see it. The dark, wet stain spreading across his clothes.

"You're bleeding."

"Is it that obvious?" he says through short breaths. "Some chick ran into me and sliced me with something—"

In the moonlight, I can see gnarly gashes in his arm. Blood has soaked all over his white jacket.

"This is going to hurt," I say, applying pressure to his wounds, hoping I'm not doing more damage than good. "You won't be able to wear this again," I add, trying to keep the situation calm.

He winces. "Not unless I want to get some seriously odd looks," he says, laughing through gritted teeth.

I force a smile. "Yeah, I don't think bloodstains are making a comeback any time soon."

Patrick groans. "Who knows? Maybe I'll start a trend."

Cam is looking out into the darkness. He's never going to live that down, not with himself. We were so freaking close. The killer was almost in our grasp. "Why did I have to fucking fall?" he whispers.

"Cam, it's fine," I say sternly. "Help me get Patrick up."

With one last look into the darkness, he obliges, though I still catch him glancing around, searching for any sign of life. Any hint that we're not alone. "What were you even doing back here, man?"

Patrick gets to his feet, assisted by our wavering grip. He winces in pain. "I texted Buffy when I got here. When she didn't respond I could tell something was wrong. Then the lights went off. I tried to speak to security but they were having none of it. They started evacuating but I managed to sneak back here to try to find you . . . and then this figure comes sprinting out of the door and slams into me." He shudders. "They were soaked in red and—"

"Yeah," I say grimly. "We know."

"What happened in there?" he asks, his eyes searching my face. "Are you okay?"

"I'm fine," I tell him, and his expression relaxes. "But as for what happened . . ."

A supercut of the last ten minutes cycles through my mind. The blood, the terror, the screams. It plays on an endless loop.

"It's a lot," I say simply.

15

JONESY

"So nice to see you all again," Sheriff Myers says sarcastically. She closes the dressing room door behind us, silencing the outside footfall in an instant. "Second body in a day. This killer is working quick."

She takes a seat on the couch. We were put in a nearby dressing room—not the one where Jeannie was attacked—so we can make statements. It seems like that's all we're doing nowadays.

"Is Jeannie okay?" Buffy asks, her voice wobbly. "And Patrick?"

The sheriff nods. "I think so—we'll hear more soon. They should be at the hospital now. They'll be shaken up, of course."

"I'd be worried if they weren't," Cam adds. I already know he's blaming himself for letting the culprit get away.

"Have you checked the security cameras?" he continues.

"The team is working on it as we speak," Myers replies. I notice a clipboard in her hand with a wad of papers embedded in it. She glances down at it before addressing us again. "I need you all to think hard about this. You were personally involved in the Graham case last year—known as the Carrington Ghoul murders. It's impossible not to suspect these killings are connected. And you seem to be carrying out your own investigation." Cam opens his mouth to protest, but she holds up her hand. "You're not in trouble for taking the evidence, but please, for the love of God, don't do it again. I'm here to help you. You can *trust* me . . . Is there anyone *you* think we should be looking at?"

We all sit in silence, pondering. A profile of the killer forms in my mind. Whoever is doing this is smart. They know what they're doing and they're happy to go the extra mile to make it theatrical—or cinematic, dare I say. God, Amber's right. We are in a horror movie sequel.

"Rick Field," Amber says at last with a shrug. "He's definitely exaggerated his involvement in the Carrington case. Murder did his career a lot of good, maybe he's already thinking about what to do for a sequel . . ."

Sheriff Myers nods and makes a note. "Do you have any proof of this?" The harsh sound of pen on paper scratches something in my brain.

Amber sighs. "No."

"But he was backstage tonight," Buffy says. "I saw him."

"Okay," the sheriff replies. "We'll look into his alibis for both attacks. Anyone else?"

I think over every interaction I've had since I've been back in Sanera, retracing my steps, trying to remember if I saw anything out of the ordinary. I return to the moment I arrived. I went and saw my mom, then met the gang for dinner, then we went to Rick's launch—

My eyes widen.

"Do you guys remember what the guy on the door of Rick's launch said to us?" I ask.

Cam squints, remembering. "That he was a big fan?"

I shake my head. "He said that there's an online forum where they discuss us, our case. Shit, they *make up their own endings*." My eyes connect with Sheriff Myers. She's scribbling away. This might be something. "He said they sometimes write their own monsters."

"Holy shit," Amber says. "Jonesy, I think this is it."

"Three murders, three different legends," Cam joins in.

"So, the Carrington Ghoul, the Lady of Haven Lake, the Crimson Witch," I repeat. That's the first connection we've made in what feels like forever.

My excitement must show on my face because Sheriff Myers raises her hand, slicing the energy in the room.

"Let's not get ahead of ourselves," she says. "But this is

a start." She clips her pen onto the clipboard with a sharp *click*. "Let's go and find this forum."

"I can't believe this is allowed," I say as the words blur past me on the page. So many ridiculous comments and titles, so many discrediting what we did. "*'Sanera Four, more like Sanera Snore'*—how old are these people?"

Sheriff Myers ignores me as she scrolls on, a compact laptop in front of her. "It seems the website is a split of theories and fan fiction." She double-clicks on one of the threads entitled *Which Is Your Fave of the Four?* A slew of replies appears, flooding the screen.

"This is insanity," Buffy says. "There's thousands of comments. All about *us*."

Cam paces behind us. He's blaming himself still, I think. First for Harry's death, now for losing the Crimson Witch. Whatever I'd say right now wouldn't comfort him. Sometimes you need to process your thoughts in silence. He'll work through it in his own time.

I turn back to the forum and read every word that comes on the screen. Every insult, every bit of praise, every theory, every single thing that happened—or didn't—is dissected. Some like us and some hate us. The emotional whiplash messes with my head. Time starts to blur after what feels like an hour of staring. It's never-ending.

"Can we not refine the search?" Buffy asks at last. "Try and narrow it down to threads that have been discussing these specific urban legends?"

Sheriff Myers turns to her. "How so?"

Buffy leans over, taking over the controls. "This is more of Jonesy's strong suit, but I've got this . . . If we cross-reference the names of the legends we've dealt with . . ." She taps away at the keys at lightning speed, then slams down the enter key. "There."

One thread matches all of Buffy's requirements. *Ultimate Urban Legends*.

FROM CANDYMAN TO BLOODY MARY, WHO IS THE BEST OF THEM ALL?

Amber tuts. "Someone watches too many movies."

We all turn to her, eyebrows raised.

"You're one to talk," I say playfully.

She nudges me. "Except I don't murder people! I may be a movie buff, but at least I know where a movie ends and real life begins!"

Myers continues to read. "There's a ton of replies, suggesting different legends that could fit the bill."

"Please don't tell me," I mumble.

"The Mothman, Phantom Clowns, Bloody Mary, the Crimson Witch, Robert the Doll, the Lady of Haven Lake . . ." Her voice trails off listing all the different answers. Hundreds of opinions. It's clear whoever's doing this has gotten their inspiration from the forum. This entire *fan site* has planned out the perfect killing spree.

"Are there usernames?" Cam asks, eyes wide.

Myers nods. "Hundreds. And we'll investigate them all, believe me. Our killer might well be on here. Or they simply drew inspiration from it—but we'll find out. Get IP addresses if we can. It takes time but we can run a background check on all the commenters. Either way, it's too much of a coincidence not to investigate."

"Can we get it shut down?" I ask. Maybe it's too late for it to make a difference but I know I would sleep a whole lot better knowing there isn't shit like that online.

"It's potential evidence, so I'll get digital forensics on the case," Myers replies. With that, she pushes back her chair and packs up her stuff. "Thanks," she adds. "This is the first breakthrough we've had."

"What now?" I say.

"Sleep," she replies firmly. "You'll need it." Her gaze lingers on us for a little longer. Then, without a second glance, she turns and heads for the door, her footsteps disappearing.

As the door opens, the world outside rushes back in. The distant hum of sirens fills the air as I spot police tape, the dark smears of Jeannie's blood staining the floor. It's a reminder that, unless we stop this, the weight of it will crush us.

16

CAM

"Thanks for letting me stay again, Maggie."

Jonesy's mom waves her hand in the air like it's no big deal. She's never had an issue with me staying over but it's common courtesy to at least thank her. "It's my pleasure, honey. I wouldn't want you holed up alone with your mom away." She shudders, clearly thinking about what happened to me the last time I was home alone with a serial killer on the loose.

"When is she coming back?" Jonesy asks.

"Damn, you want to get rid of me that bad?" I laugh, the sound escaping in a soft chuckle. He doesn't crack a smile, and I drop the act. "She's catching a flight in the morning. After last year she's not taking any chances, so she got the first flight available."

Maggie smiles warmly, the expression softening her

features. "Well, that's good to hear. But you know you're welcome anytime."

When it came to accepting my status change from Jonesy's friend to boyfriend, I could never fault Maggie. She was ecstatic for Jonesy and me when we told her we were together. Not once did she question it, not even for a second. She didn't make a joke; she was simply happy that we were happy. No judgment, only pure joy.

"Are you boys hungry?" Maggie asks now.

The thought of food makes my stomach lurch. I don't think I can face anything after tonight. "I'm all good," I say, trying to keep my voice steady. We already gave her the rundown of what happened—she forced it out of us when we turned up on the doorstep, visibly shaken. "Thank you though."

We descend to Jonesy's room, the soft thud of our footsteps echoing in the night.

"I am exhausted," Jonesy groans as he launches onto the couch, only to be immediately mauled by Macey—mauled as in lovably licked to death. I chuckle softly at the encounter, knowing full well that I'm next. And sure enough, as soon as my butt hits the cushion, her neck turns, we make direct eye contact, and she pounces. For a good few minutes, she's relentless and I'm at her mercy, laughing as she covers me in affection. But just as suddenly she loses interest entirely, and trots off to bed. The duality of dog.

"She is so . . ."

"I like to say she's the physical embodiment of whiplash," Jonesy says. He leans back against the couch, eyes closed. In the warm, low light, shadows contour his face, making his jawline pop more than it usually does.

Three months changes a lot, especially in a relationship. We speak every day, but even then certain memories fade. It's not until now that I remember the mole under his chin and the birthmark behind his ear.

"What are you staring at?"

I blink and realize I've just been inspecting his features for however long. He's turned his head now and we're looking directly at each other, faces inches apart. A smile creeps onto my face. ". . . Nothing much."

"Oh," he says in a faux disappointed manner. "I thought you were just enthralled by me."

I scoff. "Don't flatter yourself."

My smile fades after a moment as the closeness knits together a tension. I gaze at every part of his face, taking my three months' worth. But eventually, our eyes lock once again. His dark eyes are a tempting void that I could slip into.

I try to not think about today, but it's hard not to. Murder is not something you can wish away. It could have been any one of us who got hurt . . .

Jonesy's safety means the world to me, and knowing he's in danger makes my stomach twitch. It makes me ponder the eternal dilemma: Why do people even try to love when the world is so eager to threaten it? Why do we open ourselves up when we know it will end? One day, we die.

There's no winning with it, is there? Love is beautiful, but vicious. No matter what, someone is forever left behind. But we do it anyway. Fall in love. The intoxication completes us; it makes all the pain, all the fear, worth it. And in spite of everything, I wouldn't change it for the world.

"Hi," Jonesy says plainly. His voice is warm and immediately silences any thoughts I had. He has that effect on me. My world stops when it comes to him.

"Hi," I whisper as my voice croaks out the syllable. "I've missed you."

Soon, our interview should be over and Jonesy will go back to school. We'll go our separate ways once again and I'll be left alone. That is, unless this case isn't solved. No one can go back to their lives until it is.

"Stop it," Jonesy says, his voice calm but resolute. "Right now. Let's be here in the moment . . . The thing about the future"—he pauses, letting the weight of his words settle in the air—"it's always just out of reach. It's uncertain, ever-changing. But the present, right now, will slip away before we know it. If you're not careful, you'll miss it entirely."

Jonesy rests his hand on my cheek. His closeness sends

a rush through me, melting every inch of my body beneath his touch. "I love you."

Before I know it, as if drawn by an invisible string, I lean forward, my hesitation gone. Our lips meet with a calm ferocity, an intensity from our months apart. Time comes crashing down around me. Those weeks alone feel like a fable now. The world outside ceases to exist. There's only the softness of Jonesy's lips, stretching the moment into something timeless.

Eventually, we break apart, our foreheads resting against each other's as we catch our breath. The air between us is charged. A heavy sigh escapes me, and in the silence that follows, my reply flows out like water, trembling with sincerity. "I love you too."

17

AMBER

Buffy throws her phone onto the bed before flopping down beside it, face-first into the blankets. Then she turns her head toward me. "Patrick was discharged. Superficial wounds. He was back at his hotel within an hour, even though I tried to get him to come home with me. Said he didn't want to bother my mom. I doubt she would've minded . . . I mean, an attack kind of changes things."

"Yeah," I say as I rub moisturizer into my skin. "So why the long face?"

Admittedly, Patrick hasn't had a great first impression of Sanera. He's barely seen his girlfriend who he came here to spend time with, and instead, he got attacked by a knife-wielding killer. Not a great start at all.

"I feel guilty," Buffy says. "He wouldn't be here if it wasn't for me."

"Buffy," I say softly yet sternly. "You know damn well this is not your fault."

"I know, I know." She scoots over to sit beside me on the bed, and rests her head on my shoulder. This weekend is flying by, but not in a good way. The phrase "time flies when you're having fun" clearly does not apply in this situation. "Time flies when you're being hunted" has more of a ring to it in this moment.

"Do you want to see him?" I ask. I don't particularly want to go out now, but if it'll make Buffy feel better, I'll do it in a heartbeat. There is absolutely no way I'm letting her make her way alone, especially at night.

"No, it's fine. He needs the rest." Buffy offers a tight smile, but the worry in her eyes betrays her. "I can't believe this is all happening again."

"You and me both." I nudge her. "Come on. Let's try and put this aside for now. Just for tonight, let's have some fun. Or, you know, as much fun as we can manage in this mess."

We end up staying up later than we intended, hauling blankets, pillows, and an unreasonable amount of snacks down to my living room for an impromptu movie marathon. Only lighthearted, feel-good rom-coms are allowed. No tension, no thrills. Not for a while. Even I can't face a horror movie.

Our interview is in the morning and I already know it's going to be interesting. I'm glad we vetted the reporter, and

Juliet seems decent (I liked how she held Mayor Gomez accountable), but *any* reporter is a risk. They have their own agenda—but I guess so do we. They want the headlines, but we want the truth. Sometimes they don't correlate.

"I've missed being able to do this," Buffy says as our second movie, *Notting Hill*, ends. The screen goes black, casting the room in darkness before lighting up again with the credits. "Just us. I've been so wrapped up in Patrick that I've forgotten what this feels like."

I chuckle. "Oh, young love . . . so easy to get whisked away by the excitement of it all. Next thing you know, you're ditching your friends like they're yesterday's news."

My comment comes not from experience but from an overabundance of film knowledge. It's a well-known rom-com trope.

"Whatever," Buffy jokes. "But yeah, I . . . I like him. A lot." Her cheeks are slightly pink in the television light. She turns to me with a mischievous look in her eye. "What about you? Anything on the romance front?"

My eyebrows furrow in confusion, then expand as clarity dawns. "Oh, no." An awkward chuckle slips out. "I . . . Not for me."

This conversation is one that I've dreaded—one that confuses even me. I'm bisexual, that is one thing I know for certain, and my friends know it too. But since starting college, I've had time to reflect on what I really want, and not what society deems "normal."

"No one at UCLA that's taken your interest?"

I shake my head. "I don't think I want that right now," I say, the truth ringing clear in my tone. The moment the admission escapes, a weight I hadn't even realized I was carrying lifts. An invisible weight.

I carry on, surprising myself. "I think . . . relationships come with an expectation, even if it's unspoken, that I don't think I'm ready for." The more I speak, the freer I feel; the more it feels like a truth I've been avoiding.

Buffy doesn't challenge me. Instead, she gives my hand a gentle squeeze before pulling me into a warm embrace, her presence enough of a silent understanding.

"I'm proud of you," she whispers.

"Thank—"

Bang. The noise startles us both. I pull away from Buffy as my head snaps to the source of the sound. The living room is cloaked in darkness, with only the faint flicker of the television shifting shadows across the walls. My eyes dart around. Then I finally see it.

A figure stands near the doorway, motionless, almost absorbed into its surroundings. The shattered remains of a glistening vase glints faintly at their feet, only visible when the light hits it. My pulse pounds. They're dressed in full black, from feet to shoulders, with a knit beanie pulled low over their face, cut just roughly enough to reveal a pair of piercing eyes. Eyes that are locked straight on me.

Time slows. I try to scream, but no sound escapes my mouth. Buffy, however, manages to find her voice. As she screams, the figure bolts out of the room and to the front door.

Do something.

Buffy runs after the figure and pulls me with her. We fumble through the dark until we reach the light switch. In a second, warm light cascades into the room, exposing the fleeing culprit as they reach the front door. Dark hair is fastened into a ponytail that peeks through the back of the beanie. They're a slim figure, wearing a black jacket and trousers.

"What are you doing here?" I shout, my legs locked in place.

The figure doesn't take the time to answer and instead slips out into the night. I hear another faint thud as I whip around to see my parents bound down the stairs. When I turn back, Buffy is gone.

My parents' faces resemble an expressionist painting with their mouths agape in fear. Mom raises her finger to point at the open door. "Wh-what . . ."

Dad rushes down the remaining steps and halts at the open door, scanning the darkness. "Buffy, get back here," he yells. "I'll call the police," he says firmly, pushing past me to the landline.

When I reach the door, I catch sight of Buffy slowing to a stop, hands braced on her knees. Whoever was here, she lost them. As I turn away, I see her pick something up off the ground and glance at it.

"Sweetheart, who was that?" Mom asks, her voice barely a whisper.

I shake my head. Whoever was in our house was here for a reason. But the real question is: Was it the same person who's been terrorizing Sanera?

"We've got to stop meeting like this," Sheriff Myers says. By her appearance—her unkempt hair and bloodshot eyes—Dad woke her up. "Are you girls okay?"

She joins us on the couch while my parents hover nearby. They're still in their pajamas after refusing to go upstairs and change. They don't want to leave me alone, even with at least ten cops surrounding the area. I catch my mom's gaze as she pretends not to be listening in. She's worried.

"We're fine," Buffy says.

The sheriff adjusts her seating position and crosses her legs. I already know what her question is going to be. "Were they . . . dressed up?"

As in, was this another urban legend come to life? Do they fit the pattern?

I shake my head. "It was someone in black clothing, wearing a beanie over their face. I think it was probably a woman. They had long black hair in a ponytail, but as soon as we saw them, they ran."

"And you chased after them?" Myers asks, nodding toward Buffy.

"Not for long," she replies. "They were already way ahead of me."

Sheriff Myers scribbles furiously in her notepad. "This case gets weirder and weirder. If this was the killer, what were they doing here? It doesn't fit with the rest of the case. No outlandish costume, no visible weapon . . ."

"I don't think this was the killer," Buffy says thoughtfully. "It seems all wrong somehow. The killer has no problem attacking in broad daylight. This person ran off as soon as they were challenged."

"I agree . . . I think," I say, slowly nodding. "There were no theatrics. This person was just . . . lurking."

Sheriff Myers contemplates this. "I see," she finally says. "But we have to consider the possibility that these crimes might not be the work of a single killer."

My eyes go wide. The possibility of a second killer, or even more, had come to mind, but I had pushed it aside. But it's possible. Maybe the Carrington Ghoul, the Lady of Haven Lake, and the Crimson Witch are different people entirely.

"Maybe the intruder tonight is working with the killer, then," says Buffy. "The brains and the brawn."

I stare at the floor. My head is pounding—this is all too much for the middle of the night on no sleep. Clearly sensing my confusion, Sheriff Myers stands. "I'll let you all get some rest." She glances over my shoulder. "Buffy, your mother has arrived."

I turn to see Buffy's mom, Susan, hair wild, wearing pajamas with a sweatshirt thrown on top. Her eyes are filled with worry, but they soften when she catches sight of her daughter.

"Oh, honey," she says, her voice thick with relief as she enfolds Buffy in her arms. "What happened? Are you hurt?"

Buffy squeezes her arm. "We're fine, Mom."

"They chased the intruder off," Dad says. "Well, your daughter definitely did."

Susan's eyes are filled with tears that threaten to dance down her face. She turns to the sheriff with an exhausted expression. "Can you tell me anything more?"

"Only what Buffy and Amber saw. A person dressed all in black, head to toe. Long black hair. A woman, *possibly*," Myers says, recounting our description. "It's not a lot to go off but it's better than nothing."

"But they got away?" Susan asks. There's an odd note in her voice—suppressed anger.

Myers nods. "They got away."

I glance over at Buffy's mom, whose jaw is set with fury. She doesn't attempt to mask it. And honestly, I can't blame her. Her daughter and her friends have already been targeted by one killer, and now another. As a parent, she has every right to be furious.

After a brief, heavy silence, Susan turns to Buffy, her gaze flickering in my direction as well. When she speaks, her voice is dripping with determination, like a realization has suddenly hit her. "You girls should not have to worry like this. You're kids, for God's sake," she says, each word deliberate. "I will do whatever it takes—we all will—to keep you safe. No matter the consequences."

"Mom," Buffy says. Her voice is calm but firm. "We'll be fine. We've dealt with this before and we'll deal with it again. Whoever is doing this clearly underestimates us."

I can't help the way my brow lifts in response. There's a fine line between confidence and *overconfidence*, and Buffy's toeing it closely. I know she means well, but tempting fate is not something I'm particularly keen on. Still, I agree with the sentiment. I just hope she's right.

Sheriff Myers clears her throat. "Buffy, that sort of hubris is what gets people hurt. This killer is bold. They struck in the middle of a festival—the busiest Sanera has ever been. And for whatever reason, someone targeted you tonight. You need to be careful."

Susan nods. "She's right, Buff. Stay out of this, will you?"

Buffy hesitates, then nods. But I catch her eye and we exchange the briefest glance. And I know then that we're not hiding away—not when there is a killer to be found.

18

BUFFY

The morning of our interview with Juliet arrives like a punch to the gut. When I got home, I crashed straight into bed.

It's only when I'm on the way to the coffee shop that I remember the object I picked up last night. Between the police showing up, getting dragged back inside for questioning, and Mom freaking out—it slipped my mind. It looked like some kind of voice recorder. I never even got a chance to tell Amber about it. It's still tucked in the pocket of the jacket I was wearing last night, sitting up in my room. I'm not sure if the intruder dropped it or not, but it's worth investigating.

Amber's inside, waiting for me. I've never been a coffee drinker but Amber and I both order a double espresso to keep us awake. The coffee shop hums with the perfect level of noise, a steady murmur of conversation and clinking cups. A dull headache throbs at my temples, but I push through.

"I'll bring your drinks to your table," the barista says with a warm smile. Her hair is a startling bright red—she rocks it though. I glance at her handwritten name tag. *Kelly.*

"Thanks," I say, but she's looking at me like she wants to say something else.

"Do you mind if I ask you something?"

"Sure," I say, wondering what it is. Kelly could be a fan of the Sanera Four. Or a member of that forum we saw yesterday . . .

Kelly must see my wary expression, because she quickly follows up with, "Oh no, I'm not a fan or anything . . ." Her eyes bulge. "That came out wrong. I'm really appreciative of what you did for the town and—"

"Kelly," Amber interrupts, then chuckles. "It's fine. We know what you mean."

"Right." Kelly lets out a hesitant laugh. "I wanted to ask if you would pass a message along to Cam. He normally comes in every morning before work and he invited me to join you guys at the concert last night. I ended up not being able to make it but never got the chance to . . . yeah."

Oh. That wasn't what I expected at all. There's a smile on her face, and it's pretty telling. Does she have a crush on Cam? If so, she's out of luck.

"Of course, we'll let him know," Amber says. Our eyes

land on the headline of the newspaper on the counter: *Bloodbath at Séance Sisters Show—Manager Dead, Guitarist Fighting for Life.* "Though it's probably for the best you couldn't go."

"Well, yeah," says Kelly. "You four are basically drama magnets."

I don't know what to say to that. But it's pretty much the truth.

The bell at the door rings, which pulls our attention away. As soon as my head turns, I see Jonesy and Cam.

"Well, here's Cam now. You can tell him in person," I say, motioning to the boys.

When they see us, they come bounding over, taking turns to embrace us. They offer apologies for missing our messages in the night, but I reassure them they couldn't have done anything—the intruder would've been long gone by the time they got there. At least two of us four got some sleep.

"Kelly here was just saying to us that she was sorry she never got to see you at the concert," Amber says, motioning to the barista.

"Yeah," Kelly finally says, her cheeks pink. Oh, so maybe she really does like him. "Something came up at the last minute but I'm really glad you're all safe. If it weren't for all of you, I don't think we'd be looking at only three victims."

"It was a bit of a wild night." Cam scratches the back

of his head. "I'm glad you weren't anywhere near it."

"Me too," Kelly says, though she winces at her own words. I get it. It's a tricky thing to phrase. You're relieved you weren't there but saying it out loud sounds . . . off.

Cam and Jonesy order their drinks and we end up at the table in the back corner of the room. As soon as we all settle, their questions fire at us like bullets.

"What happened?"

"Do you know who it was?"

"What were they doing?"

"Have the police found anything?"

All valid questions with very few answers. We explain everything we saw. The boys listen intently.

"This is weird," Cam says eventually. "So they were just standing there, doing—what? Waiting? Waiting for what?"

We all go quiet, thinking. The possibilities are endless. Was she waiting for us to fall asleep, so she could make a move in the middle of the night? Spying on us? Or is there something we haven't even considered yet?

Then it hits me. The voice recorder I found. Maybe it's got something to do with all—

"Four drinks for the Sancra Four!" Kelly announces with a bright smile as she appears balancing a tray laden with our beverages.

Kelly carefully sets each drink in front of us. With

every cup she puts down, we offer a quiet thanks. I think back to her comment earlier. *If it weren't for all of you, I don't think we'd be looking at only three victims.*

Three victims.

Greg, the manager.

Jeannie, the guitarist.

And Patrick.

I almost missed it but now it sticks out. The newspaper headline didn't report *Patrick's* run-in with the killer. And I watched the news earlier too. They only mentioned *Greg and Jeannie.* How does Kelly know about a third victim from the concert . . . if it was never reported?

She saunters off with an empty tray now at her side and as soon as she's out of earshot, I lean in. "Hey, I think Kelly knows something."

"What?" Cam blurts out. "Kelly is a sweetheart—look, she always draws a smiley face in caramel syrup." He lifts his full cup to show off his drink.

Jonesy narrows his eyes at him. "Does she now?" he says, unblinking. I'm sort of relieved I'm not the only one picking up the vibe from Kelly.

I scoff. "Cam, I'm being serious," I say, my tone firm. "She said there were *three* casualties last night, but the attack on Patrick was nowhere in the news this morning."

Cam stares. "Maybe she heard a rumor," he finally says. "Maybe she has a family member who works at the hospital."

"You're right," Jonesy says softly. "But it's sketchy as hell, you have to admit that."

Cam bites his lip. He likes Kelly, I think. Maybe not in the way Kelly seems to like him, but he doesn't want to believe that she could be behind this.

"Let's just bear it in mind," I say eventually. It does seem a stretch that Kelly with the vivid hair and smile could be that terrifying creature from the concert.

"Yeah," Amber says. "We're not saying anything for definite. But it's something we'll keep an eye on." She looks over Cam's shoulder, where Kelly is serving a customer. Probably thinking how unassuming she looks. But then again, when has appearance ever been a reliable indicator of anything? Mr. Graham is proof of that. His nerdy demeanor, all history geekery and bad jokes, didn't give a single hint to his murderous antics.

I stand abruptly. "I think we need to focus on the legends for now. We've read up on Carrington and the Lady of Haven Lake—I say we get to the library early and do some serious research on this Crimson Witch."

Cam nods slowly, pondering. "It's weird they didn't leave a clue. The receipt, the wire . . . It's like the killer was planting things on purpose to send us to the next murder. But there was nothing by Greg's body."

"At least, from what we can tell," Jonesy adds.

Amber crosses her arms. "I think we're missing something. Something big."

I sigh. "Come on. Back to the library."

We all file into the quiet library, the door shutting behind us with a resounding thud. Cassie turns to us with a hand on her chest as she releases a startled breath.

"Geez, you all scared me," she says with a nervous laugh. Her expression grows serious. "I heard about last night. I hope you're all okay."

"Thank you, Cassie," Cam says. "And thank you again for opening early for the interview. Do you mind if we do a bit of research first?"

"Well, sure! I was just setting up anyway, so I'll be out of your hair." Cassie gestures toward the far corner of the room, where a table and a few chairs are neatly arranged. She smells divine. The scent lingers in the air and I stop myself from asking what perfume she's wearing. Now's not the time.

But the door creaks open behind us again, and a sliver of sunlight pours in, lighting the room. It's our turn to jump and turn. Then I let out a sigh of relief.

It's only Patrick. His arm is wrapped in a fresh white bandage and he's wearing a simple T-shirt and jeans and carrying a paper bag in his good hand. I don't think there's any saving his outfit from last night. Not that he would want to. He looks tired, although his glasses are doing the best they can to hide the dark circles under his eyes. He gives us his usual cheerful smile.

"Hey, everyone," he croaks.

"Patrick?" Amber hurries over. "What are you doing here? Is everything all right?"

I let out a breath. "I invited him."

There's a beat of silence. I can feel the confusion from the others. This was *not* in the plan.

Patrick clearly picks up on the tension. "I can leave—"

"No," I cut him off. "Look, we want to find out about the Crimson Witch, right? Well, Patrick's the one who knows the most about this stuff. We need him."

"Buffy . . ." Jonesy says.

I'm not done. "If we're going to figure this out, his help is crucial. That creep is probably looking on the forum right now, getting inspired by other legends. Patrick can help us stay one step ahead. Besides, the idea of him being alone does unsettle me a little."

The group exchanges hesitant glances as they all wrestle with the idea. We talked about it just being the four of us again. But deep down, they know that I'm right. Time is running out. The killer could strike again at any moment. If we have Patrick with us, maybe we'll find something that could give us an edge. Anything that might get us one foot in front of whoever is orchestrating this.

Patrick hesitantly raises the paper bag. "I brought doughnuts," he says. "If that changes anything."

"Fine," Cam says bluntly. "Patrick can stay."

19

CAM

There's a weird tension in the air as we settle around the same makeshift table as before. Honestly, Buffy should've just told us that she invited Patrick instead of letting him turn up unannounced like this. But . . . I get it.

He was attacked, and Buffy is clearly worried sick about him. I guess bringing him here makes more sense. At least she can keep an eye on him now. And if we're lucky, maybe he'll actually have something useful to tell us.

"All right," Patrick says first, breaking the silence. "You said you want to know about the Crimson Witch. Dare I ask why?" He swallows, his gaze dancing between us. "The killer at the concert . . . they were dressed as the witch, weren't they?"

"Yes," says Amber. "And they wrote the words *Crimson*

Witch on the mirror. Which makes us think this killer is reenacting urban legends—"

She breaks off. Patrick is frowning. A realization creeps into his eyes. "Wait. They wrote on the *mirror*?"

"Yes?" Jonesy replies.

"This is bad," Patrick mutters, before swiftly rising to his feet and disappearing behind the stacks. "Oh, this is *bad*." We hear him riffling through the shelves and then he reappears, empty-handed and more confused-looking than before. "Hey, that book on legends? It's gone."

"What do you mean?" Buffy asks.

"I mean . . . it's gone. I don't know how else to put it."

A wave of shared confusion stretches over us. The library isn't exactly a hot spot these days. Rick's launch is the first time I've seen more than five people in the building. But someone's taken it—checked it out, maybe.

"We need to speak to Cassie," I announce, standing up with purpose and promptly leading all of us through the aisles. We make our way to the main area of the library and see Cassie at her desk. I approach, then stop abruptly.

I see why.

Cassie has the book.

She notices us then. "Oh, hi. Can I help?"

"We . . ." I gather myself. "We were looking for a book. *That* book, in fact. The one you're reading."

Instantly, her demeanor is defensive. "I just wanted to take a look," she says.

We find ourselves on the other side of the desk. The book is open to the exact page we're after. The Crimson Witch.

My brows furrow in disbelief. "How did you know to look for that?" I don't even try to hide the suspicion in my voice.

Cassie looks up at me and is quick to explain. "I'm sure you've noticed the pattern of . . . well, urban legends. The Carrington Ghoul. And then a murder by Haven Lake—that's a famous story. I wondered if the concert killing might have been based on another urban legend—there weren't many details on the news, but I put two and two together and thought there might be some more online. So, I did some digging. And I found this forum . . ."

All our eyes widen at her words. And she notices.

"Y-you know about it?" Cassie asks, her voice slightly hesitant.

Tightly, Amber answers, "Yes,"

Cassie breathes a sigh of relief. "Oh, it's absolutely *awful* on there. I couldn't believe some of the things they were saying about you, about—"

"Cassie," I interrupt. "Can we please see the book?"

She offers it up instantly. "Be my guest."

With his good arm, Patrick takes the book and flips it around. The page is a double spread of text, with one large illustration. As soon as I see it, I recognize her immediately. The figure is unmistakable. Thick white hair, pale skin, and the bloodstained gown.

"That's her, isn't it?" Patrick breathes. "The woman who attacked me looked exactly like that."

"It sure is," I reply.

"The Crimson Witch is no joke," Patrick continues. "She's similar to Bloody Mary. Say her name three times in the mirror, and she'll appear. Supposedly, she was one of the victims of the Salem Witch Trials." He points at a paragraph. "Some say she was wrongly accused, like many women were at the time; others say she *was* a witch—and that she escaped *into the mirror.*"

"Delightful," Buffy says, her voice dripping with sarcasm.

Cassie stands abruptly, blinking rapidly as if trying to shake off whatever we're saying. "I'm going to leave you all to it, if that's okay. It's all a bit too close for comfort."

None of us argue as she steps away and heads toward a door at the back of the library, which I think is probably a staff room. The sound of her footsteps fades, and soon we're left in silence.

"Well, great," I say through gritted teeth. "I guess we know why the mirror is significant. Is there anything else we need to know about her that might be useful?"

Patrick nods. "It depends on the version of the story, but most say that when she is summoned, she always kills *twice*—both with a slit to the throat. Two victims each time. No more, no less."

The words hang heavy.

"But only one guy died, right?" says Patrick, frowning. "So the killer got that part wrong."

"She killed Greg—the band's manager," Amber says. "But she failed to kill you or Jeannie. Sheriff Myers said that she'll be fine. Besides, neither of you were intended victims—you were both in her way."

I take a breath. "Wait. We all *thought* Jeannie was just in the way and that's why she got attacked, but what if . . ."

"She was *meant* to die," Patrick adds, his voice joining in with certainty. He goes even paler than before. "Or I was. If our killer is sticking to the source material, that means they have unfinished business with one of their victims."

"Right," I say as the gears turn in my head. "That's why we don't have another clue. This particular legend . . . it's not over yet."

The quiet library goes silent as the words settle in. I'm right. Patrick is right. This legend isn't done.

"So I guess that means we can expect a second visit from the Crimson Witch," Jonesy pipes up. He tries to offer some semblance of lightheartedness with his tone, but his own fear creeps in, betraying him.

"Ha," says Patrick mirthlessly. "This is all . . . great. Best trip ever."

Buffy squeezes his hand. "We're keeping an eye on you," she says fiercely.

We all fall into a weird introspective moment as the energy tightens around us. The only saving grace is that we know what's coming—or rather, who is coming. But despite knowing what to expect, it offers little comfort. The witch's face, streaked with black tears, is cemented in my mind.

The sudden creak of a door swinging open interrupts the tense moment. We all whip our heads up to see Cassie, panic on her face.

"You need to come see this. Now."

The urgency in her voice is enough. We don't ask questions. We're up and moving in an instant.

The room we meet her in is what I expected—the staff room. Worn chairs are here and there, a table is at the center, and there's a small kitchen area. And a television.

A television showing a local news report.

My stomach sinks as I take in the figure. I've seen enough news reporters to know when they're about to dish the worst news of the day. And the reporter, ready to spill it all, is none other than Rick *freaking* Field.

"Oh God," Amber mutters.

Rick stands in front of a two-story residential home, its front yard well tended and lusciously green. From this distance, it's hard to make out all the details, but it looks like Amityville Street, five minutes away. His voice is solemn.

"We have breaking news this morning. It seems the wave of murders that is once again shaking Sanera to its core is not yet over. A fourth body was discovered at six a.m. at this suburban home."

A medley of gasps rings out around me. Patrick holds the wall with his good arm. *"What?"* he whispers.

"Number four," Jonesy says, his voice carrying a somber weight. "You were right."

"According to accounts, neighbors heard unusual noises at the rented property during the night, leading to a welfare check this morning. Upon arrival, there was no response, which forced police to make an entrance."

Rick pauses as his finger reaches for his ear. He carefully nods, as if being fed information, then his voice grows more earnest as he continues, "I can now confirm that the deceased has been identified as fellow journalist Juliet Lopez."

Juliet Lopez. All this time, this case has felt uncomfortably close, but now . . . We were supposed to meet Juliet in an hour, to sit across from her in the library and set everything straight, unravel the truth, and try to dispel some of Rick's lies—

Wait. *Rick's lies.* Rick's lies, which were about to be exposed. Would *he* do this? Had he caught wind of Juliet's interview with us and decided his fame was too precious to lose? We *did* spot him at the concert. I wasn't paying attention to him, but Buffy said that he seemed pretty worked up on the phone. Could he have been talking to Juliet? Begging her not to go through with the interview?

The thought feels absurd, yet not entirely out of the realm of possibility.

Fame does strange things to people and Rick Field enjoys it more than anyone. In a case like this, can we afford to rule him out?

20

BUFFY

"Is that you, honey?" Mom's soft, melancholic voice drifts from the kitchen as I close the door behind me.

The morning has turned out completely different from what we all expected. By now, our interview would have been underway. But Juliet—the journalist who was meant to be interviewing us—is dead. A wave of emotions floods through me, tightening my chest. Shock. Fear. Helplessness. It all rushes in at once. My heart pounds, and for a brief second, I can't breathe. It's as if a cold hand is wrapping around my throat, squeezing the life out of me.

"Yeah, it's me," I reply, my voice a little shaky. *I can't do this. I can't go in there and pretend I'm okay.* "I'll be one second."

I run up the stairs, my footsteps fleet, desperate for a minute to myself before I have to face Mom. I close my bedroom door behind me and slide down the wall, my back resting against it.

With my face buried in my hands, I take deep breaths that do little to calm my racing mind. I lift my head and that's when I see it. The voice recorder I found the night the intruder broke in, right where I left it after everyone left.

I'm quick to retrieve it, then return to my spot on the floor.

I stare at the device in my hand. Definitely a voice recorder.

I've seen them plenty of times before. We used them for projects at school, for example. But this one is new and not overused to all hell like the ones at school. Digital as well. There's even a date and time stamp. I blink, trying to make sense of it. Why would the intruder have brought a voice recorder last night? Were they spying on us? It would make sense as to why they were just . . . standing there.

I press a few buttons and realize that there's two recordings. The most recent being—

From last night.

1:23 A.M.

At that point, the intruder was in the house. Which means they were recording Amber and me.

I press play.

It's silent for a moment, then some shuffling, and finally I hear my voice. I hear Amber's voice. My eyes widen.

WHATEVER . . . BUT YEAH, I . . . I LIKE HIM. A LOT.

I gasp at the sound of my own words.

We were only chatting and watching movies. So why on earth would someone want to record us? Unless . . . they were hoping we'd accidentally let something slip . . .

Then it hits me.

Rick Field.

His face on the TV flashes into my mind. He has a motive. More murders mean a sequel to his book and more attention for him. And, oh, how he loves the attention. Maybe he didn't want Juliet to speak to us. God, Juliet was probably the one on the other side of that phone call when I saw him last night. He wanted that spotlight for himself—no. He knew we could expose his lies. He had to persuade her to drop the piece. Or else.

It makes perfect sense. The articles seem to finally be falling into place, and the picture they're creating is terrifying. But then I reconsider. Because the figure we saw last night was definitely *not* Rick. Is he working with someone? I mentally pile all my thoughts in a basket. Is there anyone else who'd kill to protect Rick? Sure, there's his publisher, but I doubt they'd go to these lengths just for another book. Is there anyone else who matches my memory of that figure?

Cassie, maybe? She has the dark hair and slim frame. And then there's the fact that she had the book earlier today when we were looking for it. I think back to when I first met her. She and Rick seemed to get along well at his event. Perhaps there's more to their relationship than meets the eye.

I huff. There's got to be something we're missing.

I click to the next recording. It's from a few hours before, at five p.m.

Without a second thought, I press play, my heart pounding as I wait for the sound to come through the small speaker. There's the sound of wind, which makes the recording crackly and indistinct. The first voice:

CAN YOU PLEASE LEAVE ME ALONE!

I press pause. I know that voice. *That's Juliet Lopez*, I think. I press play again.

NO! NOT UNTIL YOU STOP CONSPIRING AGAINST MY FAMILY!

My brows knit together, not just at the words but at the other familiar voice. The heavy wind in the recording distorts the voice enough that I can't recall how I know it. It feels so close though.

JULIET: I AM DOING MY JOB—

THEY TRUST YOU. DO NOT DO THIS TO THEM . . . DO NOT DO THIS TO MY DAUGHTER.

I gasp and quickly pause the recording. I do recognize the voice. It belongs to the person I know and trust the most in this world. The one who's downstairs right now. My mom.

But why was she talking to Juliet Lopez? What were they arguing about? *Do not do this to my daughter.* What did Mom mean by that? The questions pound in my mind, unrelenting. I feel a chill spread across me, despite the warmth of my room. My body shivers. When we talked about the interview, Mom didn't let on that she knew who was interviewing us. But this recording disproves that. *She knows Juliet.*

She didn't want me to do the interview, I think. She was scared that questions would arise—questions about Nancy. I thought I had reassured her, but now—

I need to speak with her.

I need answers.

"Hey, honey."

Mom's voice rings out as soon as I enter the kitchen. The room is lined with spotlights but they're not on. Instead, a few dim lamps cast a gentle glow over the dining area. That's where I find Mom, looking through old photographs, a tiny tear cresting in her eye.

I want to ask right away about the voice recorder shoved in my pocket, but I hold back.

Instead, I take the seat behind her. "Feeling nostalgic?"

"A little bit." Her voice comes quietly, but there's emotion behind it. I fix my gaze on the photos, all of them family memories from my childhood. The one in her hand is from our trip to Miami. Me, Mom, and Dad. We're on the beach, grinning ear to ear, so happy as a family. I remember Dad asking a stranger to take it, so we could all be present in one of our photos. A sharp pang pierces my chest as the memory washes over me.

He died a year later.

"I love this one," I say warmly, my finger grazing across the glossy finish. "I wish my hair was still that long." I chuckle, trying to cheer Mom up. Seeing her cry has always broken my heart.

Suddenly Mom's face shifts, tightens. "I . . . I heard the news. About that reporter getting killed."

I stare at her and suddenly all my questions and fears are too much. I begin to cry, an uncontrollable stream.

"Oh, baby . . ." Mom's hands slide around me, pulling my head into her chest, where I whimper, my breaths heavy. I cry so hard that breathing becomes laborious, each gasp escaping as a choked sob. It's all too much.

"Hey, hey, hey. Calm down."

Mom soothes me with gentle coos. It's a tested remedy, and eventually, it works. My breathing calms and I manage to steer myself from the brink of a panic attack.

"It all feels so . . . hopeless."

Mom doesn't respond, except to squeeze me tighter. With my head still resting on her chest, I can feel her heartbeat. Rapid, faster than mine even, as if she's hiding her own storm inside.

Slowly, I peel my face from her chest and look into her eyes. I know then that something is very wrong.

"What is it?" I say softly. I try to soften my look, trying to offer comfort, but it doesn't seem to help. She meets my eyes with a bloodshot gaze, as if she hasn't slept at all. We're all tired from last night, but Mom was fast asleep when I left this morning.

When she doesn't respond, I press again. "Mom, what is it?" Her face trembles, her lip quivers, and her eyes twitch. I pull out the voice recorder from my pocket and place it on the table. "Why were you speaking to Juliet yesterday?"

Answers. I just want answers.

"I . . ." Mom's voice croaks, catching in her throat. She pauses. "I'm so sorry, Buffy."

My voice breaks. "Mom, what is going on?" Desperation flows through me. I don't get it. I don't get any of this. "Why were you asking Juliet to leave me alone?" Silence. "Mom, *please*. I feel guilty enough about this as it is. I keep thinking if we could have solved this case, Juliet would be okay. So don't keep anything—"

"Buffy—" She stops herself. "You should not feel any guilt for Juliet's murder."

"Why?" I snap, my pot boiling over as I lose my patience. The words come out sharp, but I don't care anymore. All these half answers and strange sentences. None of this is adding up. "Tell me why? I need to—"

"Because I killed her!"

Immediately, she cups her hands over her mouth like it was a mistake. Her eyes go wider than I've ever seen, almost as if they might fall out.

No. My first instinct is denial. There's no way. Mom is the kindest person I know. I've spent my whole life with her, and I know her better than I know myself. Whenever I've felt lost, she's always brought me back down to earth. This isn't her. She couldn't have done this.

My mind races, desperately trying to think of alternative conclusions. She's being framed, I tell myself. Or maybe the killer is forcing her to say these things, manipulating her into playing some part of their game. It wouldn't surprise me, not after the things we've seen this weekend. Maybe this is all one big clue, another piece of the long-winded puzzle. This must be a hiccup or a misdirection to throw us off track.

Because the alternative is impossible. I refuse to believe it.

But as I look in her eyes, I don't see any doubt there. There's no hesitation, no flickering. Her eyes are telling the truth, ridiculous as it seems.

I edge my chair away from my mother. Suddenly it seems like I've never really known her at all. My mind struggles to hold on to the version of her I'm familiar with. Loving and protective. The mom who would never do anything to hurt me. But was that even reality?

"You—*you* killed Juliet?" I whisper. The words barely leave my mouth because as soon as I say them out loud, they become real. My voice cracks again. "Did you kill the others too?"

"No!" she cries. "Juliet Lopez was writing an exposé on you. She knew about Nancy. She was going to ruin your life. She was—"

"So you *killed* her?" I question, my voice raised.

Mom's tears well up now, a force of nature she can't control. They cascade down her tired face, dripping onto the photos below.

"Can I explain what happened?" she pleads.

"Be my guest." My voice is cold, angry. I've never acted like this with Mom, never until now.

Mom nods, clearly trying to convey that she'll get to the point. She releases a large breath, centering herself, then begins.

"I've been worried about you ever since last year. The case attracted all sorts—fans, true crime enthusiasts.

Journalists. So I kept tabs. Reading every news article, anything I can find on the web about you four. Just to keep you safe."

I stay silent, listening intently.

Mom continues. "When you moved out for college, I stumbled upon this forum." She clearly catches the shift in my expression. "You know?"

"*You* know?" I echo, but quickly wave the question off. "Carry on."

Mom nods and continues with her story. "As you know, it's horrible on there. I couldn't believe some of the stories people were inventing about you kids. So I lived on there, religiously, making sure people weren't plotting against you or anything." She fidgets in her seat, blinking hard. "A lot of it was people clearly too obsessed with the case. Most seemed weird but harmless.

"But then one user was asking specifically about you." She pauses, draws breath. "They were convinced that what happened to Nancy wasn't an accident, that it was your doing. They were asking if anyone knew anything about it. Or any theories that they could press on. They were going to find out the *truth* and expose it."

"Mom . . ."

"I'm not done," she says, her voice stern but calm. Her gaze holds mine briefly before she continues. "I need you to listen to everything I have to say. There's more to this than you think."

I nod blankly, my mind racing. "Okay."

"I got an old friend of mine, an IT guy back in Connecticut, to look into this person. The whole thing was encrypted but he managed to crack through." She tries to reach for my hand but I pull it away. "The user was Juliet Lopez. She was certain you were guilty. I think she was going to use the interview today to ruin you. Buffy, *she* was the one in Amber's house last night."

My heartbeat quickens, thudding in my chest like an unrelenting drum. Now that Mom says it, I see it perfectly. The black hair was clearly Juliet's. Why was she recording us? Was she trying to see if I would confess anything to Amber? Would she risk being caught and arrested for an article?

I find myself shaking my head, not in denial, but sheer disbelief. "So you confronted her," I say, my voice shaky as I try to piece the puzzle together in my mind. "Didn't you?"

"Yesterday evening," Mom confirms. Her voice trembles. "I was out and saw her as they were getting ready for the concert. I couldn't help myself, so I went up to her and . . ." She motions to the voice recorder. "Well, you heard it. She refused. Told me she'd go ahead with the story."

"So Juliet was only there that night to get information on me?" I frown. "We assumed the intruder was working with the killer."

"Juliet was only focused on you and the story. But there is something else." She pauses, and the tension nearly makes me yell: *Get on with it.* "Something I noticed on the forum, a user who caught my eye. They didn't post much, but when they did—well, I got a weird feeling about them. More than the others. They felt that Mr. Graham did the legend of the Carrington Ghoul a disservice, believing that they would've made a better ending. The others would suggest working different urban legends into their stories, but this user always came back to Carrington. They were consumed by it. They thought that a *redo* was needed."

A redo ... just like that first note. "And Juliet Lopez ..."

"Their paths never crossed, at least not according to their forum messages," Mom explains, her head lowered. "I don't think Juliet had anything to do with these crimes."

"Mom, how did Juliet die?" The question escapes before I can stop it. I'm not even sure if I want to know the answer, but I need to understand. Because as worried for me as she was, my mom isn't a killer. There has to be more to it.

"... It was a mistake."

"Murder is not a mistake," I say tightly.

"When Sheriff Myers called me to Amber's house last night, I had a sinking feeling in my stomach," Mom says.

"Then when you described what happened, and when you mentioned the dark, long hair... my mind went straight to Juliet. But obviously, I couldn't confirm it. I still wanted to keep this from you."

She rubs her hands over her face. "When I brought you home this morning, I made sure you had nodded off, and I went to her house... I knew where she was staying for the festival. I hammered on the door. She tried to ignore me, but once I mentioned involving the police, she let me in."

"What happened?" I say bluntly. I need her to say it.

Mom hesitates. "There was an argument. I was telling her to leave you alone, that this had gone too far, and she walked off. I followed her into the kitchen and she threatened me with a knife, telling me to leave... She came toward me..." Her eyes flick to mine, watering. "I don't want you to know the rest."

So, there it is. Now I know. And, truthfully, I wish I didn't.

The image of Mom in that kitchen, with a knife in her hand, looking over a limp, bloody Juliet is stark in my mind. It replays over and over and over. I can smell it, hear it, feel it.

There's a hesitant knock on the door. Mom's eyes widen, like she's about to be handcuffed in a second.

"It's Patrick, I told him to come over," I say. I stand up. I feel numb, like this can't be happening. "We'll go somewhere else."

Now is not the time for an outburst, not with my boyfriend outside. I need some time to process everything—the betrayal, the lies, the truth.

I go to the front door and rest my head against it to think. Juliet was always planning to double-cross us, to twist or hijack our interview—the one that was supposed to tell our truth—into something entirely different. It was going to be a hit piece. *On me.*

Now I have a decision to make. Whether or not to tell the police about my mother. How can I make that choice? Turning her in is the right thing to do, but she's my mother—

No. What am I talking about? I do have to tell the police—otherwise I'll be no better than the killer that we're chasing.

But if I tell them now, they're going to think Mom's behind all this. All the murders. And I know that's not true.

We can't risk throwing them off. Not now.

21

JONESY

"Sorry I'm late."

Buffy steps into the interview room and immediately I can tell something is off. Her face looks weathered, almost. Her under-eyes are dark, not just from lack of sleep, but seemingly from smudged makeup. Patrick looks his upbeat self, bandaged arm and all. *What's he doing here though?* I think. We all got a call from the sheriff telling us to come in—but surely, she didn't call *him*.

"I was with Buffy when the sheriff called," Patrick explains, as though reading my mind. "Thought she could use the extra support."

"That's nice of you," Amber says warmly. Cam nods. I sigh.

"Buffy, thank you for joining us," Sheriff Myers says before shifting her gaze to Patrick. "And you are?"

"Patrick," he replies. He starts to lift his hand for a handshake but quickly drops it when he realizes Sheriff Myers isn't in the mood for pleasantries. "I'm Buffy's boyfr—"

"I gathered," she interrupts. "Take a seat, please."

Both of them comply, dragging chairs from the back wall until we're all seated in a semicircle opposite the sheriff.

The room feels smaller now.

Here we are again, in that same interview room. The harsh white walls and fluorescent lights will never get less intimidating. It's the kind of place that makes you feel like you're guilty, even when you're not.

Sheriff Myers sighs, evident exhaustion in her voice. "Well, kids. Thanks for joining me. The reason I called is I think we need to get you all in protective custody. It's the only thing we can do to ensure you're all safe."

"What?" Cam blurts out. "We don't need—"

"I do not want you kids getting hurt again. Last night was proof that your homes are not secure," Myers says. Her voice is tight, stern. "And now someone else is dead. I've exhausted my options."

"I feel like we're close," Amber says. "And I can't shake the feeling the killer is planting these clues for *us*. You need us to solve this thing."

Cam nods along, agreeing with Amber's sentiment. "She's right, Sheriff."

I nod too. As much as I want to agree to hiding away,

it's the coward's way out. We've solved a mystery we thought impossible before, and I'm sure we can do it again.

I look to Buffy, who's unusually quiet. She's gazing straight ahead, like her mind is miles away. It's not like her to stay silent.

Patrick seems to notice too. He gently squeezes her thigh and offers her a reassuring smile. She snaps back and smiles, but the distress in her eyes doesn't fade.

"Buffy, how are you doing?" Sheriff Myers asks. It's clear we're not the only ones to notice her unusual behavior.

Buffy nods a few times, like she's shaking her mind from a brain fog. "I'm okay," she says. "J-just thinking."

"About what?" Amber asks.

Buffy fiddles with her fingers nervously. "The forums," she finally murmurs. She lets out a slow breath. "I can't help but feel like we've missed something . . . really obvious. Someone who believed they could have written a better ending for Carrington."

"I checked out the urban legends thread," Sheriff Myers says dismissively. "All innocent users, some of whom only posted a few times. Local law enforcement interviewed them and did a full background check. I don't think our killer is on there."

"Are you sure?" I ask.

"Unless the killer is a thirteen-year-old kid whose parents let him watch *A Nightmare on Elm Street* too early . . . then yes, I'm sure. They all check out."

Buffy nods slowly. "Maybe we're looking for someone a bit quieter," she says. "Someone whose focus is Carrington himself. Who thinks he was done a disservice. Deserved a . . . a redo. Just like the note said."

Sheriff Myers looks at Buffy for a long moment, the silence stretching on. Then she shifts her gaze to the laptop in front of her. "Well, then. Let's have another look."

She starts typing as the glow from the laptop screen reflects across her features. The light flickers, casting shadows over her expression until the site finally loads. Her face is illuminated once again.

"Search *Carrington . . . redo*," Buffy says quietly.

Myers types and then sits back. "Well, well," she says. "Look at this. *'You're all wrong. These legends are fine, but there's only one winner. If anyone deserves a redo, it's Carrington.'*"

"Who is the user?" I ask.

"Fallback2841 . . . Let's check their other posts." Myers clicks through a filter option until strings of text appear on-screen. "They don't post much," she says slowly. "But when they do, it's about the ghoul."

She painstakingly clicks on each one.

THE CARRINGTON GHOUL IS THE BEST URBAN LEGEND THERE IS. THAT'S WHY MR. GRAHAM IS SO DISAPPOINTING.

I MEAN MONEY AS A MOTIVE? BORING.

HE WAS TOO OBVIOUS ABOUT IT.

HE SHOULD HAVE KILLED TREVOR. LAME.

YEAH, THE CARRINGTON GHOUL IS THE BEST LEGEND OF ALL TIME. HE COULD DO BETTER THAN THAT LOSER.

IF I HAD MY WAY? WE'D GIVE THE LEGEND A REDO. MORE KILLERS, MORE BODIES . . .

I shiver. "That wording," I say. *"Redo."*

"It sounds like our culprit," Amber says, the first to break the heavy silence. "They don't seem to care that much about the other legends. They entertain them, sure, but they're not the focus at all."

"Like those stories are just a means to an end," Cam says thoughtfully. "Carrington is still the main player. But they need filler before the big finale? Does that make sense?"

Amber nods. "Perfect sense . . . in horror movie terms."

Sheriff Myers ends up scrolling all the way back to the very start of the user's activity. "Fallback2841 has been active since October second last year." Her eyes narrow as something piques her interest. "But a few weeks ago, they commented on this old thread from over a year ago . . ."

SANERA'S NEXT LEGEND

"Please tell me someone said unicorns," Amber says, trying to cut the tension.

Cam tuts. "*Deadly* unicorns maybe."

Sheriff Myers isn't impressed, her expression flat as ever. She reads the text aloud, her words almost echoing off the walls, which makes them even more ominous. "He only makes one reply in the thread. *'Nothing is more cinematic than the return. But even a sequel has to follow the rules.'*"

We're all silent for a minute. "Well, what the hell does that mean?" Amber says.

"Cinematic," Buffy repeats. She looks at Amber and Patrick. "You two are the movie buffs."

"He means the sequel," says Patrick. "*'Even a sequel has to follow the rules.'* We're living in this weirdo's horror sequel. Just like we suspected."

Amber nods. "Right. And they're playing by the rules. So what happens at this stage in a horror movie sequel?"

Patrick swallows. "I love a scary movie but I don't love living one . . . *anything* could come next. I don't know where we are in this loser's story. It's clear from what they've already done, they don't stick to a conventional structure—"

Buffy narrows her eyes at him.

"Look," Amber says. "A horror sequel almost always goes the same way. You keep the same location, same basic setup, but you have to add something new to keep the audience on their toes. You call back to the original killer, but then you introduce all the new shit. New location. Haven Lake. In our case, a new killer too . . . or, I guess, killers. But a true sequel always pulls things back to where it all began."

"Then what's next?" I ask.

Amber groans. "At the end of the day, this is real life. There's no script. There's no writer orchestrating what's going to happen."

"The killer thinks they are," says Cam grimly. "They believe *they're* the one writing the story . . . the redo, whatever that means."

"Holy shit," mutters Myers, her eyes still on the screen. "Look at this." We gather round. "Remember that thread we found last time—*'Best Urban Legends'*? We pulled IP addresses on the users who commented and made suggestions—but not everyone who *voted*. Well, one user has bumped *certain suggestions*.

"Carrington, the Lady of Haven Lake . . . and the Crimson Witch . . ." She looks at us. "These are the exact legends that inspired the killings. The killer's plan was on this thread the whole time. And guess which user bumped them?"

"Our friend, Fallback2841," I say.

She nods.

"Harry Lanz's murder was inspired by the Carrington Ghoul," I say. "The Lady of Haven Lake would be the park ranger. The Crimson Witch, Greg—and Juliet?"

"The Crimson Witch always kills twice, with a slash to the throat," Patrick reminds me. "How was Juliet murdered?"

Sheriff Myers's face twists. "Strangulation. There was a kitchen knife at the scene but it was unused. Seems she might have pulled it in self-defense. No fingerprints either."

"Strangulation?" Buffy echoes, going pale. I wince at the thought of it. We may have seen our fair share of corpses by now, but it never gets easier. I don't think it ever will.

"The Crimson Witch slits their victims' throats," Patrick says stubbornly. "Juliet's murder doesn't follow the pattern."

"Well, maybe they changed it," snaps Myers. "We've got two deaths for the Crimson Witch, as the legend says. And there's no more bumps, so this might all be over. They might believe they've finished their story. This has to be a breakthrough. Fallback2841 must be the killer. We need to track them down."

My head aches. All this information is crowding my brain. In spite of Myers's optimism, I don't think this is over. And by the look on the gang's faces, they're not convinced either. Nothing about this feels like an ending. It's too easy. There's more to this, I'm sure of it.

"Are you sure?" asks Amber. "What about the other suspects?"

"Like Rick," Cam instantly says. "Rick Field. His book is bogus. It's basically all lies and it's clear that he enjoys the fame."

Amber joins in. "If the fame had gotten to him, the idea of Juliet interviewing us might have been too much."

Cam nods. "We *were* going to . . . kind of expose him. That would be a big blow to his career, wouldn't it?"

Buffy finally speaks up, although she still looks unwell. "He had a motive to kill Juliet," she says, but her voice sounds strained. "And I saw him on a call at the concert—he sounded pretty angry. Maybe he was confronting Juliet?"

I nod but she glances away quickly, as though avoiding my gaze.

"Fine," says Myers. "We'll interview Rick Field about his whereabouts at the time of Juliet's murder. Anything else?"

"What about Cassie?" I say. "She was pretty interested in that book of legends. Admitted she was on the forum, too."

"There is someone else," Amber says suddenly, her voice sharp with realization. "Buffy noticed earlier at the coffee shop. This girl—Kelly, her name was—said there were *three* casualties at the concert last night... but Patrick's attack wasn't publicized. So how did she know?"

"Which coffee shop?" Myers asks.

Amber replies, "Sanera Coffee Co...."

Sheriff Myers lets out a long, disappointed sigh, though there's something else in it too. A hint of a laugh. "Right. I don't think—"

The door to the interview room creaks open. I groan. Mayor Gomez. How he's still working, I don't know. After everything he did, you'd think he'd have been long gone by now.

"We need to speak with you," Gomez says, directing his words at the sheriff. It's then I notice another figure appear beside him. It's George Pérez. What are they doing together?

Sheriff Myers glances over, brows knit. "Rookie? What is this about?"

George sighs deeply. "Another body." The words hang in the air, heavy and suffocating. Another one. Already? Myers doesn't respond right away; instead her expression hardens. She truly thought this was over.

"Go on," she eventually says.

Mayor Gomez glares at us then. "Without the kids," he says, his tone sharp.

Myers isn't having any of it. She twists her entire body so she's facing the mayor fully. "They are vital to this case, as much as I want to get them somewhere safe. Tell us, now."

The mayor hesitates, but George says, "Jeannie Ryder. Her body was found cold."

"What?" The girl from the band, who was recovering in the hospital. My heart races as I process the words. "But . . . we were told she'd be fine!"

George continues the explanation. "She was discharged in the early hours. Things were hectic at the hospital, so they let her go early on the condition that she rested. Her sisters found her body at her home. We got the call minutes ago."

"Wait," Cam says, dread in his voice. "How was she killed?"

"Apparently her throat . . . was slit."

The room descends into a heavy silence, thick and stifling. Our eyes meet and all we hear is the electric hum of the fluorescent lights.

Patrick nods rapidly. "The Crimson Witch—she had one more kill," he says. "Remember? Whoever is doing this is following the legend to the letter."

"The last urban legend bumped by our mystery user on the forum," says Amber. "So Juliet really wasn't part of it? Did she see something? Find something out?"

"*Now* all the legends are complete," Cam says.

"Well, that's good," Gomez says. "I mean, not *good*,

obviously. You still have to catch them. But . . . at least there won't be any disturbances tonight."

"Tonight?" Buffy asks, curious.

"The finale of the festival is tonight," he says.

"Are you seriously still going ahead with that?" Myers's voice captures our disbelief perfectly. She motions to us. "Have you told *them* what you're doing?"

Gomez hesitates, looking guilty. You'd think he'd have learned after his stunt the other day. Eventually, he replies, voice low. "A tribute . . . a private charity gala at . . . Carrington Manor."

"Tell me you're joking," Cam says. "Did you miss the fact there's a killer on the loose? You *just came here* to tell us about another victim."

"It's too late to cancel," Gomez fires back, his words desperate. "We have too many investors, press—there's no way we can pull the plug now. The museum is set to open next week and it's all riding on a successful launch." His voice echoes with the weight of his worry. He's clearly uncertain about tonight too.

"I'm sorry," Amber says. "Museum?"

He shrugs. "It was meant to be a surprise announcement. We've got serious investment in this. There's a lot of public interest . . ."

Carrington Manor, a museum? The idea is heartless, offensive, even—or at least it will be if Gomez has anything to do with it. The place has history, but it's not something that belongs in a tourist brochure.

Gomez steps back. "It's going to be okay," he says uncertainly. "We'll have plenty of security and there's no reason to think there will be foul play. Especially now. You said it yourself, the list is complete." He looks at his watch. "I have to go."

"Wait," Amber says suddenly. I glance at her, dark hair pulled back, eyebrows set high, focused in thought. "Was there anything beside Jeannie's body? An object of any sort?"

"Uh . . . yes," George says. "The nurse on the phone mentioned a candlestick, by the body."

A candlestick.

In an instant, everything clicks into place. The rush of understanding hits me like a shock wave, my heart pounding in my chest as the connections come together.

It seems I'm not the only one who understands. The entire gang's faces match my own, eyes wide, mouths agape with the same stunned expression. Only Patrick sits there, wide-eyed and confused.

"What is it?" he asks, bewildered.

"The killer is going to strike tonight," Cam says. "Their plan is to return to the scene of the first murders. It's all leading back to the start. The legends are finished and now they're going back to what they deem the best. The Carrington Ghoul. They want a redo."

Amber pipes up too. "They've been leaving clues this whole time, leading us to the next murder scene . . . We used a candlestick from the manor as a weapon last year. It's the sort of detail that wasn't in the press, but it leaked somehow and it's probably all over the forum. I think the killer planted the clue to let us know exactly what their next move is. Carrington Manor."

Mayor Gomez freezes, then gathers himself and tuts. His entire reputation—well, what's left of it—rides on tonight being a success. It's his last hope of winning back some belief for himself. "Supposition. You do not know that for certain."

"Oh really?" says Buffy, leaning forward, pointing to the computer monitor. "Look."

We all stumble around to the other side of the table.

The sheriff highlights a thread with her cursor. Her eyes are glaring, juddering between the laptop and the mayor. "A new thread on the forum."

I squint to read it.

FAO: SANERA FOUR

A pit forms in my stomach.

"The thread was created one minute ago," Myers says. She clicks on it.

Something pops up on the screen.

"A new post," I say, my heart racing.

Patrick grips Buffy's shoulder as he tries to get a better view. "What does it say?" he asks.

"'The end is near . . .'" Cam's voice cracks as he reads the message aloud. "User Fallback2841. If that's the killer . . ."

"Then they're online right now," I finish for him.

The room goes silent. Disbelief envelops us all.

Sheriff Myers presses a few keys, fast. "I've sent it to the team; we'll see if they can get anything from it. But I'd say this is a pretty clear sign you should cancel the event, Gomez. Our killer isn't done."

Cam turns to the mayor, whose gaze is fixed on the screen. "The killer is going to strike tonight," he repeats, voice hoarse. "At the manor. I'm sure of it. Everyone can see it but you, but I'm sure it must be hard to focus with dollar signs in your eyes . . . If you do not cancel tonight, people *will* die."

"They're right," George says. "I saw firsthand what this killer is capable of."

"Just think about how bad it'd look if someone ends up dead at an event *you* refused to postpone," Myers says. "You'd probably *finally* lose your job." She stands. "And I'm pulling rank, Gomez. You might be mayor, but this is a police matter."

Mayor Gomez glares at her, his eyes burning with anger. He huffs. "Don't do this, Myers."

"Sorry," says Myers. "I already am. You can call the sponsors and—"

"Wait," I say. A thought comes to mind. It's ridiculous and dangerous, but if it works . . . it could end this once and for all. It's a risk. But lives are on the line. I fear if we don't try, people will die anyway.

"Don't cancel tonight," I say. "*And* no protective custody."

Amber shakes her head in disbelief. "HUH?"

She's not the only one who's confused. Cam looks at me with an expression that's a mix of concern and bewilderment.

Buffy speaks up too. "Jones, what are you talking about?"

Myers, George, and Patrick share the same look of perplexity, their eyes searching mine for some kind of explanation. I'm not surprised; we were on the verge of convincing Gomez to cancel the event.

Not to mention that I'm the "shy one," who follows where the others lead. But right now, I know I have to speak up. I look around at them all, take a deep breath, and press on.

"Let's set a trap."

22

CAM

The air is refreshing as we step back into civilization. Despite the shadow of another murder hanging over Sanera, the streets are still overflowing. Festival stalls are packed with people lining up for their share of goods and games. The faint, smoky scent of cooked meats waves through the crowd. The sight is a strange contrast. Life goes on as usual, even with the stench of death lurking so close. Everyone is dressed up in costume, the freakier the better.

I have to remind myself that these monsters are pretend. Something that should be ingrained in my brain by now, but I can't help being startled when a ghoul passes by me. Thankfully, none of them resemble Carrington. I think everyone knows that's off-limits now.

Amber looks at the crowd, disgust clouding her features. "I can't imagine acting like nothing is happening."

"I bet they're all tourists," Jonesy says. "Take this mystery to *their* hometown and I'm sure they'd change their tune."

He's right on that front. When isn't he? People lack empathy until something happens to them, or someone they know. All throughout history, that's the case. And it's repeating now.

I take Jonesy's hand in mine. "What came over you in there?"

Amber chuckles. "Yeah, someone's been watching too much *CSI*. A trap? How did you even come up with that?"

Jonesy shrugs, back to his usual shy self. "I just miss life, I miss college, and we can't go back to that until *this* is over. I couldn't live with myself if we left Sanera now. Besides, if Amber's taught me anything about horror films—you *can't* hide. Protective custody wouldn't help. Canceling the event wouldn't help. That's what they're expecting us to do."

I force a smile at Jonesy's admission. I know how happy he is at college. He has big dreams and being in Sanera makes them ten times harder to reach. But it doesn't make hearing it any easier.

"I guess you're right," Amber admits. "Cancel the event, and the killer will still finish their plan—they'll just do it somewhere else."

"We know the killer is going to be there, so we outplay them at their own game." Jonesy has a hint of hope in his face, which makes me smile. I can worry, but knowing *Jonesy* of all people is confident—that settles my nerves.

And it should work. We sat there for a good few hours with Gomez, Myers, and George, thrashing out details. It turns out Carrington Manor has a few modifications that should make for an interesting night. We've been through timings, locations. It's about as thorough as it can be. We've even made sure our suspects get an invite. We want to be in control of who's in that building so we can keep an eye on them.

"I think this can work," I say as I stare at the hundreds of people. They're all in the dark to what's happening tonight but that's what we're banking on. We need to keep this on the down-low.

We've been over it all. At seven p.m. tonight there will be a coach to drive a select group to Carrington Manor, a big surprise finale for the weekend. A small guest list, a few waitstaff, the mayor, and some cops.

And our plan.

"It *will* work." Jonesy's grip tightens in mine. "It has to."

"So, they're all going to be there," Buffy says. "Should we be worried? I mean, all our suspects? That's a lot of danger in one room."

Patrick wraps an arm around her, as she still seems subdued. I wonder if this whole thing is scaring her more than she'd like to admit. "I'm not worried. To me, it sounds foolproof," Patrick says, clearly trying to keep the mood up.

"Patrick . . ." I say, feeling awkward. "I'm not sure you should come. It could get—"

"Dangerous. I know," he says simply. "Myers has already made it completely clear I have nothing useful to add to this. She wants me out of the way. So . . . I'm going to go to my hotel and keep the door *locked*."

"You are?" says Buffy, relief in her tone.

"Yeah." There's a worried smile on his lips as he turns to her. "But that doesn't mean I like the idea of you going there."

She swallows. "I'll be okay. Foolproof, remember?"

She finally looks to him, realizing this is when they part until this is all over.

Buffy and Patrick embrace for a long while, a tense silence encasing them as we all pretend to talk among ourselves. When they pull apart, he plants a kiss on her head. I hear him whisper as he leans in close to her, "Now go catch that fucker."

I open the door to find Mom sitting on the stairs, a suitcase beside her, clearly just arrived back. I said I'd pick her up, but she knew I was overrun with everything that was happening.

As soon as the door shuts behind me, she springs to her feet, and before I can say a word, her arms have encircled me, pulling me into a hug I didn't realize I needed so badly.

"Thank God you're okay." Her voice is close as her

head rests on my shoulder. "I got back as fast as I could . . ." She pulls away. "Shit, I thought if anything was going to happen it'd be on the anniversary—not that I thought it *would* . . . You know what I mean."

A smile crests on my lips. Mom being here makes me a whole lot more comfortable. Her being away was making it feel too much like a repeat of last year—another one of those unsettling coincidences. "I'm so glad to see you. It's been a *rough* few days. But Maggie has taken real good care of me."

"Oh, she's been a lifesaver. We've been texting." Rather shyly she adds, "Why don't I invite Maggie over for dinner sometime? Her and Jonesy." She beams. "It'll be a single mom–gay son dinner date!"

"Mom . . ."

"Sorry," she says, hands up in apology. "I know you're bisexual."

"Mom!" I can't help but laugh. Does every mom have no filter? "We can do a dinner date but you do *not* need to give it a weird-ass name."

"Fine . . ." She carries on through the house and into the kitchen, the lights automatically turning on as she goes. We had light sensors fitted after last year. Now we can tell if anyone's ever in the house because a light will turn on. She's also had them installed in the front and back yards. It's not perfect, but it helps settle my nerves. And I have a baseball bat under my bed. That helps too.

The house is really becoming tech-heavy, and I can't say I hate it. Our fancy security system is the only reason I'm alive today.

"Are you in for dinner tonight?" Mom asks. I hesitate, wondering what to tell her. She must see something in my expression because she follows it up with, "What now?"

"It's a . . . long story."

For what feels like an hour, I recount the last few days, every single detail. Every detail that matters, that is. She's heard snippets over the phone but it's hard to explain a situation this delicate without the face-to-face element. I start at the first body, and the first clue, and go all the way up to Jonesy's ridiculously brilliant plan.

When I finish, her mouth is agape, and her arms are splayed out on the counter in front of her. I think it's keeping her upright, stopping her from losing consciousness.

"And we thought last year was bad," she says at last.

"Which is why this needs to end tonight," I reply.

"Cam, this is so dangerous." Mom's voice is serious now. She retains her calm tone, but it's laced with a level of sternness that every parent wields. "You know I'm all for you solving these mysteries, but not if your life is on the line."

"Mom, we've been there before!"

"And you almost died, Cameron!" she cries. She puts a shaking hand on mine. "I don't know what I would do if I lost you."

"You won't—"

"You can't promise that."

I can't. But if we don't go tonight, I don't know if we'll get another chance like this. We *know* the killer will be there—if the clues tell us the truth, that is. And they have up till now.

"The killer left us a message on the forum, teasing a return. They knew we'd understand the candlestick too—that it points to Carrington Manor. It all leads there. So, for lack of a better word, this is the finale."

"I'm coming with you, then," Mom says.

"No. I can't protect you." This is the exact same reason why we can't afford Patrick to be there either. We don't need more unnecessary bodies at this killer's disposal. It's not worth the risk.

Mom scoffs. "Last time I checked, I'm the parent. I should be doing the protecting."

We lock eyes as a silence endures. In these moments, every emotion imaginable seems to play in Mom's eyes. She's at war with her own decisions and everything she's learned about being a parent. A parent's instinct is to always be there for their child, to protect them at all times. But this is not an everyday situation. There isn't a rule book for things like this.

Sometimes, a parent has to sit back and let their kids fly, let them make their own decisions—even if it means they might crash.

23

AMBER

My fingers curl around the edge of my bedroom window, slow and careful, so as to not make a sound. Mom and Dad think I'm in bed, fast asleep and safe from danger. But instead, I'm slipping away again—

Again. I pause. This feels exactly like last year—crawling out of my window and jumping down to the front yard, like I've just robbed the place. The night air slithers in and settles over my fingers. It's icy compared to the heat in my room.

What am I doing?

With a shake of my head, I let the window slide shut and I lock it tight. I'm an adult. Why am I sneaking around like it's something I should be ashamed of? Sure, my parents are not going to be happy with me. Eventually, they need to let me be my own person. Convincing them to let me move across the state was hard enough. But I did it. I managed to convince them, and now I'm thriving at the top of my class.

So, I challenge myself.

I turn with purpose, striding for my bedroom door, and make my way to the landing. The stairs creak beneath my steps, but I don't slow down; I'm not hiding anything. Not anymore.

As soon as I reach the first floor, I see my parents. They're perched on the living room sofa, half-hidden in the dim glow of a single lamp in the corner of the room. Their heads turn in unison; eyes lock onto me.

"Amber," Mom says softly. "What are you wearing?"

I look down at my attire. I've traded my jeans and sneakers for something a bit more formal. The deep red of my knee-length dress shimmers slightly in the low light. My old prom dress. It's the only thing I have that matches tonight's formal dress code.

Then it's Dad's turn. "And where are you going? We specifically said that you need to—"

"I'm going out," I say simply. My tone isn't defiant, just firm. I *am* going. This isn't up for debate. My friends are counting on me. We need all of us for this plan to work. And I won't be the one to let them down.

"Amber," Mom says again, but this time she rises to her feet. Her hands clutch at her cardigan, pulling it tighter around herself. "You can't go out at night, not with a killer on the loose. It's safe here—"

"Is it?" I reply. "Is it really? Because I was sitting exactly where you are last night when someone broke in." I move to the cupboard nearby. My hand rests where the glass vase used to reside. "They were right here."

Dad joins Mom on his feet. "Sheriff Myers has the investigation in hand."

I almost want to cry. Or laugh. Maybe both.

"Dad," I say plainly. "This is bigger than the police. It's bigger than everyone. I can't just stay here and let the worst happen."

They share a worried glance before stepping closer to me. Mom reaches for a lamp and flicks it on. For the first time, I see her face clearly. Her eyes are red and her cheeks are wet.

"Where are you going?" she asks.

I quirk my brow at her question. ". . . Do you really want to know?"

If I tell them, I wouldn't be surprised if they barricaded the door to keep me in. Sure, it's because they want me to be safe; they don't want me to risk my life going back to Carrington. But if I don't, more people will die. I'm sure of that. The killer has something planned for tonight and we have to stop them.

"Tell us," Dad replies for her.

I hesitate, the words feeling thick in my throat. I have to force them out. "Mayor Gomez is turning Carrington

Manor into a museum. There have been private investors. He's making the announcement at an invitation-only opening gala tonight at the manor . . . and we think the killer is going to show up."

My last sentence stiffens the air. My parents don't move.

"Amber, there is no way," Dad says. He rubs his hand through his nonexistent hair. A nervous gesture. There isn't any anger behind his words, just raw worry. Understandably. But I've learned that you can't let fear stop you.

Mom places her hand on Dad's arm to steady herself. "And why are *you* needed in this?"

"We have a plan," I say. "Me and the others. The sheriff is in on it too. We can finish this tonight. For good. And I'm going." My feet start taking me toward the door, but then I feel a hand on my shoulder. I turn, expecting another argument.

But instead, my dad pulls me into him. His breath is heavy against my neck.

"Be safe," he whispers, his voice thick with emotion. Then he pulls Mom into the embrace as well. She whimpers softly, the sound breaking me, but it's the closest thing to a blessing I'll get from her.

They're letting me leave on my terms. They're letting me make my own decision. One that's going to save lives.

Dad says one more thing as I turn to go, his voice barely above a whisper. "Make us proud."

This isn't like last time. We're not sneaking into Carrington Manor; we're being welcomed. We're not walking into a trap—we're setting one. And as I barrel down the street, trying to make up for lost time, I'm very glad I decided on flats. Running away from whatever monster we're going to face would also be extremely difficult in heels.

Ever since what happened last year, I've been scared walking around at night. The darkness, the unsettling feeling of not knowing if someone is watching. At college, I have these worries a lot less. Campus is always busy—and besides, it's far from Sanera. Here, it's another story.

Tonight, Sanera is buzzing. The streets are more alive with movement than I've ever seen them. The roads are packed with people, their chatter and laughter carrying through the streets. It seems that everyone had the same idea: make the last night of the festival the biggest.

I can already see the dazzling glow of bright lights piercing through the skyline. Colorful reflections dance on the buildings like man-made northern lights. The air is thick with the scent of street food and the sound of pop songs, even before I reach the main square. There is an undeniably joyful atmosphere, which is wild considering how the festival has gone so far.

But what these people don't realize is that while they celebrate in town, a select few are about to embark on an entirely different course. A coach is pulling up outside the library to take some of us to Carrington Manor. And there, we will end this.

At least, that's the plan.

If the crowds of horror fans knew where that coach was going, I'm certain they'd be desperate to get on board. But they don't realize what's about to unfold . . .

I trail behind a crowd as they slip down the infamous alley. My breath hitches and my body tenses for the worst, expecting something, somehow, to jump out at me. But nothing happens. No unseen danger, no sudden fright, just the steady rhythm of footsteps. I get to Main Street with nothing but a fresh blister.

I glance at my phone.

6:54 p.m. A flurry of people swarm me, nudging me out of the way, almost knocking my phone out of my hands. I'm tempted to curse them, but honestly, I kind of deserve it for standing right in the middle of the sidewalk. Instead, I settle on giving them a good evil eye as they march off, though, of course, none of them will notice.

I see the one woman in the white floor-length dress—that might actually be her wedding dress—drag it through a muddy puddle. *It isn't funny.* I notice the towering black-white-and-gray updo . . . Bride of Frankenstein. My gaze sweeps the crowd, and suddenly I realize they're *all* dressed up. Everywhere.

There's a killer on the loose, who is murdering people while dressed as urban legends, in a sea of monsters.

A ghostly pirate drifts past me then. A heavy black eye patch covers his left eye, and the rest of his face is painted to look like rotting flesh. He could be anyone. He might be someone I know or a total stranger.

Eventually, I manage to maneuver my way through the crowd until I reach the library. The grand building almost shines under the cresting moonlight. Cam and Jonesy are there, just outside on the sidewalk, suited and booted, equipped with a necktie and bow tie respectively. Cam's hair is slicked back, clearly laced with his mom's hair spray. Jonesy, on the other hand, looks like he always does. But I can't imagine him any other way.

Cam's blue eyes light up when he sees me, and he gives Jonesy a nudge to silently let him know I'm here.

"You two clean up nice."

"Same to you," Cam says as he straightens his tie and takes in my outfit. "Prom two-point-oh?"

I click my tongue, rolling my eyes. *"Prom Night* maybe."

"You look amazing, Amber," Jonesy says with a grin so wide, it's practically infectious. His eyes flicker down to my shoes. "And flats . . . Smart move."

"I figured we'd be doing a lot of running tonight." I

shrug. Running for our lives, maybe. "I probably should've worn sneakers."

A voice behind me says, "Sneakers with a dress?"

I spin around to find Buffy, looking like some *Vogue* model. She's dressed in a sleek black dress that threatens to touch the ground, perfectly cut for her frame. Half of her blonde hair falls wistfully on her shoulders, while the rest is tied back into some sort of updo.

"Wow," Buffy says, her eyes scanning each of us. "We look *good. And* I've managed to conceal a knife on my person, so we're winning."

Cam messes with his collar. "Smart. Okay, we established that we look *fantastic.* Is our new plan to seduce the killer or . . . ?"

Buffy raises an eyebrow. "What would you do if I said yes?"

Cam doesn't miss a beat—he was clearly ready for this one. "Well, if that's the plan then I would simply work my magic."

A smile flickers on Buffy's lips, but I can tell it's forced, a mask she's putting on for show. There's something off about her, something I can't quite put my finger on. I assumed it's the worry—over Patrick, over tonight—but now I'm starting to wonder.

"Okay!" Jonesy's voice breaks into my thoughts. "We get to the manor. We do our thing, and if it goes awry . . ." He pulls a crumpled sheet of computer paper from his pocket. "I went back over the plans of Carrington Manor we found last time and think I've identified another passageway upstairs we could use. If we have to, I mean. We can't risk getting trapped in there."

"Been there, done that," I mutter, before turning to Buffy. "How's Patrick?"

"He's cozied up with room service," Buffy says. "He'll be fine." She sighs. "Whether our relationship will survive an attempt on his life, who can say."

I squeeze her arm. "Hang in there," I tell her. "And give him the benefit of the doubt. I think he cares about you—a lot."

As the minutes pass by, more people dressed to the nines start to appear. I don't recognize any of them—probably the investors and patrons the mayor mentioned, local officials.

I spot Rick Field too—he's heading straight for us. A deep green suit clings to his thin frame, which annoyingly suits him. His red hair complements the green just right, and a matching red pocket square ties the whole look together. I can't stand the man, but unfortunately, he knows how to dress.

"Play it cool," I whisper, forcing a smile. Then, in a louder voice, "Rick, hi."

"Amber," he replies flatly, before shifting his gaze to the rest of the group. "You're all coming, I see. Isn't this exciting?" He holds up a sleek black card, its surface catching the lamplight. Gold lettering gleams across it elegantly.

YOU'RE CORDIALLY INVITED TO THE FINALE

It seems his invitation has reached him just fine. The plan is working.

A door creaks behind us, and we all turn in unison to find Cassie stepping out from inside the library. Her presence commands attention. She's dressed in a soft, pale pink dress that shimmers under the streetlights. The fabric is subtly dusted with glitter, catching the light with every movement she makes. Her eye shadow even matches the soft pink of the dress. She looks like she's stepped out of a fairy tale. She holds the same black card in her hand.

She catches sight of us, and a warm smile spreads across her face. "Wow, hello, everyone."

"You look stunning, Cassie," Buffy says.

She blushes in response. Somehow, the soft pink that flushes her cheeks completes the look. The delicate hue only adds to the charm. "You're too kind. It was a last-minute invite, so I had to pull something together... The coach should be here soon, I think."

Then, as if on cue, we spot the bright glow of large headlights. Moments later, a pristine coach glides onto Main Street, its polished surface reflecting the bright festival lights.

"Here we go," I say, a gulp forming in my throat. "Welcome to—"

"Don't say it," Jonesy butts in, giving me a pointed look.

"Say what?" Buffy asks, her brow furrowed in confusion.

"Act three," Cam replies with a knowing smile. He knows me too well. Because we're definitely in act three now—and in a horror sequel, that's when all bets are off. From this point forward, anything, everything, and anyone are fair game. We need to stay sharp.

The coach comes screeching to a halt right in front of us, sending a jolt through the air. With a sharp *whoosh*, the door slides open, and an unfamiliar scent rushes into my nostrils. It's stale and cold, as if the air is thick with the promise of new horrors. A chill runs down my spine, all through my body, settling deep in my bones, and finally reaching my toes.

"Welcome to act three."

24

CAM

Night unfurls its way across the sky, and the world slips into darkness. The drive is short but feels endless as the thought of stepping into the manor again rears its ugly head. A familiar pain shoots through me, forcing my hand to my stomach where my old wound is. *It's just in my head.* The pain is a ghost of the past, but the scars never fade. Some days they sting as if they were recently made; sometimes I forget they're even there.

I feel a hand on mine, warm and steady. I glance down and see Jonesy's hand resting there. It's smaller, the skin softer. I can't help but notice how perfectly his fingers intertwine with my own.

"What are you thinking about?" His voice is low, a breath against my ear. "Or are you too busy being dark and brooding?"

"Always," I say, the word slipping out with a chuckle—half sarcasm, half truth. "Gotta keep up appearances... and you guessing."

He meets my unwavering gaze, silently urging me to tell the truth. Jonesy loves the jokes, but beneath it all, he knows there's something I've left unsaid. He always knows, as if he can see right through me. I wouldn't put it past him.

"It's... weird." Maybe *weird* isn't the best choice of word to capture how I'm feeling, but the truth, I've found, is a strange thing. It doesn't fit into a perfect box.

"It *is*... weird," Jonesy agrees. "We're headed back to the same place we barely made it out of, knowing full well the same fate could be waiting for us. I'd be concerned if you *weren't* freaking out a little."

"Way to keep it positive, Jones," I mutter, eyeing him with a raised brow.

Jonesy chuckles, his lips curling into that familiar smirk I obsess over. "Hey, not my style. I've never been the optimistic one."

"What are you two whispering about?" Amber asks, her eyes drifting over Buffy's shoulder.

We're packed in a row at the back of the coach. In front of us, there's about twenty oblivious souls, all unaware of what they're getting themselves into. I hope we can get through this without anyone else getting hurt. But maybe that's wishful thinking.

We all had to give our names as we stepped onto the

coach, confirming we were supposed to be here. Rick and Cassie were the only familiar faces in the crowd. The rest? Complete, total strangers. Investors, presumably. A mystery waiting to be unraveled.

The killer could be on this coach. Rick is only a few seats ahead of us. This could all be another play from him. Being invited here gives him the perfect opportunity to slip under the radar, all too easily.

"Oh, nothing," I say, trying to sound casual. "Just our impending doom."

"Sheriff Myers agrees that the plan is great," Amber says. "We stick to it and we're golden."

Jonesy shrugs, his face unreadable. "That's if the killer isn't already two steps ahead of us . . ."

We all fall silent at his words. I have to remind myself that there's more of us this time. We have the police, witnesses. We can't let fear take us down, not now. This is our chance to end this.

"We can't panic and overthink. That's exactly what the killer is counting on," I say, my voice firm. "They want us at our wits' end, panicking, stressing. The more we freak out, the easier it is for them. We need to trust the plan—"

The coach screeches to a stop and my heart sinks. I don't even have to look out the window to know we're here. The way my skin is prickling is enough proof.

A murmur of voices spreads across the coach, all in

disbelief that they're at the real Carrington Manor. There's a diverse mix of reactions. Most people seem overcome with excitement. Although there are a few odd faces that try to mask their understandable apprehension—finally, some sensible people.

Cassie is one of them. She's sitting near the front of the coach, but as we stop, I catch her flicking her gaze to us, as if searching for some kind of comfort. Rick, on the other hand, is the first one to get off, eager to see what the night holds. Even more suspicious. Another story to add to his sequel, no doubt.

We're the last ones off the vehicle, letting everyone else go first. As the guests make their way toward the front gates, two members of staff stand waiting, motioning them up the path. I spot George loitering there too. But the crowd's attention isn't on them; it's on what lies above.

Carrington Manor.

It's cursed, yes, but it's also undeniably beautiful in its own twisted way. The uneven frame has a certain charm. It pulls you in. The long, winding path leads up to the dark silhouette of the building, which, if not for the moonlight, would almost blend into the night. It's a darkly gorgeous building. I just wish it hadn't nearly killed me.

We stand there, watching the coach pull away. We only wait for a few minutes, but in that time, the crowd has left us behind.

"You guys coming?" a voice calls out.

We turn. The staff have already started climbing the path. George, though, stands waiting for us.

He's smiling, his expression warm and welcoming. "Are you sure that you're ready for this?"

"No," Amber replies. "But who would be?"

"If anyone can do it, it's you," George says. He trusts us. It makes me feel guilty for ever mistrusting him.

"Thank you for the encouragement," I say, offering a small, appreciative smile.

"We need it," Jonesy mutters. "Shall we go?"

"Hang on." Buffy finally speaks up. "George, do you mind giving us a moment to pull ourselves together? We'll be right there."

He hesitates, as if weighing the risks of our request, then nods. "Of course, I'll see you soon." With that, he turns and begins his ascent toward the manor.

"So this is actually happening," Amber says. "Oh my God, we're walking fan fiction. The forums would be loving this."

"I never thought I'd be back here," Buffy adds. She tucks her hands under her armpits as she stares up at the winding path.

"That makes two of us," I say. I guess people do say to face your fears head-on. But I doubt this is what they mean.

Jonesy clears his throat and the mist of cold air appears before his mouth. California isn't exactly warm right now, but it's not *that* cold. "I swear this place is haunted."

Amber steps forward. "It's almost creepier seeing people here than it being empty... knowing what we know." She looks back at us. "Knowing one of them might be the killer."

One of them very well might be the killer. Rick is still my main suspect. But that's the thing with mysteries: They always throw curveballs. Any single one of the people on the coach could've been behind this. Or maybe the killer is already inside the manor, watching, waiting for the perfect moment. Or even watching us now at the bottom of the path...

My stomach churns and my scars ache, then my feet press forward. I'm not giving up. Not now. We're too far gone.

"For Harry," I say proudly.

"For Greg," Amber adds. "And the ranger... we really should've gotten his name."

"Bud," Jonesy says. "His name was Bud." The tight-lipped smile tells me he's looked it up since.

"For Jeannie," Buffy says quietly.

"... And for Juliet," I finish, then gulp as my sights travel down the group.

They all look off at the manor, all except for Buffy, who stares at the ground. Her eyes are closed and her teeth clenched; she looks pained, more so than the rest of us. But now is not the time to pry.

It's time to catch a killer.

★ ★ ★

The walk to the manor is brief, yet it feels like it lasts forever.

With every step, the true grandeur of the manor grows, and I start to realize how much it's changed in a year. During our planning session with Sheriff Myers, we were told things had been upgraded. Bulletproof windows replacing the old, boarded-up ones, new security systems in place, and general renovations. But this?

This is something else entirely.

Gone is the peeling paint. A fresh coat now covers the dark building and any trace of the burn marks that once marred its surface have disappeared. The cracked steps have been fixed, the railings restored. Lights gleam from the windows, chatter spilling out. I can imagine this is closer to how the manor used to look, before the fires, before the death.

Even with the changes, the moon still hangs high above, the cold light bringing me back to that fateful night. They can change the surface, but the horrors will still remain.

We all move toward the steps of the manor, our footsteps echoing in the silence, the only sound that follows us. Even those are soon swallowed by the music and voices from inside.

"Are we ready for this?" I ask.

"As much as we ever will be," Amber replies.

I step forward.

The door creaks open and I'm assaulted by light.

The manor is alive. Full of people, music, the clinking of glasses, and light—warm, flickering candlelight and some electric lights, too, tastefully disguised as gas lamps. It's like they've tried to modernize the atmosphere but keep the old charm. *At least we can see what we're doing now,* I think, *unlike last time.*

We're the last people to arrive, which means people notice us. The Sanera Four. An older gentleman hurries over, holding out his hand.

"Thank you for everything you've done for the community," he says, beaming. "The name's Mike Quinn. I must say, when I got the call to invest in something like this . . . well, I jumped at the chance. Truly great stuff. I'm so honored to be here and to meet you all."

"Thanks?" Amber says, clearly unsure how to respond. "Enjoy the night, I guess?" How joyful can a death house be? By the looks of some of these guests' faces . . . very.

With one last grin, the man steps aside. Dazed, we walk through the room. The guests fill the hallway, all of them in awe of the grand building. Each of them point, gasp, and snap photos of everything in sight with their fancy digital cameras. It's like some sort of morbid zoo, but then again, I guess that's what it is now. The Carrington Museum.

Only two officers are visible—George and another officer. I don't know his name. George catches my eye and gives me a slight nod. To all appearances they're there as a token gesture—in case anything happens, given the drama of the last few days. But we know otherwise.

They're primed and ready for the slightest sign of an attack. The rest of the backup, along with Sheriff Myers, is waiting, hiding outside until the moment calls for it. *All part of the plan.*

A young woman, her dark hair slicked into a tight bun, steps in front of us holding a tray of glasses. She's dressed in a vintage emerald dress with pleats and wearing bright red lipstick—all part of Mayor Gomez's atmosphere.

"Can I interest you—"

"Not for them." Rick appears, obnoxious as ever. "Too young for alcohol." He flashes an insufferable grin. "How about some apple juice?"

This man.

Not that I was going to take a drink, but he's always just . . . *there*. Constantly in the way.

"We're fine," Buffy says kindly to the woman, who awkwardly nods and takes no time in walking away. "Thank you though!" she calls after her.

"Well, look at us." Rick gestures to the room. "Who'd have thought?"

"Rick, what do you want?" Amber bites out.

"Nothing! I'm here enjoying the night, that's all," he responds, his tone strangely unreadable. Part of me wants to scream and ask if he's the one behind all this. But I'm starting to second-guess myself. He doesn't seem evil in this moment. He's just a douchebag.

When we don't entertain him, thankfully, Rick huffs. "Well, I can see I'm not wanted here . . ." He glances off. "Oh, hi, Jean! Pretty wild here, isn't it? Did you hear that the chandelier has been rigged to . . ." And as quickly as he annoyed us, he's gone.

"I can't stand that man," I mumble. "But is he really—"

"Look," says Buffy, pointing. "The passageway."

I turn to look—the passageway where this all began has a small cluster of people standing in front of it. We head through the crowd, who part for us when they see who we are. A red rope, emblazoned with *CM*, blocks anyone from descending into the passageway, but electronic torches have been lit all the way down. The yellow-tinged light shines brightly, illuminating the path, eventually fading off into the distance.

I never want to set foot down there again. My mind yanks me back to waking up in the dark, disoriented and terrified, then Jonesy pulling me out of that nightmare. I think about the basement room the girls found, the clues, the obsession inside. The memories come flooding back, and they're anything but welcome. Each one weighs heavier than the last. But all it does is make me more determined that it never happens again, to catch this bastard, no matter what it takes.

My gaze strays to the wall beside the opening, where a gold plaque catches the light. It reads:

TUNNEL LEADING TO A NETWORK OF PASSAGES, RUMORED TO HAVE HIDDEN THE CARRINGTON FORTUNE. THOUGH THE FORTUNE WAS NEVER RECOVERED, IT IS SUSPECTED TO STILL BE SOMEWHERE WITHIN THE MANOR.
CAMERON COTTON, ONE-FOURTH OF THE SANERA FOUR, WAS DRAGGED UNCONSCIOUS—

I stop reading. The crowd seems to be loving it though, murmuring with excitement.

"There's more over here," Buffy says from the other side of the room. She's standing by the fireplace, which looks the same, only better—polished, gleaming. The coal scuttle, the brass bucket full of pokers, and the candlesticks lining the top. There's a plaque on the wall there too.

"'The highlighted poker controlled the secret passageway on the other side of the room,'" Buffy reads aloud. She points at one of the pokers, its handle tipped in gold, clearly marked to show which one activated the faux wall.

The absurdity of it all stings.

You associate museums with the past, with things and people that are long gone. But this? Yes, the house is old—but the killings happened a mere year ago, and the four of us are indeed still alive, still dealing with the aftermath. It doesn't feel like history, it feels like exploitation.

They've thought of everything. But who? I suddenly wonder. Mayor Gomez? Did he have the brains to come up with all this? Or was this a collective effort of committees, investors, the whole shebang? This level of attention and detail seems like too much for one person. I suddenly have an uneasy feeling that there's more to this museum than we think.

"Hey, look," Amber says. I follow her pointed finger to the top of the fireplace, where the candlesticks rest in a uniform line, except . . . "One's missing."

Buffy gulps. "The one by Jeannie's body. The killer came here and took it."

So, we were right. This all feels a little more real now. We deciphered the clue correctly, and I guess we get to keep our mystery-solver status intact. We're meant to be here.

I scan the room, desperately searching for something strange, dangerous. Instead, I spot a half dozen oblivious people taking photographs of each other with Robert Carrington's family portrait. I want to laugh. Being tone deaf is one thing, but to treat this place like a theme park right in front of the victims? That takes a whole new level of insensitivity.

Then I spot a familiar face. "Kelly?" I whisper. "What is she doing here?"

She's standing with a group of people, though she

doesn't look nearly as engaged. It's like she's only with them to avoid being alone. While the others snap photos, she hangs back, distant.

"We didn't invite her," Buffy says.

I turn to her, a sinking feeling forming in my gut. "And yet she's here . . ."

"The first anomaly of the night . . . What now?" Amber asks.

Jonesy shrugs, his gaze flickering. "We stick to the plan. Act natural until they make an appearance. We need to behave like we have no idea what's coming."

"Oh, right," Amber says. "Like that's easy."

Buffy nods. "Why don't we spl—"

"NO!" we all practically say in unison, the word bursting out before anyone can stop it. Buffy's hand shoots up to cover her mouth.

"That was . . . definitely a mistake," she mumbles, her cheeks red.

"Yes," Jonesy says. "We learn from our mistakes. And last time we were here, *splitting up* was definitely a mistake. None of us are taking our eyes off each other—not for a second. Come on, let's mingle."

We blend into the celebration, our presence a strange fit amid the clinking glasses. The tension inside me is growing, building behind my ribs, tightening and threatening to burst. I don't know what to expect, what to prepare myself for. But I do know it's gnawing at me, this constant reminder that at any given moment, this night will change for the worse.

As we examine the hall, it's impossible to ignore the sheer amount of work that's been poured into the place. It feels as if we've traveled back to the years when Robert Carrington first lived here. The manor is immaculate, *too* perfect almost. Only now do I notice the absence of that familiar charred smell that once lingered in the air. In its place, heavy perfume and the sharp tang of wine fill the space.

Fresh paint coats the walls, new Turkish rugs line the stairs, and the wooden banisters gleam with a fresh varnish. It's all so pristine, so luxurious—and so odd in a place of death.

We end up standing in the center of the hall, directly beneath the chandelier that once came crashing down, its shards scattering like ice across the floor. It's been restored to its original glory. Light filters through it like diamonds.

I snatch a glance at Jonesy, whose gaze is locked on the fixture while his fingers lightly rest on his arm—right where one of the glass shards sliced through. Carrington Manor left its mark on us all, in ways both visible and hidden.

And then—

The room is catapulted into darkness.

25

BUFFY

Screams break through the pitch-black darkness as the air thickens. It's the kind of darkness that feels like it's swallowing everything whole. The kind of darkness you get when you switch off the bedroom light and your eyes haven't yet adjusted. When you're a child, and you're certain that a monster lurks just beneath your bed, and you have to make it to safety before it grabs you.

I fumble about, reaching out for anyone's hand, and thankfully, I find one almost immediately. I can't make out who it belongs to, but I don't care. Worried murmurs swirl around me. Something nudges into my side, and for a second, I panic. My hand instinctively moves to the spot, checking for injury, but there's nothing. Someone must have just stumbled into me.

Then the lights come back on.

People talk loudly, confused, before the sharp crackle of a microphone pierces through it all. I glance down to find Amber's hand gripping mine.

"Good evening, esteemed guests," a voice says.

Like headless chickens, a scramble ensues. Everyone's eyes dart frantically here and there, searching for the source of the voice. A short moment later, I feel another nudge. I turn to find Amber's finger pointing toward the grand staircase. A lone figure stands at the top, silhouetted against the dim light. For a split second, I'm assaulted by the memory of last year. Mr. Graham, standing right there. Déjà vu grips me like a tight knot and I can't shake the eerie familiarity of it all.

And then I see the microphone in the figure's hand and realize.

It's Mayor Gomez.

"Apologies," he says with absolutely no remorse in his tone. "I wanted to start the night off with a good . . . scare."

There's a smattering of relieved laughter.

"Barf," Amber mumbles under her breath.

Gomez grins, his teeth pearly white beneath the light. "I want to thank you all for attending the ever-so-exclusive grand finale of what has been an extraordinary inaugural Sanera Hallowed Fall Fest. Despite the tragic events that have occurred, we have remained resilient—*Sanera* has remained resilient. We are a town built on strength and I am proud to be here tonight with each and every one of you."

A roar of cheers follows his speech. The crowd congregates closer to the staircase, all trying to catch a better look at Gomez. He hasn't stopped smiling; clearly this response is exactly what he wants. He knows this museum is going to be a hit.

"But there are four special people here tonight who I want to truly commend . . ."

My heart sinks to my stomach. The others clearly feel the same. Mayor Gomez doesn't even need to say our names for the entire crowd to turn, their eyes locking on to us like we're another display in this messed-up museum.

"The Sanera Four in the flesh," the mayor says. "I think this calls for a round of applause."

The expected applause commences. A slow, thunderous wave that feels like an eternity of living hell. It's easy enough to walk away when people recognize me at college, but there's no escaping this. We're trapped, surrounded on all sides. Forced, faux smiles plaster our faces as we awkwardly wave. My hand is stiff and unnatural. After all, this is a part I never signed up for.

I spot Cassie clapping with a glass in her hand. She beams at us, like we're part of the show.

"Aren't they just great," Gomez says. "True beacons for what Sanera stands for . . ." He nods and leans on the handrail, his eyes scanning the room. He's in his element, loving every single minute of it. This is going a hell of a lot better than his stunt the other day. Then he softens his voice to a more somber tone.

"To celebrate, we must also commemorate. Moving forward is impossible without honoring those we have tragically lost. Yet, even in loss, we grow, and growth should be embraced. We must face the future with an unwavering hope. That is why I am incredibly proud to announce the opening of the Carrington Museum next Thursday, on All Hallows' Eve." He lowers his head. When he raises it again, his expression is proud. "And you all get to see it early. Tonight is about learning, introspection, and most importantly . . ." He beams. "Fun."

From God knows where, he produces a champagne glass, filled to the brim with a sparkling liquid that sloshes as he lifts it high.

"To Sanera!" he declares, his voice ringing through the crowd.

The lights cut out again.

But this time, the total plunge into darkness feels different. There's less shock and more embarrassment. An awkward murmur ripples through the room and there's a few hesitant laughs at the reused joke. They're uneasy though. A haunted manor whisked into darkness can never be *completely* stress-free—no matter how enthralled the people are.

When the lights flicker back on, a few muffled cheers

erupt, but instead of easing the tension, they only make the silence feel weightier. Everyone's gaze remains fixed on Mayor Gomez, who stands frozen in place, his posture unnervingly rigid as he stares blankly ahead.

"What is he doing?" Jonesy whispers.

Cam replies quickly. "I don't know, but whatever it is, it's not helping."

It's then I look closer at Gomez. His eyes are fixed, unfocused, and staring into nothingness; his expression is disturbingly vacant. Then something trickles from his mouth, red and viscous.

Blood.

As if in slow motion, the glass slips from his hand, shattering on impact. The sparkling liquid pools and spills down the staircase in a glittering trail. He stumbles forward, his body kept from crashing to the ground only by the handrail. When he finally topples to the floor, what he reveals sends a howl of screams through the manor.

The figure standing behind his slumped body.

The Carrington Ghoul.

A terrified silence ensues, a suffocating stillness in which no one dares to breathe, let alone move or run to safety. Fear takes over.

Then George raises his gun.

Everything happens so fast.

He fires—the bullet slicing through the air with a *crack*. But it misses, striking the wall instead.

The ghoul staggers, dipping low as they reach inside their ragged costume. My breath lurches. Then, another gun. Small, compact, but deadly.

Another shot rings out.

The stunned silence is shattered, and chaos breaks out. Panic erupts as we cling to one another for dear life, struggling to keep our balance as we're knocked by fleeing guests.

In the melee I look to Rick, his eyes wide, craning his neck to see the ghoul. *It's not him*, I think. It was never him.

Another shot and I hear George cry out.

"No!"

I whip around to see the other officer stumbling to the ground, his hand over his heart.

The sight is a shock. Blood seeps through the pale fabric of his uniform, spread quickly by his heart. Then he collapses.

"Ethan!" George says. "Ethan!" His face twists as he turns to the ghoul, raises his gun again—

BANG.

The ghoul jerks their hand and this time George falls to the floor, his body hitting the wood with a dull thud.

No.

No.

No.

It wasn't meant to be like this.

As the ringing in my ears fades, I realize the crowds

are gone. Cassie. Kelly. Rick. *Everyone.* The noise. It all fades away to just . . . us.

The four of us and the ghoul. The only ones left standing in the manor.

"Where are they?" I mutter through gritted teeth, my pulse quickening.

Then I hear the heavy thud of boots pounding on the stairs outside the manor—Sheriff Myers and the other officers storming up, like we planned.

I look back to the ghoul, and to my surprise, they don't flinch. They stand unwavering, careless. The gun is gone somehow, vanished into their costume.

"Run," I whisper.

Then my stomach drops.

A thunderous slam reverberates through the manor, the walls seeming to tremble with the force of it. An instant later, a sharp click. The unmistakable sound of a lock snapping shut.

Then another.

And another.

"What?" The words leave my lips in confusion.

"They're locked outside," breathes Cam. "The officers are locked outside."

And we're the ones trapped in here, with the ghoul.

The plan . . .

When they told us about the new locks—electronic, high security, installed at the suggestion of a potential investor to keep the place safe—Jonesy had the bright idea to use them to our advantage. The plan was simple: activate the locks once the officers were inside, trapping the killer in the manor.

But now...

Instinctively, we all falter backward, still in our same clumped formation. We sprint for the front door. Officers shout from outside, their voices muffled, their fists pounding against the door in a frenzy.

"How the hell did this happen?" Cam says through choked breaths as his hand rattles the handle with little success. He lets out a bitter laugh; sarcasm is thick in his throat. "Always expect the unexpected, right?"

"Leaving so soon?" The voice is gruff. Low but carrying.

I spin around, heart racing. At the top of the staircase the ghoul still stands, unmoving. Gomez's blood now trickles down the staircase, pooling at each step before spilling over in a silent stream.

The panic rises as I realize how defenseless I am. Then I think of the pocketknife in the waistband of my pantyhose. It's not much, but it's something.

Cam rattles at the door handle again.

"There's no use in trying to open it," the ghoul's voice cuts through the cold air. "*Grade-one dead bolts* . . . great suggestion of mine though, if I do say so myself." It pauses, letting the words hang in the room.

Suggestion? Who is this person?

Then with a chilling breath, it adds, "There's no use in delaying the inevitable. You can't get out. The police? They're not going to save you. You're going to die the way you . . . were . . . always . . . supposed . . . to."

I gulp, like a stone is lodged in my throat, choking me with my own fear.

The way you were always supposed to . . .

"Why are you doing this?" Cam steps forward until moonlight spills over him from an upper window. "Why bring us here? If you wanted to kill us, you could've done that without dragging us all back to this hellhole."

A slow, maniacal laugh escapes the ghoul's mouth in return. Only a glimpse of their eyes is visible through the charred scarf encircling their face, and it's enough to send ice straight through my veins, just like it did a year ago.

"Isn't it obvious? I needed *you* to make a better ending."

A better ending. It all makes sense. So we were right. It was the user on the forum. The one who felt Mr. Graham was an awful ghoul. They theorized how they would fix his mistakes. Correct the things he got wrong and make the best ending they could . . . no matter the cost.

Give the Carrington Ghoul the ending they deserve.

"So you are redoing last year," I say quietly.

"Rewriting," the ghoul spits back. I'm sure I catch something familiar in their voice then. "If life imitates art, why shouldn't I choose how it ends?" The words hang in the air, icy and final.

We find ourselves back in the center of the room, our footsteps slow and steady.

Amber shakes her head and her voice trembles. "If everything is about the ending, about the four of us here, in Carrington Manor—then why murder all those innocent people? What do they have to do with any of this?"

"The ending doesn't come out of nowhere, Amber," the ghoul replies in a cold whisper. Her name on the ghoul's lips sends a shiver through me. "You have to build to it. Work in some twists and turns. Some good set pieces. C'mon, you know this stuff. Those other legends . . . they really made for a great story. But in the end, nothing beats this." The ghoul raises their arms, displaying themself like a trophy.

It's a twisted sort of logic, I suppose.

"You're out of control," Cam says.

"I'd rather be 'out of control' than a coward . . ." The ghoul moves then, as they finally begin their descent down the staircase. Each creak of the old wood echoes. "You weren't very brave in that alley, were you, Cam? And the way you didn't immediately contact the authorities the moment you felt something was wrong about Harry's absence . . ." The ghoul pauses, head tilting. "That's hardly the spirit of the Sanera Four . . . is it now?"

I see anger flare in Cam's eyes. Jonesy tightens his grip

on Cam's hand. Sometimes Cam's anger overtakes him. And right now, we need him calm.

"What . . . do you want?" Cam forces the words out.

The ghoul reaches the bottom with one last resounding step. They play with the knife in their hand, the blood still wet and dripping onto the floor below. Tiny, crimson echoes of death.

"I want to finish my story."

26

JONESY

The ghoul studies us as we stand in a line. Fear keeps us frozen, our breaths shallow, knowing full well what a blade can do.

I steal a glance at Cam and catch the flicker of something shifting in his expression. A thought clearly whirs through his mind, and then it clicks. His eyes become focused, all the rage gone.

The moment the ghoul turns their back on Cam, he pounces. A guttural yell rips from their throat as he slams into the figure, his full weight crashing into them.

But the ghoul is ready.

Their bodies twist and writhe, all while the knife flashes wildly between them.

The ghoul is strong, frighteningly so. In an instant, they have Cam in a headlock, the blade hovering just inches from his throat. My breath hitches and my body trembles. Not Cam. Not again.

Cam grunts, struggling against the blade.

I realize the banging at the door is louder now, each impact more frantic than the last. The culprit darts a look toward it. Then the sound shifts, sharper and more forceful, as if the police have switched to using something heavy to break through.

But these doors were reinforced for a reason. The bulletproof windows too.

Grade-one dead bolts . . . great suggestion of mine, if I do say so myself.

I see it then. The ghoul was the very one who suggested these so-called safety measures in the first place. An investor. That would explain everything. How they knew what security systems were in place, and how they managed to hack in. They didn't simply plan around the security, they used it to their advantage.

The police are going to need a hell of a lot more than a battering ram. They'll have to hack their way back in.

"The police will be inside soon," I say slowly, with no credibility, my eyes locked on Cam as he squirms, his body twisting in a desperate attempt to break free. But the cold press of the knife stills him. I see blood trickle down his neck.

"Oh, I don't think we need to worry about the police." The ghoul moves then. My breath catches, muscles tense.

But the blade doesn't falter as it drags Cam along the floor toward us. "You have the sheriff's number, don't you? Dial it."

Shaking, I take my phone out, my focus locked on Cam.

"You tell them to back off," they command, voice dripping with menace and urgency. "Or your little boyfriend won't see the morning."

The phone is cold in my hands, but I click on the sheriff's number and press it against my ear without question. My gaze floats to the girls. Their eyes are wide. Amber gives me a faint nod.

I hear a voice. "Hello?"

"H-hello?" I respond, my voice barely steady.

"Jonesy, is that you?" Sheriff Myers's voice crackles through the speaker, edged with panic. "Jonesy, we're trying to get in—are you okay?"

"No, you can't," I say quickly. "You need to stay out. Cam's life depends on it."

"Jonesy . . ."

"Please," I beg, desperation tightening my throat. "Stay away—"

Before I can say another word, the phone is ripped from my hand, knocked to the floor.

The ghoul chuckles, the sound thick with amusement. "So easily played . . . I'm stronger than you, faster than you . . . smarter than you. You think you're so important, the Sanera Four? Wrong. You are *nothing* in here."

They laugh. "You were mightily pleased with yourselves, playing detectives. I had *great* fun leaving you all those clues," they almost hiss. "That officer handing you the clue to Haven Lake was incredible . . . really holding up the law there, George—*oh*, I forgot—he's dead."

Another chuckle.

"Why did you kill Harry?" Cam asks beneath the knife, his voice stretched thin.

"Did you say something down there?" The ghoul tightens their grip, causing Cam to wince as blood trickles down his neck. It takes everything in me not to jump forward. But this monster has the knife. And they have a gun somewhere on them too.

Cam's not done though. "H-he was only a kid."

"Ah, I just couldn't help myself," the ghoul sneers. "I was waiting for my first victim. And then I saw the Sanera High colors. The setting was too perfect to pass up. The same place where Trevor Ward was kidnapped? C'mon, that's perfect sequel material there. Amber, you agree, right? Always good to have a callback."

She's silent. Her mouth tightens into a thin line.

"You're no fun . . . I was worried you wouldn't find those security cameras by the lake, but I knew I could always count on you, Cam, to notice even the slightest of details."

"Fuck. You." Cam's voice is thick with rage. "You went through all that trouble rewinding the tapes, and murdering an innocent person . . . just to set up your movie?"

"You're finally getting it!" The ghoul laughs. "What is an ending without a setup? Without a good mystery to carry it? How many times do I have to repeat myself? I didn't care who I killed at Haven Lake; I needed a body for the legend, that's all. You have to respect the original story. The ranger has made his rounds at the same time every day since I was a kid. Once in the morning, once at night, so I was ready." They laugh again. "And the wire. I thought that would be a puzzler for you, but you got there in the end. A little faster than I'd hoped—your move at the concert did throw a wrench in my plan. I didn't expect you to clear the stage. George again, sticking his nose in. That obnoxious manager ended up getting the brunt of my anger after that . . . Still, it worked out in the end. It was always meant to be *two* that night. I had to honor the legends, you see? A true fan doesn't skimp on details."

I rip my gaze away. *Jeannie.* Bile rises in my throat. Greg and Jeannie. Patrick got hurt also, but he was just in the way as the Crimson Witch escaped. But . . . Juliet? What is the deal with Juliet?

"You were going to kill them in front of the town, weren't you?" I ask.

The ghoul chuckles darkly. "Bingo! Well, only two of them. The legend only kills twice."

I swallow hard. Two of them were meant to die, but one was meant to survive—to witness her sisters be murdered. The horror of it settles in my mind. This person is absolutely twisted.

"Was it you in my house?" Amber asks, her voice low.

The ghoul fixes their gaze on her. Their face is covered by the singed scarf, but a soft chuckle escapes, and I can't help but picture the smile it must be hiding. "That isn't a question for me . . . but I think Buffy might have an answer. She's hiding a lot more than you realize. Aren't you . . . new girl?"

We all turn to Buffy, whose head is lowered. Her breath catches, followed by a sudden, sharp sob. What does she know? What is she hiding? All my old suspicions come flooding back. We'd moved past that. Hadn't we?

"Buffy, what . . ." Amber says. "What is this freak talking about?"

Through stifled sobs, Buffy raises her gaze to reveal black streaks forming beneath her eyes, her makeup smearing from the tears. "I . . ."

"Buffy," Cam says, concerned, even with the cold steel of the blade pressed to his skin. "You can tell us."

She nods, but it's tentative, like whatever she's going to say is going to change everything. It's in the way she holds herself, the tension of the words she's left unsaid. "Juliet Lopez was the one in your house, Amber."

Amber frowns. "What? How do you know that?"

Buffy rubs her eyes with the back of her hand. "My

mom . . ." Her breaths are short and heavy. ". . . My mom killed Juliet."

Stunned would be an understatement. Questions rear through my head. *Buffy's mom killed Juliet?* Is she in cahoots with the killer beside us? Why would she—how could she?

"Buffy, tell me you're joking," Amber pleads. But this isn't something you joke about.

Buffy shakes her head in response, though it clearly pains her to. "I found out this morning. When I chased Juliet out of your house, she dropped a voice recorder. I picked it up and forgot about it in all the chaos. I meant to show it to you. But when I listened to it, I found recordings—of us, but I also found one of my mom . . ."

Buffy lets out a soft whimper, her face falling to pieces. And then it makes sense. She's been acting strange all day. Because she's been carrying this terrible secret.

"They were arguing because Juliet had been planning an exposé on me. She was using the interview as a ploy to get closer . . . She believed the rumors of me pushing Nancy down the stairs, she thought I did it and—"

Buffy's hand shoots to her chest as she gulps back air. Her breaths become even more hasty, like she can't stop herself, like the emotions inside are too big. The floodgates are open.

"She's having a panic attack," I say. My attention is on Buffy but, out of the corner of my eye, I catch the ghoul make an involuntary movement, almost as though . . .

"Buffy!" Amber's instincts kick in. Her hands gently press against Buffy's back, offering steady coos as she pats softly. "Hey, hey. It's all going to be okay. I just need you to breathe . . . Breathe for me, yeah?"

Eventually, Buffy's breathing steadies, still rapid but under control. "Thank you," she manages to get out. "I was going to tell you . . . I was going to tell Sheriff Myers when this was over. I just didn't want the other killings to get pinned on her—"

"That's enough!" The ghoul holds up the knife-wielding hand. "When this is all over . . . let's just say none of it will be important." They shove Cam forward and jerk their head toward the staircase. "Up . . . My ending starts now."

I walk to the stairs and the others follow. I stumble on the first step, landing heavily on my hands. When I get to my feet, I see the red clinging around my fingers.

"What about your grand reveal?" Cam says in an almost mocking tone as he follows behind me. "Isn't this when you take off your scarf, we all gasp, and you get off?"

"Silence!" the ghoul snaps. "All will be revealed in due time."

We walk in terrified quietude. When I crest the top floor, I see Mayor Gomez's slaughtered body. His eyes are open and if they weren't unblinking, I'd think he was alive. They bore into me like a warning until I'm forced away.

"Keep it moving . . ."

My eyes scan my surroundings for anything that can be used as a weapon, anything that is remotely sharp. Instead, I'm met with some sort of contraption to the right of the staircase. A rope is connected to something...

My eyes follow the rope to the chandelier in the middle of the hall. It's a re-creation of Mr. Graham's device that dropped the chandelier down and sliced my arm open. It's surrounded by a red rope that's similar to the one in the passageway below, and accompanied by a golden plaque. It's hard to tell from here, but it looks almost... functional. A lever sits in front of the contraption, gleaming and golden.

Before I can inspect it more, I'm pushed along once again and I find myself on the upstairs landing. An all too familiar sight. A long corridor with rooms leading off it. Way at the end lies the infamous bay window, overlooking the entirety of Sanera. But there's something on the floor that intrigues me more. Two white outlines.

"What is that?" Cam asks as he reaches my side.

"Those are the body outlines of Bradley Campbell and Shelley Jones," the ghoul says, their voice flat. "Seems I am not the only one with a morbid mind... The mayor did go to some extreme lengths to stay in the spotlight."

I look away, the bile returning. *This is not how we die.* Despite the dire circumstances, despite our foiled plans, this is not it. I refuse to lose my life. We've escaped before and I'm determined to do it again.

Without looking to the others, I weigh my options.

The door to my right is closest, but the ghoul is beside it and there's no way out once I'm inside. Too risky. The one to my left is farther away, but I discovered a passageway when researching the plans earlier today. I never wanted to be in this situation again, but somehow, I always expected this. Now I'm thankful for that intuition.

Police lights flash through the bay window then, cutting across the darkness and momentarily pulling the ghoul's attention away. I don't take a second to consider it. Every instinct screams to act. I bolt forward, rushing into the room to my left.

"STOP!"

I hear the crack of a gun, but it misses. I slam the door behind me and sprint to the bookshelf.

With nimble fingers, I press the mechanism that opens the secret door and slip into the secret cubby behind the shelves. Darkness greets me with its clawing hands, and I embrace it. I manage to drag the door back into place just as the main room's door flies open

I watch the shadows stretch through the cracks below the bookshelves, stopping for a long, silent moment right outside. *Shit.*

More footsteps.

The Carrington Ghoul releases a guttural cry as Cam, Amber, and Buffy make their own run for it. Their feet bound in the direction of Robert's bedroom—another passageway. And they link.

I scuttle through the dark, knowing my footsteps, no matter how light, will cause loud creaks to echo through the manor. There's no time to lose.

In the background, I can hear the slamming of doors, followed by frustrated grunts. The others must have gotten away. But there's no time to think I'm safe. The ghoul is a Carrington expert—they must know all about the passageways. And we'll have to come out at some point.

All we're doing is delaying the inevitable.

A large creak sounds before me as something brushes against my face. My hands flail in front of me, only to find a swinging piece of string. A light cord. I waste no time in pulling it down. A soft hum of a light cascades out, illuminating the passageway and revealing my friends, hunched over a few feet away, where the passage is lower.

They make their way to me so they can stand up fully, and I feel better now that we're together. But the question is: How the hell do we get out of here?

"Cam, are you okay?" Amber whispers.

There's a thin gash on his neck, trickling with blood. But it doesn't look serious. "I'll be fine."

There's a silence as we all look to one another. Buffy's face is marred with black mascara and I can't help but wipe under her eye. She offers a small smile as I do so. It's enough for her to know that we've got her. We always have, and always will.

Another frustrated wail sounds through the top floor,

the sound presumably carrying through the ventilation ducts. "You can't hide forever!"

Another shot. Clearly meant to intimidate.

Cam turns to us. "Apart from the front door, are there any other ways out?"

"We can break a window," Amber adds.

"Bulletproof," I say. "It'll take too long, make too much noise . . ."

"COME OUT, COME OUT!" I can hear creaking. The ghoul is close, I think. They'll find us soon enough—they know there are passages here. It's a matter of minutes at most.

"There must be a remote that controls the lock or something," I suggest. "Sheriff Myers had one, so why hasn't she gotten it open?"

"The ghoul has somehow hacked into the security system," Buffy says. "Does that mean they have a control too?" She shakes her head. "We need to buy the police some time."

Frustrated, Buffy throws her gaze the way she came. When she turns back, she has an unreadable look on her face, like she's conjured up a plan that's as dangerous as it is uncertain.

"I have an idea," she says, her voice low. "But you're not going to like it . . . I should be right back."

27

BUFFY

Here we are, doing the one thing we swore we wouldn't do again . . . splitting up.

I stand at the back of the bookshelves we entered through, my heart racing. The others don't like my idea—neither do I, if I'm honest—but it'll work. If I let myself get caught, it'll give them time to get away. Try to break a window, hide, anything. Buy the police some time to get in. If it means my friends will get a chance, I'll do it. I must undo Mom's wrong somehow and this is the way I've decided.

"Buffy, you don't have to do this," Amber whispers.

"I do" is all I say before I motion them back into the dark. ". . . I love you all." My words go out into the void. Now that the light is off again, it feels as though I'm speaking to no one, just the lingering ghosts of

Carrington Manor. But I know they're there. Hidden.

My breath hitches as I slide the bookshelves aside, praying none of the books will fall and alert the ghoul. I can't give away their hiding spot. We only know about this entrance because it's where Cam's mom was hidden when she was taken. The thought sends a chill through me, knowing how close we are to repeating that dark history. The entrance Jonesy found gives me a glimmer of hope, however. If the ghoul doesn't know about it, at least it's an advantage of some sort.

Robert Carrington's bedroom is silent, ominously so. We ran in here so fast, I didn't even take in the room, but it's different from last year.

It's stale, the air riddled with the stench of heavy-duty cleaning products—whatever they can do to mask the smell of death. Like the rest of the manor, it's been tidied up, staged, as if trying to re-create the way it might have looked when Carrington was alive.

Portraits line the wall, the eyes unnervingly cold, almost as if they're staring straight into me. At the center of the room sits a four-poster bed, pristine and seemingly untouched, as though frozen in time. Not a speck of dust in sight.

With one last glance at the room, I close up the bookshelves behind me. They slot into perfect place and I double-check for any telltale signs. We're good. No one would know. Not even a murderous ghoul.

I don't have to even travel a few steps before I hear it. Echoed thuds coming my way. My chest aches with dread, but I push it aside, forcing myself to breathe. Play it cool until they're out. That's the plan. Keep it together and give them time.

"Here I am!" I say loudly as I step into the center of the room. Flashbacks of the last time I was here flood me, the sight of Amber driving a knife into Mr. Graham ingrained in my brain. It's been a year, but I remember it like it was yesterday. The terror, the dread.

The thuds grow louder, practically shaking the floor beneath me, until they abruptly stop. And there it is. The Carrington Ghoul standing in the doorway, gun in hand.

I expect a twisted remark, or some clever quip, but no. The figure is on me in seconds. My hand goes up in defense as a scream rips from my lips.

My world goes dark.

Light comes back to me in small pieces. At first, everything blurs with flashing spots, as if I've been staring at the sun for too long. Then I remember where I am.

My head pounds and I go to raise my hand but—

I'm tied up in the same place Cam was last year. Ropes constrict my arms and legs, keeping me in place as I throw my gaze around the room, searching for the ghoul. A bead of sweat rolls down my forehead that I'm unable to wipe away.

"You've got me," I say. "... What are you going to do?"

A floorboard creaks behind me, then a hand brushes the back of my neck. I can't turn to see, but I feel the glide of gloved fingers tracing against my skin, their touch sending a wave of revulsion through me. Then something cold. The blade. It's wet with Cam's blood.

"What am I going to do? Now that's a question with a lot of answers," the ghoul whispers, their low voice making every hair stand on end. They could end everything right now. Before I take another breath, my life could be over.

"I'm not going to tell you where they are," I say.

Without another word, the ghoul removes the blade. I catch my breath while I can. They walk slowly until they're standing in front of me. A familiar scent hits me. It's subtle but once I catch it, I can't shake the feeling that I know that smell.

The ghoul bends their knees, lowering themself until we're face-to-face. Their features remain obscured beneath a thick, charred scarf, the fabric frayed and torn. The color is almost indistinguishable through the grime and soot. The air grows cold with the uncomfortable closeness, then the ghoul whispers in a voice that's barely more than a breath.

"They can hide in the walls all they want. It's not going to change anything. I'm still getting my ending."

All this time, we thought we were one step ahead. We

were wrong. Every time we think we've got the upper hand, the rug is pulled out from under us.

"You're not going to get away with this," I say hopelessly. It's an empty statement, one made out of desperation more than certainty. This can't be how it ends. The knife in my pantyhose presses against my thigh, but I can't get to it. And even if I could, I'd be dead before I could make it count.

"But I already have." The ghoul shifts, their eyes focused on mine. A chilling pause before they speak again. "This is my moment of triumph, Buffy. And I want you to join me."

A confused *"What?"* claws from my throat.

"I always meant to involve you." The words echo in the air. "I planned to kill Juliet after all this *for* you . . . but your mother got there before I could. I underestimated her." The ghoul cackles at their own words, but I've never been more confused.

"Why would you want to kill Juliet for me?" I ask, my brows arched. Questions flood my mind. *"Why?"* I choke out. "What do I have to do with any of this?"

Instead of replying, the ghoul takes a deliberate step back, breaking the suffocating closeness. A hand reaches up and grips the end of the dirtied scarf.

"I can explain," the ghoul whispers in response. "But first . . ." Slowly, they begin to unwind the countless layers of the scarf. A mix of confusion and anxiety swirls inside me. *Expect the unexpected.*

The scarf falls to the floor in a silent motion.

Patrick.

Patrick stares back at me.

But it isn't the Patrick I know. Gone are the soft, innocent features that I fell deeply into. His jaw seems harsher now and his eyes soulless.

Why? is all that comes to mind. I struggle to form words, as if I'm learning how to speak all over again. I feel like I should cry, but the tears don't come. Maybe it's because the person I once knew feels unrecognizable now. "It was *you*? Why, Patrick?"

"Why? I told you . . . to rewrite the ending that old Graham fucked up. He took one of the best urban legends there is and he cheapened it. The ghoul deserved more!" His words are laced with an anger I didn't know he had in him. Goes to show how well you really know a person. "But *this* ending," he says. "I want you in it . . . You're my final girl, Buffy."

I shake my head. He thinks we're living a real-life movie. At least Mr. Graham wanted money. Something tangible, material. But this? This is pure delusion.

"We can walk out of this . . . together." He lowers himself again, till he's kneeling by my side. There's a softness now when he talks to me, a faint glimpse of the Patrick I knew. But did I really?

"Was I part of your plan all along?" I ask, frantically casting my mind back. "Is this why you asked me out?"

"I admit I got close to you on purpose, though us joining Stanford at the same time . . . that was pure divine intervention. The world works in mysterious ways." He pauses, his expression loving, but the effort is hollow. Now that the facade has crumbled, there's nothing left to disguise the void beneath. He may *look* like my Patrick, but it's not him.

"I'm a horror buff—you know that. I became obsessed with what happened in Sanera last year. I read everything there is to know on the forums. The Carrington Ghoul is one of the best villains there is. But Graham . . . he was just so *disappointing*. I formed my own theory of how Graham should have ended things. He was shallow—only out for himself. He didn't understand how cinematic true horror could be. Money is the lamest reward . . . a true waste of the legend of the Carrington Ghoul. Carrington deserved so much more. And when we met, I saw my opportunity to rectify things."

He smiles. It sickens me.

"You were my way in to the Sanera Four. My ticket to Sanera itself . . . but then I fell in love with you, Buffy."

I don't respond.

"I fell in love and I know you did too." He lowers his head. "Don't fight it. You can't fight a love like ours. You can help me. We can finish this *together*."

I have to stop myself from scoffing. I loved Patrick, sure—but this is a far cry from *my* Patrick. I can *fight a love like ours* because it's been two months. Sixty days is not enough for me to abandon my friends and discard all my morals.

But I don't let my scorn show. I watch him carefully, like I'm seriously considering this. I have to buy time somehow.

"Think of the stories they'll write about us. The sole survivors of the Carrington Ghoul 2002 . . . doesn't that sound great?" His eyes are fixed eagerly on mine. He's so oblivious to actual human emotion that he thinks I'd go through with his evil plan. It's absurd—another twisted fantasy to add to his ever-growing list.

But what if I oblige? Or at least convince him that I will?

I need to play along, to buy my friends time to escape. If they haven't already. Have they run for it yet? I haven't heard anything. No footsteps. No creaking. But maybe they slipped away when I was knocked out.

I can only hope.

Keep him talking, I think. "How did you do it?" I ask, my voice light, almost sweet.

"Which part, my love?" His lips curl into a terrifying smile.

"The costumes." My stomach twists as I replay everything we saw. The Lady of Haven Lake. The Crimson Witch. Unrecognizable. "I—I don't get it."

"Aww, Buff!" Patrick's hand strokes my cheek, cold

and deliberate. "I thought you'd have put that together by now. You have met my sister, after all."

His sister? The time I met her was brief. She'd just come back to town after a work trip. She'd been on a shoot where she was... the special effects makeup artist...

I blink at the realization. "She's in on this?"

Patrick laughs again. "Lois?! No, no! But her makeup expertise definitely helped. I used to complain about being her practice model growing up, but turns out, I picked up a lot of tricks along the way."

I stare at him. "That was all makeup?"

"Honestly, the best horror effects are pretty simple," he continues, his voice closing in on giddy. "In case you haven't noticed, I'm not a withering old ghoul, so I had to play around with the height. It's all about perspective. But I knew you'd only see the Lady of Haven Lake on CCTV—my parents' security system, by the way. The Crimson Witch was the toughest one, because I was going to be close to you—but I think I got there in the end. Wouldn't you agree? Oh, and yes—I was the anonymous investor."

The pride in his voice makes my stomach churn, but I have no other choice but to nod, pretending. Playing along.

"You're right," I say, my voice carrying the same sickly-sweet tone as I force the words past the tightness in my throat. "So Harry Lanz's murder was just . . . opportunistic?"

"You could say that," Patrick replies. "I was waiting around the alley and it seemed like fate. When a perfect victim falls into your lap like that . . . you have to seize the moment, right?"

The perfect victim. He's totally delusional. This is an innocent kid he's talking about. It gets me thinking about all those moments he was absent.

"What's on your mind, Buff?"

I blink. "I'm just . . . how did you kill Bud?"

"Poor Bud. He's been working at Haven Lake since I was a kid. He was a lovely man, but he was the easiest target for the Lady of Haven Lake. No kids, his wife long gone. No one would find out he was missing until . . . you found him. And why'd you think I couldn't grab food with you and Jonesy?"

I shake my head. He said he was busy. He said he was going to see his parents—who live only an hour away. The realization hits me like a strike to the gut. Oh my God.

"C'mon, Buffy." Patrick laughs, like it's all completely obvious. "The plan was perfect. I decided when you found things, the order you found the bodies. It's the same with Jeannie. I did that hours before her sisters found her . . . Tragic, really. But being with you when they found her kept me off the suspect list. And all it took was a text pretending to be their mom, to get the timing just right."

I smile but I feel sick. This whole time we've been trying to work things out, we've done it right in front of him. He's been one step ahead at every moment.

"I'm impressed," I lie. "I knew you were smart, Patrick, but this is something else . . ." I straighten my posture. There's only so long I can hold him here—I need to do something to keep him occupied and let my friends escape.

"I *do*," I suddenly say. The thought comes to me and I quickly decide it's the way forward. I need him to think I'm on his side. "I—I want to be . . . in your ending."

Patrick's uneasy smile broadens.

"I knew you'd come around to the idea," he says. "Turns out we have more in common than we thought." A breath later, he plants a wet kiss on my cheek, lingering far too long. Then he starts to untie the ropes that bind me.

"Patrick?" I say as he loosens the ropes. One last thing gnaws at me; it's like a shadow I can't run from. It confuses me, unsettles everything.

"Yes, love?" He stares back at me, eyes wide with affection. I want to puke.

"How did you post on the forum?" I ask. "You were with us the entire time."

What he does next surprises me. The ropes drop to the

floor, and he goes silent. Any trace of joy at me joining him falters on his lips. "That . . . wasn't me."

I swallow hard. *What do you mean it wasn't you?* I want to ask. But I don't. If I push now . . . I don't know what he'll do. He thinks I'm on his side. I can't afford to screw this up.

"Some kid with too much time on their hands, then," I say nonchalantly as I stand up, breathing slowly and counting my blessings. But the thought never leaves me . . . Who else knows about this? Is someone just messing with us?

But I have no time for that. Not right now. One wrong step and he'll know I'm playing him. If this really is the ending of Patrick's messed-up movie, it's time to act my ass off.

28

AMBER

"I'm so glad you told me the truth," Buffy says as we listen through the walls of the hidden passage.

"I'm glad, too," the ghoul says sincerely. "I was worried you'd be loyal to your friends. But I should have known you'd understand. You always have."

"They're nothing to me," Buffy says. "If it means I get to be with you . . . I'd do anything." Her voice is sincere, sweet, and I see right through it. She's playing along like her life depends on it—it does.

Patrick. It was Patrick all along. My mind races back to the past few days, from the first time I met him, hurrying into the diner, to the library this morning. He was so unassuming. He was even attacked by the Crimson Witch—but no. He must have discarded his costume and then attacked *himself.* Anything to throw himself off the suspect list. A true, twisted killer.

But a few things don't make sense. How was he online on the forum when he was right there with us in the interview room? And the timings of the murders—do they line up?

In the shadowed passage, I glance at the boys, whose faces are struck with betrayal.

"What is Buffy doing?" Cam mutters.

"She's buying us time." I point toward the passageway. "We need to go. Now."

The boys don't question anything further and instead follow my silent steps. Patrick knows we're in the walls but I don't think he knows how to get in, otherwise he would've done that ten minutes ago. At least we have our safe zone, even if we're about to leave it.

And then my phone rings.

Everything in me screams as I fumble for it. I yank it from its hiding place in my dress, frantically pressing every button I can to silence it. It's then I see the caller. Sheriff Myers. Jonesy told her to stop. She could've killed us.

I hit accept, clamping the phone to my ear.

"Amber? Are you okay? What's going on?" Her questions fire off hastily. She sounds both relieved—she must have thought we were done for—and terrified.

I look to the boys, hoping the volume isn't too loud, even with the phone pressed close. They nod, signaling for me to carry on.

"We're trapped in a secret passageway upstairs," I whisper. "Can you break in?"

"The security measures Mayor Gomez installed have been hacked. You're in a manor-sized bank vault, Amber." Myers's voice is thick with guilt, like it's her fault this has happened. But this was our idea—to trap the killer. And it has backfired majorly. "We're doing our best—we've got our top people trying to reboot the system. We just need you to hang on."

"We know," I say softly. "It's not safe to talk anymore."

I hang up then.

For now, we're on our own.

"What did she say?" Cam whispers.

"Nothing good. We're stuck here till they can hack the security system."

"But . . ." Jonesy falters before he can finish his sentence. "Buffy is out there. With him."

Cam joins in. "We can't leave her."

Jaw clenched, I nod. "And that's why we're going to draw him away." *For Buffy.* "If we manage to escape, who knows what he'll do to her. She'll be his only hostage."

I stop behind a bookcase, the wood rough against my fingers. I feel around for a catch and quickly find a groove that I can dig my fingers into. I glance back, give a thumbs-up, then slowly reveal the empty room.

One by one, we exit the secret passage and close it back up. Just in case.

The old plan is out the window. Buffy should never have gone. But we couldn't stop her. She shouldn't have to pay for what her mom did. The Sanera Four do not split up. We've learned that enough times now.

My heart pounds as we creep out of the room, barely a few yards from the staircase. We need to create a distraction—run, make noise, anything to get him away from our friend. I don't know what comes next or how we'll get out of this mess. But I do know that we can't leave Buffy. We won't leave her.

I hold up my hand, hold the boys' gazes, then use my fingers to count down.

Three.

Two.

One.

We race toward the staircase, our footsteps a cacophonous herd, when—

Bang.

We skid to a stop.

I turn to find Patrick at the top of the stairs, standing by Mayor Gomez's body, with the small pistol in his hand. A wisp of smoke circles the gun before fading away. Buffy is beside him, her expression calm, like she's not affected by this at all.

Keep playing your role.

"I knew this would come in handy," Patrick says, waving the gun. "I've never been a fan of these things in horror movies. Always thought they were too easy. But sometimes . . . necessary."

"Put it away, then," Cam says. "Fight us like a real man."

Patrick snickers. "So now you're the tough guy."

I shrug for him. "Wouldn't it make a better ending?"

Jonesy nudges me to shut up, but an idea forms in my head. And this time, it might just work. But I need Buffy, which might prove difficult when we can't communicate with her.

Patrick blinks. "You know, if you weren't so insufferable, you'd make a great killer, Amber. Oh wait"—his lips carve into a sideways smile—"I almost forgot how you gutted Mr. Graham . . ."

I swallow. The image of blood slices itself into my mind once again, something that I'd managed to forget for at least a few months. All that work, undone.

"But you're right . . ." Patrick lowers the gun and slips it into the folds of his costume, exchanging it for the knife. He walks down the stairs until he's standing only a few feet in front of us. "Since I met you all, I've wondered what it would look like when you bled."

Buffy stays at the top of the stairs, her eyes wide. Which is exactly what I need her to do. Stay back. Be ready.

Knife raised, Patrick inspects the still-bloody blade, a twisted smile playing at the corners of his lips. ". . . *This* would make for a much better ending." His eyes are locked on his weapon, giving me time to look up at Buffy. Our eyes meet and there's instant understanding. She's still with us.

I dart my eyes toward the rope tethering the chandelier. It's a ballsy move but it has to work. Buffy gives the smallest nod.

"Your loyalty will be your downfall," Patrick says. His voice drips with malice. "I'm sure you could've found a way to escape, but instead, you stayed. For what? To save Buffy? She wants *nothing* to do with you."

I flinch, like his words hurt.

"You can't do this," I say. I edge backward a touch, subtly positioning myself under the chandelier. Careful, hoping not to give myself away. We need to tempt him closer.

"Come on, already." Jonesy's voice rings out. He's obviously picked up on my plan too. "Or are you just going to *talk* about killing us all night?"

"Yeah, we haven't got all day," Cam adds with a dramatic yawn. "Or aren't you up to the job? Talk about all bark, no bite."

Patrick laughs. "You don't think I'm capable? You have no idea what I'm willing to do. Besides, Cam, you bleed so well." He leaps forward, his knife flashing in the air, slashing with jagged, sharp slices. *It worked.* His eyes burn with a newfound intensity as he barrels toward Cam.

"Cam, watch out!" I scream, narrowly dodging one of Patrick's swipes. I stumble back, but Jonesy catches me. His face is pale with fear, his eyes locked on Cam as he prepares to dance with the devil.

Cam ducks the first *whoosh* with ease, then dips for the second. The third slash comes with a guttural scream from Patrick, raw and frantic.

Cam lets out another quip. "That all you got?"

The lights start to flicker around us. Are the police trying to reboot? Shutting off electricity?

"You wish," Patrick growls, not holding back. He becomes animalistic, frenzied almost, a far sight from the relaxed, cheerful guy I met. He's like a physical embodiment of his own rage.

Cam plants his feet suddenly, unwilling to move back farther. I look up and understand why. Cam is out of the chandelier's way, while Patrick is nearly underneath—just one more step and he'll be in the perfect spot. But Patrick doesn't budge . . .

If this doesn't work, we're out of ideas—and Patrick has a gun and a knife. And then I see Cam's expression harden and I know what he's about to do.

Jonesy sees it too. "Cam . . . please," he whispers. "Don't—"

Cam locks eyes with him and mouths something that looks a lot like "I love you." Then with his next breath, he shouts, "NOW!"

Buffy sprints toward the lever that controls the rope and Cam launches himself at Patrick with all his strength, crashing them both to the floor.

The chandelier plummets, sending cascades of light scattering down the walls, but then it halts midair with a jarring clang. *It was only for show*, I think.

Patrick glances up and laughs, a sick sound that makes my skin crawl, pinning Cam down with frightening ease. "You thought you could take me down with *that*? It's nothing but a museum attraction." He sneers, getting to his feet with a wicked grin, making sure to kick Cam as he does so. He throws a glance at Buffy, whose hand is still gripping the lever.

A look of betrayal crosses his features. "You've chosen your side," he spits. "You could've had everything, but now you will all . . . die."

"No," Cam says, his voice cracking. "Just . . . us . . ."

With a sudden burst of strength, he grabs Patrick's leg and yanks him down. Patrick topples, losing his balance, before crashing to the floor. Cam doesn't waste a second, straddling him. His breath is ragged, but he does everything in his power to keep Patrick down. Urgency blazes in his expression as he locks eyes with Buffy.

"BUFFY, NOW!"

The next moment is a blur.

A sharp *pop* echoes through the manor. The next thing I know, the chandelier falls in a dazzlingly beautiful torrent. My heart stops as thousands of crystals shatter against the floor, sending shards skidding across the tiles. I throw my arms up to shield my face, bracing against the storm of glass.

When the noise settles, I force myself to look up. Buffy is at the top of the stairs, eyes wide with shock. In one hand, she grips a pocketknife so tightly her knuckles are white. From the other, a cut rope dangles limply. She drops both, then bounds down the stairs.

When I look down, the floor is a mix of red and crystal.

Patrick is on his back, a large shard of glass lodged in his chest. Blood trickles from his mouth as he struggles to move his lips. He's trying to say something.

But then something moves beneath the glass.

"CAM!" Jonesy shouts as he drops down beside our friend, unbothered by the jagedness of the once-grand chandelier beneath him.

We all follow, ignoring the stings of cuts as we kneel down and drag Cam from the shattered remains. He's face down, sputtering as he struggles for breath. We carefully turn him onto his back, hands trembling, relief washing over us when we see no large shards piercing his skin, just a scattering of tiny fragments and cuts. His eyes are closed, though, and his breathing is shallow.

"What do we do?" Jonesy asks, panicked. "He's unconscious. We need to . . ."

"Jones . . ." I grab his hand. Tight and comforting. "We need to call Myers."

All of a sudden, Cam's eyes snap open wide, and he coughs violently. As the coughing subsides, relief rushes through me. He's okay. Jonesy helps him up to a sitting position so he can catch a breath.

Cam clears his throat, raising his hand to cover his mouth. "That hurt like a motherfucker."

Jonesy laughs, pulling Cam to his chest. "You are such a goof."

"Watch it!" Cam warns. "I think I'm gonna be sore for"—he looks down at the thousands of tiny cuts covering his skin—"a while."

"You need to stop getting yourself in these situations."

Cam winces. "I don't think this is what my therapist meant by facing my fears head-on."

Then comes a faint groan from the right. Patrick's still breathing. He's not dead—not yet, at least. Buffy is the one to stand up and slowly walk over to her boyfriend. Her eyes are narrowed.

"Buffy," he murmurs faintly. *"How could you?"*

She squats down beside him, her voice nothing but a whisper. "If you thought for a second that I'd betray my friends . . ." With a firm grip, she grabs him by the hair, pulling his head up to make him feel every bit of her anger and betrayal. "You don't know me at all."

She drops his head, as if he's a crumpled-up piece of paper.

"Oh, and it's over, by the way. I've realized we have *nothing* in common."

Bad. Ass.

"Please . . ." Patrick chokes out, blood accompanying the words as they spill from his lips. There's regret and pain in his eyes—not for the murders, but for losing Buffy. His gaze never leaves her, the intensity in his eyes almost pleading. "We can still . . . you can still be my final . . ." But before he can finish his sentence, the words falter and die in his throat.

"Good riddance."

29

JONESY

Patrick's last breath escapes him in a puff of air, a fragile, metaphorical wisp that hangs in the silence for a brief moment. It's as if the very essence of him evaporates with that breath.

Buffy doesn't move, her face still. Her frame is stiff and she's obviously doing everything she can not to fall apart. The shock is there though—her eyes give it all away. Her world was just flipped upside down and back again. First, discovering her mom is a killer, then her boyfriend is also a murderer, and now, watching him take his final breath.

"Buffy," Amber says softly.

But Buffy drops to her knees and before we can stop her she's rummaging through Patrick's pockets—the pockets of the Carrington Ghoul. She hisses at the shards of glass digging into her skin but pushes through. Then her fingers halt and all of a sudden she pulls something free.

A remote.

She holds the tiny device up to the front door and presses the button. In an instant, the familiar sound of clicking locks reverberates through the tainted manor.

It was that easy. It was all that easy.

The next thing we know, the door bursts open and blinding flashlights pierce the dim room. I squint in the harsh glare. The sound of footsteps grows louder, followed by the sound of voices.

Arms envelop me.

"Mom?"

"Oh honey," she says. "It's all going to be okay."

More figures come into view—it's not just Mom. It's all our parents.

Cam's mom.

Amber's parents.

And . . . Buffy's mom.

Susan pulls her daughter into a hug. I wonder. She could easily get away with it. Patrick is dead. Buffy could—*we* could—put it all on him; we could make him out to be Juliet's murderer without a second thought. Myers already said there were no prints at the scene. Patrick murdered enough people; what's one more?

But the thought of it makes my stomach knot, and then knot again. I don't know if I could live with myself, knowing that I'm protecting a killer. That goes against the very core of everything we stand for. We take on these mysteries to make Sanera a safer place for everyone. A lie would betray that. I wonder if Buffy feels the same.

"Honey, honey, honey . . ." Cam's mom falls to her knees beside him, stroking his bloodied face. His eyes are closed now. "Can you hear me?"

"Sure can," Cam says in a sarcastic tone, tapping at his ear like she's talking too loud. As always, he will find a way to make a serious situation a joke. This boy was just assaulted by a hundred-pound chandelier and he's acting like it was nothing.

His mom tuts, shaking her head. "There's nothing wrong with him." But she still holds him close, as if he were a kid.

Cam's voice softens, losing the sarcastic tinge. "I told you not to come. It was too dangerous—"

"You told me not to come *alone*," she says. "I brought the best backup I could find." She laughs softly, glancing around at the rest of our parents.

"She got you there, Cam," I say, climbing to my feet.

Amber's now on her feet too, basking in the embrace of both her parents. Her eyes are closed but her smile could blind a hundred people. From the way her parents look at her, I know that however angry and worried they might have been, that's now in the past. Amber's safe and that's all that matters.

I'm sure we'll face wrath from our parents at another time, but that isn't now. I let Mom hug me tight, my head on her shoulder. Her head plants itself on top of mine. Her hair is pulled back out of her face, but some wisps fall onto mine. She doesn't say a word, but we stand there, in silence, and savor this moment.

Officers surround us, waiting to question us about everything that transpired, their eyes locked on to the kid dressed up as the Carrington Ghoul who is being examined by paramedics. Myers stands off to the side, looking down at the bodies of her fallen officers. George and his partner, I think. I swallow. George didn't deserve this. He helped us. From the start.

Suddenly Myers's face changes.

"Pérez?" Her voice croaks as she drops to her knees. "Can I get some help here! We've got a live one!"

I stand at the top of the hill, the silhouette of Carrington Manor looming behind me like a silent witness. I wonder if its creaks and groans are more than just the old house settling. It might be a warning—one that we clearly don't listen to.

As we wait for the sunrise to spill out over the desecrated night, I keep my eyes on the house. There's a morbid respect I can't shake for the manor. Through all the deaths, it has stood strong, a pillar in the town's history. It makes me understand why Mayor Gomez wanted it preserved as a museum. In a way, perhaps he was on to something.

I tear my gaze away as Cam is lifted into the ambulance, the bright lights hazy from up here. His mom is at his side; her hand hasn't left his since they put him on that stretcher. I'm pretty sure I even see Cassie among the people still lingering.

From here, it's all so surreal. It feels like at any moment I'll wake up and still be at college. Not many people can say they've survived a serial killer one time, let alone twice.

What does that say about me?

Do I return to college like nothing ever happened? I realize that the answer might be . . . yes. I love college, and it's the place where, for this moment in my life, I'm meant to be. I will always worry about my mom, but she's an adult, and so am I. I've learned that I can make my own decisions. And Cam . . . no matter how much time we've spent apart, we'll always be together, really. That's the one certainty in all this.

Eventually, life in Sanera will go back to normal. This will soon become a distant memory—for everyone else. We'll remember. One day, someone will write a book or release a documentary all about this weekend and reinvigorate the case for a while. And then the cycle will continue.

Just like that, a news van pulls up beside the police

cars, its engine still rumbling as the doors swing open. Out steps a familiar figure. Rick Field, back at it, ready to do what he does best. Quickly, a camera is on him and he begins his report.

I chuckle softly, shaking my head as I turn my gaze away from Rick and watch a few birds fly across the sky as the moon nears the horizon, my thoughts racing with the inevitable questions. Maybe *I* should be the one to write that book, and not Rick, or another journalist like him. Maybe I'll get our story straight once and for all. We've had enough of the journalists. Enough of the press spewing nonsense. Maybe it's finally our turn to tell it on our own terms.

Mom's head rests on my shoulder. "What are you thinking about, honey?" Her voice is soft, like a light breeze that graces your skin on a summer morning. I can imagine it as she speaks.

Her question has a million different answers. "Everything" is the only response that fits and it leaves my lips with a warm smile. The future is uncertain, but everyone I love is safe, and that's all that really matters.

Buffy stands a few feet away from us, alone, and I only now notice a single tear trickling down her cheek. Her mom is nowhere to be seen. I saw them talking earlier, voices lost in the distance between us, but the exchange was clearly emotional. Tears and whispered words, something private.

Buffy catches me looking and offers a bittersweet, closed-mouth smile. I offer a similar smile in return, then she looks away, her sights fixed at the bottom of the hill.

I finally see her mom.

Sheriff Myers is in deep conversation with her. As I watch, I see the sheriff nodding, listening.

Then, as the sun finally breaks the horizon, Buffy's mom offers her hands, palms up, and Sheriff Myers secures handcuffs around her wrists. I swear it happens in slow motion. I can see every breath, every step.

Buffy breaks, the flood unstoppable as her grief takes over her. Amber and I rush to her side and throw our arms around her. I'm sure our parents are bewildered. They'll know soon enough; everyone will. But right now, it doesn't matter.

Buffy needs comfort. She needs us. Her friends. The Sanera Four. She needs the space to grieve. She lost two people tonight, no matter what they did. She lost two people she thought she knew, she thought she could trust. And in this moment, she deserves to feel that grief however it manifests itself, no matter what the rest of Sanera might say.

Two black body bags are carried past us by four officers. I shield Buffy's gaze from them with my hand. She doesn't need to see this.

Buffy wipes her tears away with a trembling hand. She straightens up, her voice suddenly clear. "I said we'd keep it a secret," she says, her voice heavy with guilt. She looks away like she's disgusted with herself. "Mom wouldn't let me. She wouldn't let me live my life a lie. She said that it wasn't fair to me, or to all of you."

The sun hits Buffy's face, casting a golden hue over her pale skin. "She was right. I just . . ." She shakes her head. "I don't know what I was thinking."

"Hey," Amber says as she wipes a tear away before it can reach Buffy's mouth. "I think you'll find a lot of people would've had that first reaction. Especially with what you've gone through tonight."

I nod. "More than anyone deserves to go through . . ." I say. "In their entire life, let alone one single night."

Buffy chuckles, easing some of the tension. But then her face hardens as a shadow of doubt crosses her features. "He said something. Patrick. I don't know what to make of it."

I lean in slightly, a nervous edge creeping into my voice. "What was it? We couldn't make out much in there."

Buffy hesitates, as if trying to piece together the memory in full. "The post on the forum—the one earlier today when we were all with Myers—that wasn't him," she says slowly.

Amber frowns, visibly confused. "What do you mean?"

"I asked how Patrick managed to post it while he was

with us," Buffy explains, "and he said it wasn't him."

I nervously snort in disbelief. "He was obviously lying."

But Buffy shakes her head firmly. "No, he seemed genuinely confused."

The thought settles between us and it's sour. My heart pounds harder with the idea that someone else might be involved in this mess. Patrick never mentioned having a partner. Not that we're aware of, anyway. And I trust Buffy's conviction. So, if he was telling the truth . . . then who was behind the post?

Amber pulls Buffy in. "I think we've had enough mysteries for one day," she says gently. "You've got a whole life ahead of you for that."

Buffy lets out a shaky breath. When she replies, there's a hint of uncertainty in her voice. "I don't know where to go from here."

Amber smiles and squeezes her tight. "Anywhere you want." Her voice is warm like honey. "The future is up to you."

EPILOGUE

CAM

One Week Later

"Someone wants to say goodbye!"

Maggie rushes past me, Macey wriggling in her arms, desperately trying to break free. As Maggie reaches Jonesy, who's packing his suitcase into the back of the car, Macey leaps at him. He catches her just in time, and the love fest begins.

"She's going to miss you," his mom says, watching with her arms folded.

Jonesy comes up for a breath to reply. "I can"—he gets licked again—"tell. Goodbye, girl."

I hope he visits soon. Let's pray next time we can avoid murder.

After a while, he passes Macey back to his mom and shuts the trunk.

"I think it proves that you need to come back more often," Maggie says in a playful tone.

Jonesy eyes me before responding. "I think I might just have to."

Maggie smiles, seemingly thrilled at the thought of seeing her son more than once a quarter. She plants a kiss on his forehead, then glances at me. "I'll go take Macey back inside."

Once Maggie's out of sight and the door closes behind her, I turn to Jonesy.

"Visiting more often?" I say, brows raised. "Is that so?"

Jonesy envelops me in a tight hug. "I'm gonna miss you." His touch brings a bittersweet sort of pain. Bittersweet partly because I'm still sore after last week, but also because I know this is the last time I'll see him for who knows how long. My physical pain pales in comparison to the thought of not seeing his scruffy hair or hearing his absorbing laugh every day. But I want what's best for Jonesy and, at this moment, college is that. I'd never stand in the way of something that brings him so much joy.

"Are you being serious about visiting?" I ask in his ear.

"Only if you visit me too."

"Is that . . . allowed?" I ask. "Being a dorm and all."

Jonesy pulls from the hug into a shrug. "I think we've broken much worse rules." He breaks into a soft laugh. Once a rule follower, now a rule breaker. That's character development if I've ever seen it. "Back to school on Monday, then?"

I gulp. I haven't told him yet. "I handed in my resignation," I rush out. "I've learned, yet again, that life is far too short to spend any time doing something I'm not passionate about. I love helping those kids, but I'm not doing it for myself, I'm doing it for them—"

"Cam." Jonesy stops me. "You don't need to explain yourself to me. Where is that big heart of yours pulling you now, then?" His hand rests on my chest.

"Well, the committee behind the Carrington Manor Museum is going to need some help."

Jonesy's face distorts. "You're kidding."

"No, actually, believe it or not." I could almost laugh at the irony. Never have I ever wanted to go back to that place, but here we are. A lot can change when you cheat death. "Carrington Manor is going to stay open, whether we like it or not . . . might as well be entrusted to someone who isn't going to glorify it all. Maybe I'll get Kelly involved. At least then I'll have a friend."

Kelly. Finding out she's Sheriff Myers's daughter was extremely embarrassing—especially after we thought she might be the killer. Turns out Myers didn't even know she was at the manor that night. She'd snuck in even though she'd been told to stay home. But Kelly was worried for her mom. I know the feeling.

Jonesy looks at me, clearly struggling to hide the mix

of emotions inside him. He wants to be happy for me, of course he does, but he's worried. And I'd be worried if he *weren't* worried. It's an . . . unusual step.

"Do you think you can handle that?" he asks.

"I guess it's one way to face this fear," I reply. "Better than being crushed by a chandelier."

"You strange, strange boy," he says in reply. "Still, I can't think of anyone better to take it on than one of the Sanera Four." Jonesy leans in, pauses just long enough to make me impatient, then kisses me right there in the middle of the street. It's quick but the most unforgettable kiss of my life. It's full of mixed emotion and ends before I can fully savor it.

"Wow," I say. "You're getting better at that."

"I've been watching a lot of rom-coms." He laughs as his lips tickle mine. "The only thing that would make it better is if the heavens opened and . . ."

He pauses and looks up to the sky. I follow his gaze, sort of expecting rain to crash down in full-on rom-com style, but all I see is bright blue Californian sky. After a beat, we both lower our gaze and it's impossible to stifle our laughter.

"Okay, you're not *that* good," I say.

"Sure, but imagine if it did."

"Keep on dreaming . . ." I lean in again just as the front door opens and Maggie's voice carries across the front yard.

"Jones, you forgot—oh!" She pauses. "I can come back."

"Mom, it's fine," Jonesy says, before kissing me on my nose. "I have to get going anyway."

He meets his mom by the car door and squeezes her tight. Stanford isn't that far away, but goodbyes like this make it feel like there's light-years between us. With phone calls, we can make it work though. We always do.

"Make sure you take some rest stops," Maggie says. "I do wish you had someone going with you."

"I'll be fine." He leans down and opens the car door. His mom's car. She let him borrow it because Buffy had left already; she wanted to get back as soon as possible.

She needed to get away from Sanera, away from everything. College is her one escape, even if it imposes its own struggles. Buffy's grief is a strange thing because she's mourning two people, almost. Her mother and her boyfriend. And there are reminders of both people in both places she calls home. Everywhere she turns, she'll find a reminder. Whether it's an old sweater or a postcard or even a familiar scent. It's not something she can avoid. Grief doesn't have an off switch; every memory is something she can't forget. Rather, she will have to learn how to carry it with her.

Amber left a few days ago too—she couldn't miss any more time. Being a big-shot nursing student requires her attention. Once she made sure the forum was shut down, she said goodbye. It doesn't stop another one from being made, but it brings me a little peace knowing that stuff isn't easily accessible anymore.

But anyway. It's clear Amber's destined to be incredible at whatever she does. I've never met anyone so genuinely caring, who forever puts others before herself. I'm constantly learning from her.

With final kisses blown—one for myself, one for his mom, and then a third for Macey, who's panting at the front window—Jonesy opens the car door and clambers in. He sits there for a moment, deep in thought. It makes me wonder what's on his mind. I can see his bright red sweater through the closed window; I can almost hear the sound of the material scratching against the car seat.

Eventually, the car rumbles to life, and lurches forward. The little blue car barrels down the road before shrinking into the horizon.

I stay there for a while, long after Maggie has retreated inside. Even as the car disappears from sight, my lips remain upturned, an eternal smile. The distance may grow, but something tells me there's more adventure waiting ahead, closer than it seems.

ACKNOWLEDGMENTS

I can't believe we're here again. *Be Right Back* is the book that almost didn't exist. But when *Let's Split Up* resonated with so many people, everything changed. I love these characters with everything in me, and it means the world that you do too.

To my brilliant editor, Polly—thank you for your support. I couldn't have done this without you! And to Gen, Wendy, Judith, Mollie, and Isabella—your insight is unmatched. Tina, Ellen, and Lauren—I am so lucky to have you on my team. Team Scream forever.

A huge thank-you to my wonderful agent, Lucy, for always being such a champion.

Jamie, thank you for another incredible cover—I think this is my favorite.

Emma, thank you for joining me every night for

writing sprints as I wrote, edited, and edited again (and again). Writing can be a lonely thing sometimes, but you make it so much less so. I can't wait for everyone to read your brilliant books.

Joe, for always being there . . . and for being the first to read my writing when I'm spiraling.

My family—Mom and Dad, I love you. Thank you for everything. To my siblings, Ted and Charl, and of course, the most important girl, Macey. You can't read this, but yeah.

And to the rest of my family, especially Weasel (her real name, yes)—thank you for being my biggest supporter.

And finally, thank you to the readers for making my dreams come true. It's been a wild couple of years. There's so much more to come.

ABOUT THE AUTHOR

Bill Wood writes mysteries for young adults. After earning a degree in film and screenwriting at Birmingham City University, he worked as a bookseller while writing his novels and building a presence on TikTok. He currently lives with his family and Staffordshire bull terrier, Macey. His first novel, *Let's Split Up*, was the UK's fastest selling YA debut of 2024.